LIGHTVILLE

BOOK 2 OF THE INSPECTOR DALTON FILES

Editing by Miranda Miller of Editing Realm
Cover by Tom Edwards
Interior design by Colleen Sheehan
Proofreading by Paula
Published by Quantum Edge Publishing

ISBN: 978-1-7327422-7-7

www.AdairHart.com

To get updates on new books and other notifications, sign up for my mailing list at
www.AdairHart.com/MailingList.aspx

LIGHTVILLE

THE TEAM

DALTON KINGSTON

An evolved human who traveled through ten other alternate Earths before coming to this one. Most of his technology came from the first Earth he visited, where he was a Scout-spectre, or space inspector. He has fair skin, slicked black hair, and the sides of his head are shaved.

TECHNOLOGY

Nanosuit: He wears a nanosuit that has three modes: default, chameleon, and Scoutspectre. Default is his everyday casual wear, which is usually black boots, beige pants, and a dark-gray T-shirt. Default is also what spawns his official suit. Chameleon allows him to blend into his environment. Scoutspectre forms an armored suit and allows a nanoshield to be spawned. He can also vibrate the whole suit or parts of it.

Multipurpose handle (MH): A hilt-shaped device that carries an energy cell. It can extend morphable metal to form various weapons, such as a stun baton. The energy cell can carry one hundred charges. A light stun uses one charge, medium uses two, and heavy uses three.

Ranged Stun Gun (RSG): A ranged stun weapon that forms around the right hand. It carries twenty-five charges and can fire light, medium, and heavy stun beams with similar charge usage to the MH.

Augmented Reality Interface (ARI): An interface only he can see that overlays information on the environment. He can interact with it by using his hands.

Augmented Right Palm: He has a ring embedded in his palm that allows for scanning or pulsing bright lights.

ENHANCEMENTS

Super cells: Biologically engineered cells that provide rapid cellular regeneration.

Cosmic energy: This allows him to use Evaran-sense and provides enhanced strength and speed as needed. While using his Evaran-sense, he can read life auras and has peripheral awareness of up to fifty feet. When he focuses, time slows down.

Torvatta-touch: An ability granted to him by Evaran's ship, the *Torvatta.* He can open, close, or permanently seal any existing portal. His connection ability allows him to open a new portal to an existing one if he can sense it. His recall ability lets him open a portal back to this timeline if he is in another.

EVOT

An artificial intelligence who resides inside Dalton as an augment. Evot has taken on a female persona and manages detachable secondary control units in Dalton's upper arms. Each secondary unit controls a nanoswarm that allows her to morph into various forms. Her usual ones are a cat and a crow. She was an enhanced virtual intelligence until Dalton was infused with cosmic energy. Evaran and V stabilized her, and she evolved into an AI.

BRAD WASHINGTON

A human with Wildborn energy that allows him to talk to technology. Although human in appearance, he is classified as nonhuman. He has dark skin, and his casual attire consists of black shoes, black pants, and a shirt with a metal or punk band on it. His head is usually shaved, and he has small tattoos on his arms.

He arrived from a cyberpunk alternate Earth and has only been on this Earth for a few years. Since joining the team, he has been gifted a prototype hunter drone he named Gizmo.

VALERIE SIMMONS

An outsider who came from another dimension. Her species is referred to as Zikarian, and on this Earth, she is classified as a vampire. She has pale skin and black, shoulder-length hair. Her casual outfit is combat boots, jeans, a comfortable shirt, and a tactical jacket.

She crossed over in AD 1906 and used to be an assassin. Due to a promise to Dalton, she is no longer one.

TODD ARMANI

A human who used to be a slayer in the Faith Militia. He is a second-generation Persian-American with light-tan skin and a shaved head. His casual wear is made up of tactical boots, camouflage-patterned pants, and a shirt with camouflage-patterned sleeves and a solid-color middle.

He has previous military experience and became an ex-slayer after encountering Dalton. Rick Westmoreland helped Todd adjust to his new life.

RICK WESTMORELAND

An ex-slayer human who has been enhanced through experimentation. He has fair skin with a shaved head and a well-trimmed red beard. His casual attire consists of black boots, camouflage-patterned pants, and a tight black T-shirt.

He is known as Executioner by most and was considered a legendary slayer. After Blake Brown broke his mental conditioning, Rick left the Faith Militia to help nonhumans and those who also left the Faith Militia.

He has Special Forces training and served as an elite mercenary in his past. His executioner suit has multiple layers and armored fiberglass-like pads, with a tough under-suit. It supports dual blades and an assault weapon on the back, pistols on the thighs, and a helmet that has cutouts for the eyes and ears. The helmet also has a technological component to it.

CHAPTER
ONE

Inspector Dalton Kingston despised necromancers, especially those who preyed on teenagers and holed up in an abandoned insane asylum. Although he normally took challenging cases, he sometimes did nearby local missions. This one was just north of Columbus, Ohio. It was near the regional Earth Ward center, so he made use of that by bringing their response team. He stood in the asylum's overgrown parking lot and enjoyed the midday cool breeze.

Next to him stood Brad Washington, Valerie Simmons, Emily Snowden, and Evot in humanoid form. Her crow scouted the surrounding area. Having Emily along had made Dalton's day despite the task ahead of them. He trained with her on Tuesdays in the *Torvatta*'s holo room, but he had to cancel due to this case popping up.

It was 1:00 p.m. on August 24, 2013, just two weeks after Emily had completed an outing with Evaran. Something to do with a giant, cosmic plant being. She wanted to come along today, which was in line with her fierce yet kind personality. Her advanced survival suit, Personal Support Device—or PSD—and sliver of cosmic energy made her a formidable ally. Evot had been all smiles at working with Emily again.

Dalton gestured at a team of four Earth Ward agents. "Cover the back side. Evot will show you where."

"Yes, sir," said one of the men before taking off.

Dalton pointed at another group. "Don't let anything escape through those front doors."

The agents moved into position behind their bulletproof SUV, which was parked parallel to the entrance.

Dalton commanded two more groups to move, then faced his team. "All right. Nothing's going to escape, and now all that's left is to go in and grab Sidrual. He won't be much of a fight, but his minions will."

"Necromancers," said Brad, shaking his head. "I read some on them, but what are we expecting?"

Dalton nodded. "They use Displaced as scouts, zombies as guards, and vampires for retrieval of corpses. Necromancers are Daedrould, and they are classified as linkers, meaning they can extend a Daedrould tendril to the head of a dead body and control it."

"And, of course, we can't *see* the tendril," said Brad.

"You can sense it but not see it."

"All we have to do is slice off the head," said Emily, smiling.

Valerie crooked a thumb at her. "I like the sound of that."

"Wait…you said Displaced were used as scouts?" Brad looked around. "Any out now?"

Emily pointed ahead. "Two near the entrance, but they'll leave when we approach."

"That's…great," he said.

Dalton chuckled. This retrieval was good experience for Brad and Valerie, and Dalton made sure to take the opportunity for live training. He wished Todd had been around, but he had been at home when the call for the case came in. Although he was on his way, this case was time sensitive, as there were reports Sidrual might be moving. Emily made up for that and then some. She had been Dalton's partner in crime when fighting the immune system of a sentient dimension. He had no worries about her ability to handle herself. He waved forward.

"Let's do this!" said Emily.

"Yes, we will!" said Evot.

The group laughed.

Dalton loved that Evot interacted more with organics, as she called them. Emily had been one of the first faces Evot saw when she became an AI. He grinned when Emily's PSD formed a baton. It could shoot stun, repulsion, heat, and mist beams as well as sticky globules. Her survival suit was highly advanced—designed by Evaran himself—and she had cosmic senses.

Valerie had on her new Earth Ward suit. On her back were a blade and a stun baton. Her left thigh had a holster for her SP-8, which was used for stunning, and her other thigh held a pistol in case things got lethal.

However, it was Brad whom Dalton had his eye on. In addition to Brad's new suit, he had Gizmo, a hunter drone, that roamed the area. Brad also had been provided with twenty stickbots. When folded up, they resembled a thin, rectangular bar that fit onto his belt, and when expanded, they formed a stick figure. It was a small swarm that could be tactically used.

Brad and Valerie also had headsets and miniature earpieces. Advanced contact lenses allowed them to use an augmented reality interface, or ARI, and they could view a heads-up display, or HUD, and information from Dalton or Evot.

The group paused at the entrance.

"That's odd," said Emily. She looked at Brad, then Dalton. "I think the Displaced are scared of Brad."

"Huh?" asked Brad.

"I see it too," said Dalton.

The two Displaced out front looked like they had been in a car accident, as parts of their body were missing. Bones, blood, and guts were on prominent display.

Dalton interacted with his ARI. "Relaying what I see in regard to the Displaced."

"Now, that's cool," said Valerie, staring ahead.

"Are you kidding me?" asked Brad, stepping back. "I think you got the whole scared thing flipped around."

Dalton smiled. "Take two steps forward."

Brad sighed. "Sure, step *toward* the disembodied floating corpses." He took a step. "Wow, they're retreating. They really do fear me. How about that?"

"Brad can be quite scary," said Evot.

He laughed. "Thanks."

Dalton scrutinized the Displaced's bizarre behavior. From what he understood, they did not feel much of anything other than some malevolence and not wanting to be purged. They must have seen Brad as someone who could purge them. That gave Dalton an idea of how strong Brad's Wildborn energy was. He was not a conduit—someone with more Wildborn energy than flesh—but he was close to that line. Dalton planned to review the footage in detail later.

The group entered the asylum.

Dalton had the layout already thanks to Evot's scouting around. Sidrual was on the lower levels, but the elevator was out of commission, so they needed to take the stairs. That was where he expected the fight to begin. The trip there did not take long. Despite the dirty hallways, lack of light, and strange noises, the ten-minute walk had been uneventful.

As they went two levels down, groans and moans filled the air.

Emily formed a bladed staff from her PSD. "They're coming!"

Dalton sensed six zombies approaching. They moved slowly, and although they might prove a challenge to a normal human, he was evolved. He activated his Scoutspectre mode, which gave him an armored suit. His nanoshield spawned on his left forearm, and with his right hand, he grabbed his multipurpose handle, or MH, and formed a blade.

The zombies approached in a horizontal line, then charged.

Emily spun into two of them and decapitated them.

Dalton dashed forward and, in one motion, sliced the heads off the next two.

Valerie jumped ahead and took care of the last two zombies.

Brad looked at Evot. "I guess we'll just observe. With that said, time to test these stickbots out." He tapped his belt.

The folded stickbots fell to the ground, then transformed into stick figures.

"Awesome," said Emily.

Brad smiled. "Yeah, and this is my first real run with them."

"You'll get a test soon. I'm sensing a lot more zombies ahead. Let's go," said Dalton.

The group advanced past a few undead until they reached a long hallway. A large octagonal room sat at the end, and on the sides were multiple open doorways.

Dalton counted thirty-three zombies, four vampires, and Sidrual. The zombies cluttered the hallway ahead, with some in the side rooms. The vampires and Sidrual were not in his line of sight, but Dalton suspected they were in the room at the end.

"All right. I'm gonna charge through. Once Sidrual is down, the zombies will be too. Emily, you've got the rear. Valerie, you'll be behind me and behind her, Brad and Evot. Brad, you can test out your stickbots."

Gizmo beeped at Dalton.

"You can protect Brad."

Gizmo vibrated.

"Here we go," said Dalton.

He lowered his shield and charged into the zombies that faced the group. The ones in his way were easy to bowl over. Valerie made quick work of them. As they moved past the doorways, some zombies lurched out.

Emily handled the ones closest to her, but one zombie grabbed Brad by the neck and slammed him into the wall.

His stickbots swarmed the zombie but had little effect.

Gizmo hopped up and tried to yank the hands off Brad's neck to no avail.

Evot grabbed the zombie's wrists and vibrated her hands to chew through. Once Brad was free, she gripped the zombie's neck, then tossed it into a side room.

Although Dalton could have stopped and gone back to help, he trusted his team to deal with it.

The group burst into the large room at the end of the hallway. Emily turned and fired a repulsion beam, which cleared out any remaining zombies.

The four vampires rushed forward, but a stun volley from Dalton, Brad, Valerie, and Gizmo took them down.

"No!" said Sidrual, pointing at Dalton. "You can't do this!"

Valerie smirked. "I'm pretty sure he can."

Sidrual pulled out a gun and fired.

Dalton's kinetic shield lit up. He raised his nanoshield.

Sidrual backpedaled and shot a few more times.

"Enough," said Dalton. He rushed over and tapped Sidrual with his stun baton.

He collapsed.

"Mission complete."

"A decent workout," said Emily. She glanced at Valerie. "You're quite tough."

Valerie winked. "You're not so bad yourself." She gestured at Evot. "That vibrating hands thing worked. It looked just like when Dalton does it."

Emily swatted Dalton's arm. "I see you're passing on some tricks learned from traveling with us."

"Sure did," said Dalton. He looked over at Brad. "I guess stickbots are only effective against living opponents."

"Yeah," said Brad. "Gizmo tried as well. At least I have an idea of what it might be like to fight a living opponent that could shrug those attacks off."

"We can upgrade your stickbots," said Evot.

Brad nodded.

Dalton surveyed the scene. Sidrual was out, as were a lot of corpses that needed to be cleaned up. The four vampires would go to the local Earth Ward center. Although Dalton never doubted the outcome of the mission, it provided him with some insights.

While Brad's stickbots might have been useless against zombies, with some tweaks, they could be more capable. Evot's using the vibrating hands approach surprised Dalton. It was a last resort move, and he suspected that Brad being harmed made her choose an action she might not have otherwise.

It was good to work with Emily again, and Dalton would miss her when she went home. She was one of his closest friends, and he felt better knowing she was around. Now that the mission was over, he would head back to the team's new base. Todd would be arriving soon, and although he had missed coming along with them, Dalton was sure the others would be eager to fill him in.

He picked up Sidrual. "Good job, everyone. Let's get out of here."

Brad placed his hands on the wooden railing of the platform out back of the team's new base. It was 7:30 a.m., and he had gotten a cup of coffee. He stared out at the forest that had a slight mist rolling around it. The fresh air and sounds of animal activity embraced him. Definitely a far cry from the zombie mess he had seen yesterday.

His throat constricted. He never imagined he would be able to see something like this. Life in an underground city on his former world was brutal. Living in a trash-infested living area with the smell of piss or rotting corpses was ingrained in his mind. He welcomed every day on this Earth as a gift. Waking up in a comfortable bed, getting a cup of coffee, then standing outside and gazing at nature without fear of being hunted was more than he could ever ask for.

A squirrel caught his eye. It roamed around and paused to look at him. It reminded him of a crat—an extremely aggressive rodent the size of a cat. They were known to attack anything out in the open on his world. Sometimes they would invade poorly built shacks or housing and wreak havoc. Sentcom, the AI collective, let them exist to keep humans in a state of disarray. The squirrel would run for its life if a crat were present.

He connected to the domain awareness system Columbus, Ohio had. With closed-circuit TVs, or CCTVs; drones; and platform-based monitoring such as cars, phones, laptops, and the like, he could see everything going on in the city. The only places that showed as black dots were Earth Ward facilities like the one he was in and other sensitive, high-security government areas. On his world, this would be a treasure trove ripe for plundering by Sentcom.

Thankfully, this Earth had protections against rogue AIs. V, the AI who traveled with Evaran, did periodic sweeps with Evot. Although this Earth's AIs were primitive, there had been a few incidents where an AI became more aware than it should. Brad had watched V decimate an AI that tried to get into a missile defense system. Evot did not participate, but she watched. V was ruthless, and he not only boxed in the AI with himself, but he also destroyed both its digital and physical footprint. His red orb was like a wrecking ball. Afterward, an Earth Ward response team visited the facility the AI originated in.

Despite that, Brad liked perusing the city. He respected others' privacy unless they were doing something criminal or being assholes. Most people would probably riot if they understood how much data was gathered on them. The data points for any individual blew him away when he first arrived. He had kept his ability hidden since he had sensed an AI presence. That turned out to be U4, another AI companion of Evaran's and also V's predecessor.

AIs on this Earth seemed restricted to Evaran's approval. Brad had gone to a recent cookout where he had met another version of Evaran called Sivaran, who had an AI companion named Q. Unlike V or Evot, who both had some form of organic interface, Q was a pure AI. Brad appreciated talking about Sentcom with Q and understood some of its decision-making from Q's insights.

Brad recalled when he had stumbled into this Earth in a state of confusion. After gathering his senses, he found an ATM and got some cash. No terminators had come to exterminate him. That was when he knew he was somewhere else. The sun, fresh air, and lack of people wearing armor also helped paint a picture that this Earth was vastly different than the one he arrived from.

He turned his head as footsteps approached.

Valerie joined him. "Hey."

"Hey."

She took a deep breath. "It's nice out here. You've been out here every day since we moved in three weeks ago."

Brad chuckled. "I'm just soaking it in. I love this place. It's northwest of Columbus but not too far, is surrounded by a forest for privacy, and has a landing pad we can use as necessary."

"And a support staff that provides security and food."

He smiled. "That too." He eyed her. "This is the first time I've seen you out here this early."

She shrugged. "I went to bed early; now I'm wide awake. I checked the calendar and saw we have a meeting later this morning for a new case."

"Yeah, saw that," said Brad. He sipped his coffee. "What do you think it's about?"

"Not sure, but Lord Vygon and Hermes are coming over to present it, so it must be important."

He nodded. "How are you getting along with the ancient vampires now?"

Valerie grinned. "Surprisingly well. I talk a lot with Mikhail."

"Oh really?" asked Brad with a raised eyebrow.

"It's nothing like that, although it could be, and we'd both be okay with that. He wouldn't break down and get puppy dog eyes after one encounter."

Brad laughed at the thought of Mikhail, a beefy ancient vampire, having softened eyes when looking at Valerie. He was tough, and with his speed and strength, few could handle him.

"I heard Rick is coming today," she said.

"Really?"

"Yeah. I don't know why, and neither does Todd. Maybe Rick will be joining us on this next mission."

Brad nodded. "No problems with that. I like Rick."

"Me too."

They stared off into the forest.

"This is nice," said Valerie. "I should do this more often."

Brad gestured at some concrete tables. "We could probably get something a bit more comfortable to sit on."

"Yeah," she said.

Their first case together had brought them closer, even if they were split up for about half of it. Over the last three weeks, Brad had gotten to know her better. While she could kill at a moment's notice by using whatever was around her, she had a very easygoing personality. If she were human, she would probably be labeled a sociopath. From what he had learned, Zikarians processed emotions differently. To others, it might seem like she had a death wish, but she truly did not fear death.

Another aspect that surprised him was that she did have a softer side. She placed a strong emphasis on her friends, and to be included in that circle was an honor. That extended to animals too, dogs in particular, which seemed out of place for someone who could ruthlessly slaughter another person. She was complex, and he looked forward to learning more about her.

Lord Vygon coming to give a case was a first. Brad liked him, and they had become good friends. Lord Vygon sometimes sent Brad a text for technical help for a trivial issue. He did not mind, and through that constant communication, he had come to learn more about Lord Vygon. Sometimes they chatted via phone, or Brad connected to the system at Lord Noskov's base.

On Evaran's last outing, the ancient vampire origins had been revealed, and Brad was honored to have been included in that knowledge. Like him, they originated from someplace else, although he arrived from another timeline and they from another universe.

Hermes would be someone new from the Greek pantheon. After some research and poking around in the Earth Ward logs, it turned out he was also close with Evaran.

Hermes had also assisted Lord Vygon in the past, so his involvement in presenting a case was not as strange as it sounded. Perhaps Hermes had an insight that went beyond data.

Brad sipped his coffee. It was going to be an interesting day.

CHAPTER
TWO

Rick relaxed on the drive up to Dalton's team's new base. It was nestled back in the woods and was close to a highway. There had been some traffic around I-270, which ringed Columbus, Ohio. After taking an exit north to I-71, it was a short distance to an exit leading to a country road. From there, it was a quick trip to the base. He liked that their team could get to Columbus fairly quickly, but he also recalled the Earth Ward had some fancy ships that could hide themselves.

Rick had been surprised Dalton called the previous day. There was a new mission coming up, and although Dalton did not know the particulars, he had invited Rick to join the team. He had expected to get freelance work every now and then, and the pay from the first case had done him good. It had been a while since he had seen that type of cash, and on top of that, he got to hang with Todd and experience some crazy things.

Rick reached a guard booth with a banner across the road.

A man in a security uniform studied him. "You're cleared." He smiled. "Your truck does have a sound."

Rick wrinkled his brow. "Todd say that?"

"He said we could identify you by a truck that sounds like it's about to die."

They laughed as the banner rose.

"Just take a right at the split for the parking garage," said the guard, pointing down the road.

"All right," said Rick.

He shook his head as he continued on. With the money from the first case, he had fixed up his truck, but it still made some noise. It was old, but it had served him well for so long. In time, he might get a new vehicle, but for now, this would do.

When he reached the split in the road, he observed the left side going to a roundabout in front of a large three-story building with big windows. A flagpole flew the Earth Ward flag, which rustled in the light breeze. The drones flying around were to be expected. The right path angled down into a subterranean parking garage.

He drove in and parked near the end where a large ramp sat.

Dalton, Evot, and Todd waited at the ramp's base.

Rick hopped out of his truck and approached them. "Hey, 10:00 a.m. on the dot."

Todd laughed as they slapped hands. "At least your truck sounds like it has better legs now."

"Still works." Rick shook Dalton's and Evot's hands.

"Glad you're here," said Dalton. "Part of me didn't expect you to accept my offer."

"Well…things have been sorta bad for the group I ran," said Rick.

"For what reason?" asked Evot.

Dalton cleared his throat. "Evot, you only ask that if they want to discuss it."

"I see," said Evot, smiling at Rick.

He waved dismissively. "It's cool. The group I formed of ex-slayers was meant to protect the area. I wanted a refuge. They now want to go to war with the Faith Militia. That's not why I created the group."

Todd shook his head. "They'd be badly outnumbered."

"Yeah, and it would make the area a war zone, which it isn't now."

Dalton rubbed his chin. "The retaliation efforts would be nonstop. Plus, you have families involved at that point."

"Exactly," said Rick, gesturing at Dalton. "I had a meeting with the council that manages the group, and they voted to go to war. I told them I couldn't be a part of that. Then you called a few days later with an offer to join up…so here I am."

"We're glad you came," said Dalton.

Todd eyed Rick. "Sounds like you might be here for the long haul, then. Plenty of space here."

He looked around. "Yeah, I'm getting that feeling. This sounds like a five-star hotel to me, and I'm still in the parking garage."

"Todd can show you to your room, then we're meeting for a case briefing. I need to go greet our other visitors," said Dalton.

"All right," said Rick, shaking his hand again. "I got a few things to unload."

"I will take care of that," said Evot.

Rick nodded. "Works for me. Truck is unlocked."

Todd smiled as he clapped Rick on the back. "You came just in time. Let's go, brother."

The warm greeting from Dalton and Evot was what Rick had expected. Dalton seemed like a fair person, and he was beyond tough. He had earned Rick's respect in a short amount of time—not something Rick gave easily. He directed Evot as to what needed to be unloaded from his truck, then followed Todd up the ramp.

"Sorry to hear about your group," said Todd.

"I tried," said Rick. "Seems like the bigger they got, the cockier they became. The idea was to protect one another, not start a war we couldn't possibly win without heavy casualties."

"I hear ya," said Todd.

Rick ran a hand over his shaved head. "I'm surprised Dalton called me, but you know what? Maybe this is what I'm supposed to be doing. That last case was balls out crazy, but I liked it. Dalton's a capable leader, and I respond well to that type of leadership. To be honest, I was kinda getting tired of all the meetings with my former group."

"I bet. I sorta like all the meetings. Dalton's made it official that I'm a deputy inspector."

"The ole SIC," said Rick. He punched Todd's arm. "Now I know we're in trouble."

They laughed as they entered a large hallway.

Rick easily saw why Todd was made second-in-command. He had a good temperament and had led before. This would be nothing new for Todd, although with the type of cases the team dealt with, it would be a different experience for sure.

"I wasn't in on the briefing of the original case, but sounds like we have one here shortly," said Rick.

"Yep, and Lord Vygon and Hermes will be presenting it."

Rick scratched his jaw. "I haven't met those two before, but I look forward to it. Hopefully, there's no issue with Lord Vygon, ancient vampire and all."

"Nah, I think you're fine," said Todd.

They reached an atrium.

"Holy shit," said Rick.

He surveyed the area. Sunlight filtered in from all levels, and he suspected the glass was bulletproof. A desk resided out front, and behind it was a large concourse. A set of elevators sat off to the left of the reception desk. Above him were various floors with walkways and guardrails. Exploring the new base would be an adventure unto itself.

They took an elevator to the second floor. After exiting, they reached a room near the end of the hallway and entered.

Rick's jaw dropped. Not only were his living quarters comprised of several rooms, but they also had two levels. The main area had a lot of glass on one side with a decent entertainment section packed with technology and comfortable couches.

Todd pointed at a nearby stairwell. "Your bedroom is up there."

"This is all mine?" asked Rick.

"Yep. Earth Ward doesn't skimp when it comes to accommodations at their bases."

Evot arrived, pushing a cart with Rick's belongings. She grinned at him. "I hope you like your living arrangements."

"Oh, hell yeah," said Rick with a laugh.

"Do you need assistance with unpacking?"

"I think I'm capable of that."

"Of course," said Evot. She walked over to a button on the wall. "There are several of these around. Press it if you require me for anything."

"Cool," he said.

Todd slapped hands with him. "All right, man. Meeting is at 11:00 sharp. I'll swing by at 10:45, and we can go down together."

"Works for me," said Rick.

He closed the door after they left, then walked onto the spacious balcony. The fresh air and sunlight did him good, and he could see himself getting used to this. The fact he could live here rent-free while collecting big paychecks made joining the team even sweeter. On top of that, he got to utilize his skills, and he did not need to do it from the shadows. This was yet another chapter in his life, and so far, it seemed to be starting off on the right foot.

Valerie studied the half-circle briefing room. The curved front section had a wall with a screen that covered most of it. An elongated podium with some interface sat in the center of the front area. A three-step platform, with a row of comfortable chairs on each level, resided in the middle and back. The tablet devices that could extend out from the beefy right chair arms intrigued her. There was even a small table-like area on the left side. This was a far cry from the conference room where they held their first mission briefing, which had been a pitch to join the team.

Dalton stood up front with Lord Vygon and Hermes. Lord Vygon had greeted her warmly before the meeting. He wore his black armored suit like always and relayed that Mikhail was curious when she would be out next. She suspected that, like her, he did not have any qualms about physical intimacy. Now that the team had a base, she told Lord Vygon that Mikhail could stop by anytime.

Hermes rocked the business casual look in his comfortable shoes, slacks, and short-sleeved T-shirt. She had interacted with the Greek pantheon in the past, although she had never met him personally. When he arrived with Lord Vygon, Hermes had been a fountain of jokes and smiles and had even flirted with her a bit. That was to be expected, given what she knew of his reputation.

Rick caught her eye. Evot mentioned that Dalton had extended a team invitation, and Rick had accepted. Dalton would probably announce it in the meeting. She was glad to have Rick back and loved his rough personality. Todd sat next to him on the third row on the right side. Brad was in the middle of the first row on the left with Evot in her humanoid form.

Valerie sat by herself in the second row on the far left. The scattered seating gave everyone space, but she had liked the cozier conference room they had first met in. This room seemed like it was meant to deal with larger meetings.

Dalton gestured for everyone to quiet. "All right. All right. I'm glad everyone could make it. Welcome to our first briefing in our new base. With me are Lord Vygon and Hermes, and they'll be giving the briefing. This is an informal setting, so if you have questions, feel free to ask them, but you may want to wait until the briefing is finished first." He gestured at Lord Vygon and Hermes.

Hermes smiled and motioned at Lord Vygon.

"Fine, I can begin." Lord Vygon interacted with the podium.

The screen changed to show a map of Louisiana with a red dot in the southern part of the state.

"This case will take you to Baton Rouge, Louisiana. Inspector Sean Chalmers and his two associates were killed there a few days ago. They were investigating an unusual case regarding people not being who they used to be. Several bite job bars across the nation have been reporting some regulars going from nonhuman to human, and for those who hadn't, they went from tasting normal to bad."

Valerie eyed him. "What level of bad?"

"The few vampires who reported it said they were literally repulsed. The few who went through with a bite job said the blood tasted strange and the semen smelled odd. Yet when Inspector Sean followed up to talk with some of the unusual people, they were nowhere to be found. It was like they vanished."

"That is strange," said Todd.

Lord Vygon nodded. "One time, sure. Over fifty…yeah. Inspector Sean's team took lead on the case, and after some investigation, they determined that all of the people who were reported as strange had one thing in common: Baton Rouge. Something is going on, and I suspect Lightville, a suburb in southwest Baton Rouge, may be involved. It's the most advanced city in the state and is populated almost solely by lightmires."

Valerie's blood chilled. Lightmires made her nervous. They could not be detected by other nonhumans, and they could use their natural gifts to stun as well. They also hated vampires.

Lord Vygon changed the screen to show several tan-skinned individuals. "The Genucian family has been around since the Roman days when lightmires came into existence. They control the city completely. Lightville is but one of several cities where lightmires congregate, and nonhumans are not allowed in any of them after dark."

Brad raised a hand. "I've heard of lightmires but haven't read much on them."

"They're our opposite," said Lord Vygon. "Vampires feed on humans; lightmires heal them. They possess our strength and speed, but instead of Daedrould energy, they have Alkarin."

"How do they heal humans?"

Hermes's face lit up. "Unlike our fanged friends, lightmires have a feeding spike that shoots out from their palm. The spike acts as a tether while Alkarin energy seeks out and eradicates disease. They can also use their genitals as a tether, and, yes, it can be a surprise to those not expecting that."

Brad drew his head back. "They're disease eaters."

"Yep, they are. The kicker, though, is that they appear as human to other nonhumans. Also, if they try to heal a nonhuman, it will either stun or kill them. Well, usually anyway. Sometimes it can actually heal them. Not much is really known about it since most nonhumans avoid light-mires if they detect them."

Todd sat up. "Really? That's quite an advantage."

Lord Vygon grimaced. "Yeah, tell me about it. They're our natural enemies." He glanced at Valerie. "They really won't like you."

"Tell them I have a waiting list," said Valerie, shrugging.

Everyone chuckled.

Dalton looked around. "I don't know much about them either, but if we need to deal with them, we will."

Lord Vygon pointed at various members on the screen. "The family is led by Marcus. His wife is Adrienne, and along with his brother, Julius, and his wife, Portia, that's the ruling council. Marcus has three children. The two sons are Decimus and Septimus. The daughter is Camilla. Julius and Portia's son is Tiberius."

"Like a royal family down there," said Rick.

Hermes smiled. "I may have had an…incident with Adrienne. Marcus still hasn't forgiven me after eight hundred years."

Rick laughed. "That's some grudge right there."

"Yeah."

Dalton cleared his throat and changed the screen to show a map of Baton Rouge. He pointed at a red dot. "This is where Sean's team was killed. The manner of his death was as strange as this case. Three pinpoint holes in each of their heads. The bodies have already been picked up by the Earth Ward center in New Orleans, and I've reviewed the footage. Those were shots from a laser gun."

"Does the Earth Ward have those?" asked Rick.

"They do," said Lord Vygon. "However, each weapon is registered."

Dalton raised a finger. "I had Evot do a quick check, and all weapons are accounted for. Wherever the weapon came from, it did its job. I think Inspector Sean had worked some things out, but like me, he didn't keep notes where the Earth Ward could reach them during a case. One of his associates always carried a laptop for notes, but that was missing."

"Any leads?" asked Brad.

"Per the homicide report, the South Boyz," said Lord Vygon. "They're a street gang or, as the local law enforcement calls it, a faction. Their leader is Crayzo, and they have denied any involvement."

Hermes pointed at the map. "South Baton Rouge has areas of extreme poverty. The mentality there is that of survival mode. If there was a bounty on an Earth Ward inspector, that's just asking to be taken out." He looked at Dalton. "I have faith in you and your team, but you're walking into some hostile territory."

"Wouldn't be the first time," said Dalton.

Brad rubbed the back of his neck. "I bet the local police shit their pants when they saw the bodies. No way a street gang has laser weapons. Unless…"

"We'd have heard about that," said Lord Vygon.

"I figured."

"All right," said Dalton. "The primary goal of this case is to find out who killed Sean and his team and bring them to justice. The secondary goal is to complete Inspector Sean's team's investigation."

"What's your gut telling you?" asked Todd.

"Unregistered alien technology."

"You think Lightville might be involved in some black-market stuff?"

Hermes snorted. "Not a chance. They make way too much money being legitimate."

Lord Vygon raised a finger. "As a side note, everyone is watching to see how the Earth Ward responds to this. It's why I asked Dalton to take it. Killing our inspectors and their teams can't stand. The Earth Ward regional headquarters in New Orleans can provide limited support, but they have their hands full with the voodoo queens and other groups."

"So outnumbered, outgunned, hostile territory, unknown assailants, lack of information, and who else knows what," said Valerie. She smiled big. "When do we go?"

Rick laughed.

She peered back, and he nodded at her.

"Later today," said Dalton. "Obviously, there are some new uniforms and gear, and we'll be traveling via a ship that can transport the SUV. Oh, and before I forget, I invited Rick to join the team, and he accepted."

Everyone turned to look at him.

He gave a thumbs-up.

"I suspect his services will be much needed on this case, just like they were on the last one," said Dalton.

"Ready when you are," said Rick.

Dalton pointed at him. "That's what I like to hear. All right. It's almost lunchtime, so we can do that with Lord Vygon and Hermes in the cafeteria. After that, we'll check out our new gear, then Jake will drop us outside Baton Rouge. The first step will be to secure accommodations, and, yes, we will be staying in a nice hotel."

Brad shook his head. "Security might be an issue there. One advantage of a motel outside town is no one knows you're there unless they're looking hard. Hotels have security systems that can be utilized."

"I will monitor the systems," said Evot.

Dalton gestured at her. "There you go. We'll try it, and if it becomes untenable, we'll fall back somewhere else. All right, any questions before we go?"

"I got one," said Valerie. "I assume we'll be talking with the Genucian family at some point. If they don't allow non-humans into the city after dark, how's that gonna work?"

"I can answer that," said Hermes. "Nonhumans can't live in the city, and they have to be out by sundown."

"A sundown city except for nonhumans," she said, shaking her head. She recalled sundown cities, and even counties, in the past where those who were not fair-skinned had to leave before the sun set.

"I don't like it, but it is what it is," said Dalton.

Todd raised a hand. "I know it's been mentioned that lightmires have cash and one of the most advanced cities. How do they do it?"

Lord Vygon grinned. "Due to what lightmires are, they offer their services to the rich. With that type of cash flow, they invested heavily into technology. It's said they have a very advanced city underground, although we've not been able to detect anything like that. They have never had to resort to anything criminal since their services are in high demand and they can bill at high prices. They made two hundred million when a billionaire wanted to heal his cancer-stricken wife. Yes, she was saved, but then she died ten years later of a heart attack."

"Wow," said Brad. "That's crazy."

Lord Vygon grinned. "Yes. Vampires can only offer bite jobs. It doesn't really compare."

Valerie laughed. Her appreciation for Lord Vygon grew the more she was around him, and she wished she had met him earlier instead of fearing him from a distance.

"All right, lunchtime," said Dalton.

Valerie stood along with the others. This case, like the first one, was interesting. She avoided lightmires like the plague, and now she might be walking into one of their bastions. Human factions would need to be accounted for as well. Despite all that, the upcoming trip sounded fascinating.

CHAPTER
THREE

Todd loved the armory at the new base. It was packed with all sorts of equipment. There was even a research room where gear could be tweaked and experimented with. There would be some good times ahead when he and Rick tried out various ideas.

The large open area had lockers on one part and tables and cabinets on the other. In the center were more tables with numerous devices that could hold objects like weapons or clothing.

Lunch had been fun, and Todd really enjoyed talking to Hermes, whose historical perspective blew both his and Rick's minds. Hermes was old, yet he resembled someone in their late thirties. The advantage of being an Outsider, or a Greek god in this case. He cracked one-liners and joked effortlessly. Between that and his physical appearance, it was easy to see why he had no trouble finding mates.

Lord Vygon had also been fun to talk with. He was even older than Hermes and had chimed in to give some historical context. Todd cherished these occasions. Hearing them speak about their involvement in the fall of Rome had been fascinating. Not many could say they knew people like them.

Dalton gathered everyone around one of the tables in the center. "If you recall our last case, there were moments when better gear would have helped ease the situation. To that end, we have some new equipment, so I'll begin with those that are usable by all. Check out the undersuits in your lockers."

Todd opened his and pulled out a dark-gray undersuit. A uniform hung in the locker, but he was sure that would be covered. "Same design as our last ones but a different color."

"Show him, Evot," said Dalton.

"Of course," she said. She grabbed a claw from the table, then struck Todd's suit.

His pulse quickened as he flinched. "Whoa. Not a scratch."

"It's been reinforced, and you're looking at the prototypes for other inspector teams," said Dalton.

Todd laughed at Rick's astonishment when Valerie changed into her suit. Her personality was sorta like Rick's, and Todd noticed that while everyone else faced away, Rick had taken a little longer than the others to do so. When he turned back around, she winked at him.

"That was…something," said Rick.

Valerie smiled. "Oh, you'll get used to it."

"Sure…" he said with a grin.

Todd sensed some chemistry between them, but then again, they were both seasoned killers with a different mindset than most.

Dalton walked over to a locker and pulled out several devices, then placed them on the central table. He pointed at the first one, which looked like a small cylinder with a bigger flat end on one side. "These buds can fit inside your ear and are wireless. They are essentially invisible and will allow us to keep in contact. Brad and Valerie have already tested these in the field."

"That's awesome," said Rick.

"If the signal is rough, I will act as a relay," said Evot.

Brad nodded. "She's like a mobile cell tower except with much more power."

Rick gestured at Evot. "What exactly is your power source? I can only imagine it must be strong enough to allow you to fly and morph."

Evot glanced at Dalton, then at Rick. "I can't discuss that other than to say it's beyond the technological level of this planet."

"Oh," he said and raised his eyebrows.

Todd wondered about some of the tech he had seen on both Dalton and Evot. It had to be far more advanced than they let on, and from what Todd understood, Dalton had only been able to bring and use equipment he had on him when he came to this Earth. Todd was not sure who made that rule or enforced it, but Dalton and Evot kept the internal aspects of their technology secret outside of a general description.

"What she said," said Dalton. He opened a small container. "These are specialized contact lenses that will give you an augmented reality view and interface. The undersuit collar has sensors that detect your hand motions relative to what's projected and determine what action you're doing."

"They're really cool," said Valerie.

"We can see what you do?" asked Rick.

"Not quite as much, but it can be configured," said Dalton. "Your augmented reality interface, or ARI as I call it, is powerful and will allow us to tag points of interest to one another and relay information in a stealthy manner."

Brad rubbed his eyes. "Contact lenses bother me, but I don't need them anyway. The others can definitely benefit from them, though."

"Yeah, they're a pain in the ass for me too," said Todd.

Dalton smiled. "These won't be. They're unlike any you've ever used before. Between the earbuds, contact lenses, and a collar that has a throat microphone, we'll have a good team's communications infrastructure. Using your ARI, you can configure what chat groups you're in and which one you speak and listen to. There was a headset at one point, but its functionality is now covered with this new equipment."

Rick snorted. "I've seen setups similar to this in my former merc life but nothing quite this advanced."

"What if we don't want to move our hands around like magicians when out in public to use the ARI?" asked Todd.

"A good question," said Dalton. "Your undersuit has a flexible slide-out screen from your forearm. You can pull it out and use your palm to support it."

Todd grinned. "Awesome.

"Good," said Dalton. "Now that we have that established, you'll find your official uniforms in your locker as well. It's a pair of black slacks and a light zip-up jacket that functions as a long-sleeved shirt for the most part. The right upper arm has the Earth Ward insignia, and the left has the inspector team one. Your names are on the top right of your chest."

"Loving all this. It's all official," said Brad.

"There's more," said Dalton. He projected a holographic display of some symbols and labels. "The Earth Ward is trying something new this time in terms of command structure. The inspector department doesn't really have ranks other than an inspector and their team. However, some command is needed. On your collar is a silver hollow circle with a letter in it that reflects your position. Brad, Valerie, Rick, and Evot have a blue "A" for associate. Todd has a silver "D" for deputy inspector, and I have a gold "I" for inspector. Yes, it's official now that Todd is second-in-command."

Rick and Todd slapped hands while Brad, Valerie, and Evot cheered.

"Don't celebrate just yet," said Dalton, eying Todd. "There's some training you'll need to undergo."

"I'm ready," said Todd.

"Why does your circle have another segmented circle around it?" asked Valerie.

Dalton tapped his symbol. "That's used to establish who has rank in terms of inspectors working with other ones. It's awarded by the ruling Earth Ward council, and there are ten ranks, each with their own qualifications. But the main purpose of them is to indicate who takes lead on an investigation or case. If two have the same amount, there are other rules that are applied."

Rick pointed at the symbol. "You have ten segments."

"That means I take lead when it comes to dealing with a case involving other inspectors. I'm the only one currently with rank ten."

Brad laughed. "Yeah, it helps that you're Evaran certified."

Dalton shrugged. "The last thing the Earth Ward would want to see is me sidelined by another inspector for any reason. There are almost a hundred inspectors now with more in training. Each country will be getting one eventually, and some will have multiple per country. Of the current inspectors, almost all are one to three segments. Inspector Sean had four, the first one to receive that."

Todd's eyes widened. "Wow, so his death is a much bigger deal than I thought."

"Yeah, and he was also my friend," said Dalton. "If another inspector had taken this case, I would have probably stepped in, but Lord Vygon knew to give it to me."

"Makes sense," said Todd.

"All right," said Dalton. "You'll also find your badge wallet in your slack pocket. There's a hook in all pockets for your badge wallet, but if you lose it, we also have GPS in it."

"We're being tracked," said Todd.

"That's a part of this job. You'll thank me if you ever get captured and we have to locate you."

"Oh, no complaints here," said Todd. "It's easy enough to just be out of uniform if we don't want to be tracked. But while on the job? No sweat."

"Agreed," said Rick.

"That's your call. As for specific enhancements for each of you, we have those as well." Dalton gestured at Brad.

"He's already tested his stickbots out. He can carry twenty of them, and they're essentially small humanoid robots when they transform from their folded-stick state."

"That's cool," said Todd.

"Yeah, but useless against zombies, and I guess anything tough," said Brad.

Rick's eyes narrowed. "Did you say zombies?"

Brad cleared his throat. "Yeah. Before you came out, we did a quick local mission. Had to fight zombies, vampires, and a necromancer. It wasn't as exciting as it sounds. My stickbots didn't do much against the zombies, but they would be useful against those who can feel pain. I can also use them for surveillance or doing utility and support stuff."

"He's right. In addition to Gizmo, Brad has his own little army," said Dalton. He motioned at Valerie. "She wanted a filtration system, so we have a tactical mask that can be worn. As for illumination, there are flashlights that attach to the wrist or are worn around your waist. They can go from one hundred lumens up to ten thousand, although I would suggest only going that high for pulses. One hundred is the default."

"Lumens?" asked Valerie.

"A measure of light output," said Evot. "A one-hundred-watt incandescent bulb is about 1600."

"Wow, so ten thousand is not something you want to look right at."

Evot smiled. "Correct. You can blind someone temporarily with three hundred lumens in daylight, but prolonged exposure or higher lumens can cause eye damage."

"Got it," said Valerie. She swatted Dalton's arm. "You weren't kidding about getting some light output!"

Dalton nodded. "As for weapons, Rick will be getting an SG-5 and SP-8 as well as stun batons. Of course, like Valerie and Todd, Rick will have some lethal options in his handgun and blade." He faced Rick. "We've also made some enhancements to your suit. It still has the dark-gray aesthetic but with stronger material for your pads."

"Look forward to seeing it," said Rick.

"Evot will take you to it after we're done here. Okay, I think we're good now. We'll leave at 8:00 a.m. tomorrow, so take some time to try out the suit and all its functionalities. I'll be around if anyone wants to run something by me or has questions."

Todd loved his upgraded undersuit, and his new role excited him. There would be much to learn, and he was thankful that, in addition to the courses and training he was sure he would receive, he had Dalton as a mentor. Even if Todd became an inspector, he would carry the honor of being trained by Dalton. The rest of the day promised to be an exciting one.

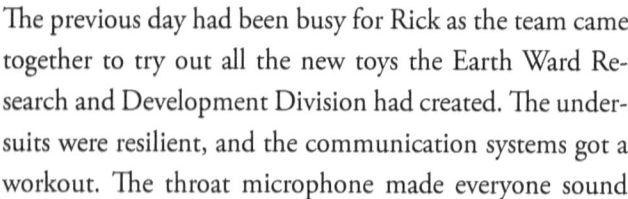

The previous day had been busy for Rick as the team came together to try out all the new toys the Earth Ward Research and Development Division had created. The undersuits were resilient, and the communication systems got a workout. The throat microphone made everyone sound clear, and the earbuds provided background-noise-free audio. The tricky part was working with the ARI.

The contact lenses did not irritate his eyes as he thought they would, and the various data labels popping out everywhere he looked surprised him. He had learned to slow down the onslaught of information, but he did like the small screen that showed video from another person's perspective. Brad had gone on about bandwidth and the compression used, but that was beyond Rick's knowledge. Group communication management had been as simple as selecting a channel, then tapping in the air.

The slide-out screen from the wrist was the backup, and part of him liked interacting with that instead. One pull, and out came a flexible screen. He was not even aware that type of technology existed, but Evot mentioned that it would be everywhere in a decade or so. While the ARI was nice, it was a bit busy for him. It was not that he could not keep up with everything, but he preferred a clear field of view with minimal information.

The undersuit had slipped on like a glove, but it was the uniform that he was most proud to wear. He had a natural skepticism about anything so formalized, but the uniform allowed for good mobility and provided instant recognition to others that he was Earth Ward. That could both be a good and a bad thing. He would keep a set of casual clothes.

The changes they did to his executioner suit were phenomenal. He no longer needed the first layer of clothes, as the undersuit provided that. A stronger material had been used for the pads relative to the old ones, and they easily withstood a Dagothian claw. However, it was the helmet he appreciated the most. It could close in a hazardous setting and provide filtration support. It also had built-in light modes and projected the outside environment along the inner face plate. That made the helmet appear to vanish from his perspective when he had it on.

It was 7:30 a.m., and everyone had assembled at the concrete landing pad out back. The building provided shade from the rising sun, and it was a bit chilly out. He never tired of the fresh air and the sounds of the nearby forest coming alive. Breakfast had been quick, and the team seemed to be in a good mood. It was cool to see them in uniform, and they looked like a solid unit. Brad had been a chatterbox with Evot, and Valerie was as relaxed as always. Dalton and Todd stood off to the side and talked.

After fifteen minutes, a ship landed.

Rick fully understood now how advanced the Earth Ward was. Spaceships blew his mind, and although he had heard stories, he had never seen one until Todd had been picked up by one that could cloak during the last case. This ship was bigger than that, most likely since it was to transport the SUV along with everyone else.

After the ship landed, the rear part folded down into a ramp. Dalton backed the SUV in and secured it, then he hopped out and motioned for the team to board.

Rick surveyed the ship's interior. It reminded him of a cargo plane. The SUV had been clamped into place by something underneath. He was not sure how that would hold it, but he figured it was a spaceship, so this must be common when carrying things.

He passed the SUV as the back ramp closed. Up front was a large room that had a pilot area with a merged passenger cabin. Jake Melkins sat in the left seat closest to the front, while Brad took the right. Everyone else sat in one of the various rows of seats behind them. Rick recalled Jake from when he had picked up Todd.

Jake and Brad talked like old friends as the ship took off.

"I still can't believe these things exist," said Rick.

Todd laughed. "Yeah, me neither, but, man, they make travel easy."

Jake peered back. "We're in stealth mode, so we'll be okay. It won't take long to drop you off near Baton Rouge."

"Cool," said Rick.

Dalton looked around. "I mentioned this before, but we'll be staying in a hotel this time. It's less secure, but we need to present ourselves as if everything is normal."

"I hope we're not too exposed," said Valerie. She glanced over at Evot, who was in humanoid form. "I suppose you've already checked their security systems out?"

"I have, and it does not have surveillance systems in the rooms," said Evot.

Valerie grinned. "Brad won't be able to peep in on me."

Brad looked back. "What?"

Rick laughed. He loved that Valerie teased everyone.

"There may be surveillance that is activated upon arrival, but I will scan the rooms," said Evot. "You can be assured Brad will not be getting a peek."

Brad shook his head.

"We won't have to stay there long," said Dalton. "We'll arrive, check a few places out, ask some questions, then see where we stand. This may be an easy open-and-shut case, but I suspect it will be more than that. Did everyone go over the case packet Evot and I put together?"

Everyone but Jake indicated they had.

"Wish I could come with," said Jake, sighing. "These cases are more my speed."

"You mean you don't like chasing down someone who can send others back through time?" asked Dalton.

Jake laughed. "Yeah, that's not exactly at the top of my list."

Rick was not sure whom they referred to, but he understood Jake and Dalton were close with Evaran. They sometimes made inside references to cases or events Rick had no knowledge of. He was positive he would learn more as he accumulated time with the team.

After a few hours, they approached a forested area to the east of a hospital in east Baton Rouge. North of it was I-12, which would take them to their hotel in the city. It amazed Rick to be able to fly around like this in complete stealth. There were even noise dampeners. He scrutinized the hospital as they flew above it. The cars and people scurrying below had no idea what was above them.

They landed out of sight near a road that went around the hospital.

"All right, let's get in," said Dalton, gesturing back at the SUV.

Rick grinned as everyone hustled. He felt it too. It was a bolt of excitement at the thought of starting another case. Hopefully, this one had fewer aliens, shifters, and witches in it. He opened the door for Valerie, who winked at him.

The SUV had been expanded, and a third row had been added. He suspected the seat was made for him since it was large and comfortable, but he also had part of the metallic cabinet next to him.

Once everyone was in place, Jake released the clamp and lowered the rear ship door. He flashed a thumbs-up at Dalton, who started up the SUV, then drove off.

Rick peeked back when they drove around the grassy corner. The ship was not visible, but he knew it was still there. No one would have seen the SUV appear out of thin air due to the hideaway they had landed in. No wonder the Earth Ward could travel so fast. He kicked back and smiled. This was how he imagined things could be.

CHAPTER
FOUR

B rad relaxed on the ride over to the hotel. Everyone was healthy, the team had new equipment, and Rick had joined up. This case seemed like it would be challenging. Brad smiled at Evot on the dash in her cat form. She studied the world outside, and he did too as they drove west on I-12. Their hotel was about thirty minutes away, so he figured he would check on the city's technical capability.

Baton Rouge had a form of city-wide surveillance, but it was not fully implemented. Thanks to the SUV's wireless connectivity, Brad could see the city from the satellite and drone view as well as from the various CCTVs scattered around. There were a noticeable number of areas that had no surveillance. Lightville, to the southwest, had a black shape over it. That meant there was an active jamming system of some type. Not unusual if what he had heard about their advanced city was true.

The highway led to I-10, and their hotel was a short ride south of that. Brad examined their lodgings. It was a highly rated place in terms of service and a far cry from the motel they stayed at on their last case. He connected to a wireless system in their network, then to a desktop PC in the lobby. From there, he accessed their local network and security system, then checked the group's reservations.

He grimaced. It should not have been that easy, even with his ability. Anyone with a laptop and an above-average hacking skill would be able to see they were staying there.

The players for the case were still unknown, but Brad suspected that if there were any bad factions, they probably knew the Earth Ward sent another inspector team. Checking the audit logs showed no unusual activity, but it was like looking for a needle in a haystack. Although he appreciated the hotel, he would feel better in a motel with less technological capability. He disconnected when Dalton swatted his arm.

"Surveying the city?" asked Dalton.

Brad looked out the window as they drove over a stretch of wooded area, with a residential one to the north. "Yeah. I just wanted to test the hotel's security system."

"How'd it go?"

"Anyone with some hacking ability will know we're there. I realize I probably sound like a crazy person, thinking someone is out to get us when we haven't even arrived."

Todd chuckled. "Not crazy at all. An Earth Ward inspector team was investigating something and died. Now another inspector team appears on the scene. Maybe whoever did the first killing has us in their sights now."

"Then whoever they are will be in for a surprise," said Valerie.

"Damn straight," said Rick.

Although Brad wanted to feel confident about their prospects, they entered into a much more populous environment than their last case. There would undoubtedly be more factions and players to deal with. Maybe not, but he suspected the high-profile nature of the group would contribute to any issues.

They merged onto I-10.

"Hotel looks decent, though," said Brad. He peered back. "They have a drinking lounge."

Todd and Rick slapped hands while Valerie smiled.

Brad laughed as he faced front. He figured they would probably spend some time there. As for him, he was not much of a drinker. Being in a state where he did not have full control of his faculties was something he avoided due to his experiences on his cyberpunk Earth. It paid to be able to react with precision when needed.

Thirty minutes later, they pulled into the hotel parking lot. Everyone hopped out and assembled near the back.

"Okay. Get your things, and we'll check in, do a quick lunch, then head out to the Genucian compound in Lightville," said Dalton.

Brad grabbed his wheeled luggage and put his laptop bag on top. After the SUV was locked, everybody followed Dalton. Brad scoured any nearby systems. Many cars had some technical system of some type with a wireless access point. There were also people walking around with cell phones and some with laptops ahead in the lobby.

He unfocused and studied the sunny lot. It was nice out, and sometimes it was good to stop and focus on the environment, even if it was a concrete parking lot.

He smiled as they entered the lobby. The drinking lounge was off to the right and seemed more like a mini restaurant. Todd and Rick took a quick detour to peek in but rejoined the group before Dalton reached the front counter. The woman behind the counter verified their check-in and handed out five key cards. Brad could easily change them to work for any of the other doors in the hotel if required, but he doubted he would need to.

He entered his room ten minutes later. He stayed with Dalton and Evot, while Valerie had her own room. Todd and Rick shared one, and Brad figured this would be their usual traveling arrangement. The accommodations were much nicer than he had expected from the photos he had browsed earlier. Two plush beds separated by a night table were on the left side, and the right had a dresser with a large flat-screen television. The bathroom was off to the right. A mini fridge sat in the back next to an area with a sink and mirror, and there was access to a balcony.

"This is nice," said Dalton.

Evot scanned around. "There are no surveillance bugs in the room."

"Good. I think we're safe for the moment."

"I hope so," said Brad as he plopped down on his bed.

Evot sat next to him. She pretended to wipe sweat from her forehead, then smiled at him. "Me too."

Brad laughed. He loved Evot trying out various adaptations. She really worked hard at trying to fit in, although from his perspective, she was fine the way she was. Her presence made everything feel better.

The upcoming trip to visit the Genucian family at their compound raised his blood pressure. He had never encountered lightmires before, and walking into a bastion of unknown, powerful entities was not something he aspired to do often. However, his curiosity was piqued. Thankfully, he had a tough group to go with.

Edward Carrington, known as the Facilitator, studied the basement of the dilapidated house he had bought. It was on the outskirts of Baton Rogue, Louisiana, and it would serve as a good meeting place to do what he did best: facilitate contracts between dangerous entities. There was no electricity, and a sewer tank sat out back. Everything was shut off, and he intended to keep it that way. Places like this could be reused for future meetings.

One thing he planned to install was a solar power generator. It could provide enough power for a surveillance system. He would probably build something underground as well, a place he could phase through the ground to. As a Wildborn, that option ensured he never had to worry about any of his places being compromised. If they were, he usually phased away, and the entire area was incinerated.

He checked his light-gray business suit and adjusted his fedora. His outfit had changed with the times over the last few centuries, but he always enjoyed his current look for these meetings.

It was 11:15 a.m., and the three people he had contacted anonymously would arrive soon. Normally, he would contact each one individually, set up a meeting, deliver the contract, and explain any limitations. He could be reached anonymously as well for those in the know. It worked out in that, in most cases, contracts would be exchanged, and the only thing involved outside of him was the flow of money.

In this case, the contractor wanted the three men to see one another. That was not too unusual and meant there was a shared goal and they would know whom not to interfere with. It would still be a competition between them, but they were considered off-limits to one another. Some worked together but not often, as the egos involved usually did not like to share.

Some would balk at the thought that he bought a neglected house just to have a meeting. However, he made money by taking a percent from whoever contracted him to facilitate. Buying a house for under $100,000 was a minor pittance in the grand scheme of things. To him, it was the cost of doing business, and he could ensure it was a safe place to meet.

He exited the house and stood on the covered porch. The first vehicle to arrive was a green SUV that blared bass and hip-hop. It had custom rims, tinted windows, and three passengers. Although Edward had specified only one person could enter, he suspected the other two were muscle.

It was easy to determine who had arrived when he stepped out of his ride. It was Crayzo, leader of the South Boyz, a notorious criminal faction in south Baton Rouge. He had dark skin, shaved sides on his head, and a short dreadlock-like hairstyle. His khaki pants, red polo shirt, tattoo sleeves, and white shoes were one of the more colorful approaches Edward had seen.

Edward motioned for him to approach.

Crayzo sauntered forward as he looked around, then studied Edward. "So you're the Facilitator, huh?"

"I am," said Edward. "There are two others joining us."

"You didn't mention there would be others."

"There's no need to worry. I'll explain when they arrive."

Crayzo lit a cigarette. "This better be worth it. Drive up here is some crazy shit. Through the woods…damn. I'd hate to kill someone before lunch."

"I understand," said Edward, smiling. "Your presence here indicates you realize the opportunity."

"We'll see."

A beat-up sedan arrived.

Edward scrutinized Viktor Sokolov as he stepped out. Even on a sunny day, his black boots, pants, and shirt were no surprise. Known as Marksman, he was famous worldwide for sniping notoriously hard targets. There was no doubt he had probably scoped out several ways to take out Crayzo's

SUV and anyone else if things went south. Viktor's silent but ruthless approach to life and his work was legendary.

Viktor stopped short of the porch and examined Edward and Crayzo, then faced Edward. In a thick Eastern European accent, he said, "We meet again."

"Indeed," said Edward.

"Who are you?" asked Crayzo, who gestured at Viktor.

"Names aren't important here," said Edward. "It's probably best kept that way. We have one more coming."

A man walked around from the right side of the house.

Edward nodded at Damian Wu, a member of the Star Lotus ninja clan. They were an ancient organization that had adapted to the modern world. Damian wore black boots, baggy pants and shirt, and a hood. Armored pads were spread throughout his body, and various weapons were on his belt and back.

Damian, like Viktor, paused before the porch and bowed slightly, with his right fist pressed into his left palm.

"Welcome," said Edward. "Let's all go downstairs."

Crayzo eyed Damian. "You look like a damn ninja."

Damian stared at Crayzo.

"Let's keep the chatter to a minimum, shall we?" asked Edward.

He opened the door and led them downstairs to a basement illuminated by several lanterns. Three stacked envelopes resided on a table in the center.

Edward checked each one, then handed them out in a specific order. "The contract is in the envelope. You've already given me a place to deposit the advance if you showed up, and that has been done. $10,000 as promised."

"Aight," said Crayzo as he tried to open the contract.

Edward raised a finger. "The contract's content is not to be spoken of here. What is to be spoken of are the terms. Complete the contract, and two million dollars will be wired to your accounts. You three have been chosen specifically. As you all are here, it's meant to ensure you don't interfere with or attack one another."

Crayzo sneered. "I ain't working with these bitches anyway."

"You talk too much," said Viktor.

"Yeah, whatever."

Edward cleared his throat. "You can all work together if you want or not. That's your choice. What's important is the contract is completed. When it's done, contact me. Once I've verified with the contractors that the conditions have been met, I'll contact you."

"Who are the contractors?" asked Crayzo.

"Anonymous, as it should be," said Edward. "That's why they give me the details anonymously. Even I don't know who they are."

Crayzo sighed. "And how we know you ain't trying to play us? We could do this shit, then you bail."

"The Facilitator doesn't do that," said Damian. "He has honor."

"He's unknown to me."

"Nonetheless, you have your contract in hand," said Edward. "Again, don't contact me unless it's to say it's completed."

Crayzo sucked on his teeth and exited.

Damian bowed to Edward, then left.

Edward and Viktor walked up to the porch and watched Crayzo drive off like a madman. Damian had already disappeared.

Edward grimaced. "I don't know the contract's content. I pride myself on that, but this one is unusual, both in money amount and the meeting requirement." He laid a hand on Viktor's shoulder. "Be careful with this one. An Earth Ward inspector was recently killed in the area. I suspect another one is coming, so this contract's timing is…unusual."

"I'm always careful," said Viktor. He looked around. "Interesting place."

"One of many, as you know."

Viktor nodded, then left in his car.

Edward took a deep breath and stared off into the grassy fields. The area needed some work, and he must secure it from prying eyes. He used contractors in the past, but all that did was leave a trail. He had become an expert at securing areas like this, and even in cities, he had safe places. Some were permanent like this place, while others were temporary.

Another contract had been facilitated, and he already made $20,000 just for the contract delivery. Another $180,000 waited for him should the contract be resolved. He loved being Wildborn, living far beyond a human's lifetime, and collecting easy money because he could make himself intangible. The lavish lifestyle also helped. He whistled as he walked toward his car.

CHAPTER
FIVE

D alton studied the sign that said they entered Lightville. It was 1:00 p.m., and after a quick lunch, the team seemed refreshed. Now that they had their hotel rooms, they had a base of operations to work from.

He was not sure what to expect from this trip. Inspector Sean had mentioned in his reports that he followed a lead that might be connected to Lightville, but that was it. Unfortunately, his team never made it out of south Baton Rouge. Dalton wondered if Inspector Sean kept details obscured because he did not know who could be trusted. That pointed to something potentially bigger.

The main road into Lightville had a security checkpoint. It was a large guard post, and a multitude of drones flew above. Additional smaller defensive structures peppered the area. Some had large turrets on them, while others, based on Brad poking into their systems, were meant to shut down the road by raising barriers and ejecting large tacks and strips that would disable a moving vehicle. The lightmires took access into their area very seriously.

A chain-link fence extended off both sides of the entry point, and every twenty feet, a thick, rectangular post stood prominent. Brad had determined that each one not only contained sensors but also some type of jamming mechanism. Apparently, the team was expected, as the guard waved them through without issue. The Earth Ward had already notified the Genucian family on behalf of Dalton and the team, so he was thankful for that.

Dalton thought he sensed life-forms under the road, as if it had been built on top of a subterranean tunnel. Maybe the idea of an advanced city underground was not as crazy as it seemed. The drive to the Genucian compound was short, and when they arrived, he marveled at how the structure resembled something he might see on a planet with a colony. The domed, rectangular building had a spacious parking lot, so he had no problem finding a spot to park.

After he got out, he motioned at Evot, who morphed one servbot into a crow before launching. She would provide an early warning system. Her other servbot was in human form, and she wore her new suit with pride. He smiled at her, and she returned it. It warmed his heart to see her happy, and he knew she sensed that.

The stairs to the compound lit up with each step the group took. At the top and sides of the stairs were pillars that ringed the building. Dalton sensed tech in them and figured they provided some type of security he was not immediately aware of.

"This place really sticks out," said Rick.

Brad's eyes narrowed. "There's tech everywhere. Something's off, though…"

"You detect an AI," said Evot. She glanced at him. "Another AI unless you were thinking of me."

He eyed her.

"They're not supposed to have an AI, right?" asked Valerie.

"No, they're not." Dalton sighed. "One thing at a time. Let's go."

The two guards in blue-and-white tactical suits and black boots waved them inside where another guard waited to escort them.

The assault weapons they carried were on prominent display. They did not seem to mess around with sending a message. A quick check on the group showed they were as curious as he was. The embedded screens on the walls appeared as part of the wall. The tiled floor was shiny— maybe it had been permanently waxed. Overhead light strips provided illumination.

Other people paused to stare at the group before moving on.

The team arrived at a large room with a crescent-shaped table in the back. In front of it was a row of seats that resembled some type of formal interrogation room. To the sides were more seats. The guard escorting them motioned for them to sit.

Dalton studied the eight people seated behind the table. The four in the middle looked older than the others. They all had light-tan skin and wore a mix of white-and-blue bodysuits. The elder ones had white sashes with elegant designs over their blue long-sleeved tops. The pale woman standing directly behind the center seat made him narrow his eyes. She had no heartbeat. A quick glance at Brad, Evot, and Valerie indicated they detected it as well.

The elder man in the middle raised a hand, and everything went silent. "Welcome. I'm Marcus Genucia, president of the Lightville city council." He pointed at the others around him, starting on the far right. "That's Decimus, my son. Next to him is Camilla, my daughter." He laid a hand on the woman to his immediate right. "This is Adrienne, my wife." He motioned to the left. "This is my brother, Julius, and his wife, Portia. The final two are Septimus, my other son, and Tiberius, my nephew."

"A family affair," said Dalton. He gestured at the woman behind Marcus. "And she's an android."

Marcus drew his head back. "How can you tell?"

Dalton's eyes glowed. "I'm an evolved human, and, yes, I can see you're all lightmires."

Marcus ran a hand over his mouth. "The reports are true, then. You're one of a kind."

"Indeed, I am. Androids and AIs are technically not allowed on Earth," said Dalton.

Septimus smirked. "Then maybe the Seceltor slave raiders should have thought about that before trying to attack us. They brought us Amelia, a generation three android from Fredoria."

"A G3," said Dalton.

"You know of them?"

Dalton smiled. "I possess knowledge of what's beyond Earth." He gestured at Evot. "She's an AI, as I'm sure Amelia already detected."

"I did," said Amelia in a quiet voice.

Evot smiled at her. "Hello."

Amelia looked down.

Evot tilted her head.

Dalton was not sure what was going on there, but he sensed Amelia was nervous, or what passed as such for an android. He would verify with Brad and Evot later.

"Don't worry," said Dalton. "If she had accessed any systems our AIs were on, it would be known. We'll keep this to ourselves for now."

Marcus cleared his throat. "Thank you. As to why you're here…I heard about the Earth Ward inspector and his team who died. The inspector had scheduled a meeting with us before his death. I assume you're here to pick up on whatever he wanted to talk to us about."

"I wish that were the case, but I don't fully know what he was pursuing other than he planned to come here." Although he had read Inspector Sean's notes, he did not want to give anything away.

"We'll help in any way we can," said Marcus. He eyed Dalton. "We had an understanding with the Helians, but we don't have much of anything with the Earth Ward."

"They'll be more than glad to establish a relationship. I understand the Helians gave you free rein in this and other bastions across the world. While the Earth Ward may be more active, exceptions can be made, I'm sure," said Dalton.

Marcus smiled. "It does me good to hear you say that. You're the first Earth Ward person that we've had a direct talk with. I assume this visit is part of your investigation."

"It is."

"Where do you plan to go next?"

Dalton studied the ground for a moment. "We'll visit the crime scene next, then we'll need to talk to the crime investigation bureau, in particular the homicide and crime scene investigation divisions. Then we'll go from there."

"Then you have a busy schedule ahead of you," said Marcus. He raised a finger. "A word of caution. The city police have factions in them, and some are corrupt. I don't think they'll be of much help. They were less than helpful when Lightville was being established."

Dalton nodded, then glanced at the others. "All right. Anyone have any questions?"

They shook their heads.

Dalton smiled at Marcus. "Do you have any for us?"

"I have a few," said Julius. He looked around the table. "Perhaps Marcus and I can talk to you about them in private."

"Sure, but Todd, my deputy inspector, should come as well," said Dalton. He gestured at the rest of the team. "Take five. I won't be long."

He stood along with the others. As he walked over to a side room with Marcus and Julius, he observed Brad and Evot going to talk with Amelia. The rest of the Genucian family made a direct exit, leaving Valerie and Rick by themselves. It seemed the rest of the family was not in a talkative mood.

Evot's interest had been piqued when she discovered Amelia was an android. Per the Earth Ward rules, androids and unregistered AIs were not allowed on Earth. Only she and V were registered. The standard response to Amelia would be to deport her off-world.

Dalton had exited with Marcus and Julius to a side room, and Evot determined they were going to go over more sensitive topics not meant to be overheard by others. She wanted to talk with Amelia, and it seemed Brad was interested as well. Rick and Valerie had already separated off to discuss things.

Evot followed Brad over to Amelia. His curiosity probably drove him, and one thing she had learned about humans, Wildborn or not, was they were a curious species. Most organic life seemed to be if they had time and were not in a fight-or-flight situation. She enjoyed the team's curiosity and wondered if Amelia had come to the same conclusion. Meeting another AI interested Evot, as V and Q had been her only points of reference up to this point.

"So…you're an android," said Brad, extending a hand.

Amelia smiled and returned the handshake. "Yes, I'm a generation three android created on Fredoria. Also known as a G3."

"Fredoria. That's the planet where humans go if they're abducted from Earth, then rescued."

"Yes. All Earthborn are relocated to Fredoria per the Kreagan Empire rules for abductees."

Brad grinned. "I read some about Fredoria, mainly due to Blake Brown who was exiled from Earth via a Seceltor slave raid."

"He would have gone to Fredoria, then."

Evot was fascinated by the ease with which Amelia conversed with Brad. Her mannerisms were hard to distinguish from a human's, and her appearance seemed to please Brad based on his accelerated heartbeat, slight temperature increase, dilated eyes, and rapid blinking. He could be nervous or scared to death, but everything suggested Amelia's beauty was a factor.

"Yeah, probably," said Brad. "So the humans there created you, then?"

Amelia grinned. "They did. My generation was built for generalization, and I have morphable skin to adjust as needed."

"You're an AI tied to this form," said Evot.

"Yes," said Amelia. She studied Evot. "You're an AI as well. Are you tied to your form?"

Evot changed into a cat, then a crow, then back to her human form. "I'm not. My main processor is in Dalton, but I control two servbots, which have a supporting nanoswarm."

"You can morph into anything," said Amelia. She looked at Brad. "This must please you."

Brad furrowed his brow. "Um, yeah, I guess. I think it's great Evot can be whatever she wants to be."

Amelia gestured at Evot. "Is this form to please Brad?"

"It's to blend in with humans," said Evot.

Brad wrinkled his brow. "Yeah, she wouldn't choose something just to please me."

"I apologize," said Amelia. "I thought you two were in a relationship. That's something I have learned more about since coming to Earth."

"Relationship? Um…no. We're just friends."

Evot had considered Brad as a potential boyfriend to learn about relationships, but it seemed he was not interested, based on his clarification of their relationship as a friendship.

Brad wagged a finger. "How did you come to Earth?"

"I was captured a while back by a Seceltor slaving group," said Amelia. "They used me on the ship for entertainment."

"I'm going to guess that's not singing and dancing."

"It wasn't. They put a collar on me and used me for sexual gratification."

Brad's eyes widened. "Oh! I'm sorry to hear that."

"It's okay. I was happy to please them. They treated me nice. However, when they tried to do a raid on Earth, they ran into Lightville. Their ship was captured and the crew killed, and Marcus took me in as a bodyguard. He has been very good to me and treats me like a human."

Evot calculated that Amelia must have a different set of goals in her programming. Being used as a sex slave did not bother her, whereas Evot's goals would be strictly against that. They both had been created by humans from vastly different places and had very different programming.

"Marcus sounds like a stand-up guy," said Brad.

"Yes, he does like to stand up," said Amelia.

Evot smiled.

Brad laughed. "I meant he's a good person who does right."

"Oh," said Amelia. "You used Earthborn slang. Even to this point, I'm still mapping that. It is quite elusive and seems based on geography or event."

"Yeah, it can be," said Brad.

Evot had formed her own internal mapping dictionary. Most slang she ran into was difficult to find meaning for via her data sources, so she used an algorithm to determine the context. She understood what *stand-up* meant due to Brad referring to Marcus's actions after Amelia said she liked how he treated her. Evot's analysis showed her to be slightly more advanced than Amelia.

"Marcus seems like a good person," said Brad. "I guess you won't tell us about the rest of the family out of loyalty."

"Marcus has asked for silence on that matter," said Amelia.

Brad puffed his cheeks. "I bet."

"You seem comfortable with the fact that I'm an android," said Amelia.

"I came from a cyberpunk world ruled by an AI collective. They had exterminator androids, so I grew up with them. They hated that I could talk to technology. Obviously, you're no exterminator, although with your strength, you easily could be."

Amelia tilted her head. "You must be Wildborn, then."

"Yep."

"Interesting," said Amelia. She examined Evot. "He would be an interesting companion for a relationship."

Evot smiled. "It would seem so."

Brad's eyes narrowed as his gaze alternated between them.

"Perhaps we can talk more in my unsecured space," said Evot.

"Okay," said Amelia.

Evot noticed Brad's heart rate had increased again when the topic of being a companion was brought up. Perhaps the idea or suggestion caused him stress. She did not want to be a source of that. However, she agreed with Amelia's assessment. The offer for the unsecured space was meant to provide a safe environment for Amelia to discuss things she might not say in public. It was as much investigation as it was social, but Evot was curious how Amelia viewed herself digitally. It also did not hurt that Evot could see Brad's mental state clearer in the space.

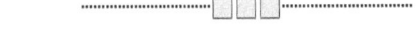

Dalton surveyed the small side room he had entered. It was a comfortable area with bookcases along three walls and a small lounge section filled with couches and chairs. There were ashtrays filled with cigar stubs as well as a mini bar in the corner. Marcus sat in a plush chair and lit a cigar, while Julius went to get a drink.

Marcus gestured at a couch on the right. "Please have a seat."

Dalton and Todd did so, and when Julius returned, he plopped down in a chair to the right of Marcus.

"Inspector Sean wanted to discuss something with us, and I truly don't know what about," said Marcus.

Dalton gestured at him. "I understand that lightmires, especially your family, avoid dealing in criminal activity simply because you don't need to."

"Then you have read up on us." Marcus cast a sidelong glance at Julius. "We make more money being legitimate than not."

"That's the truth," said Julius with a laugh.

"How much we talking?" asked Todd. "I'm just curious."

"It's okay if you know. It's all public," said Marcus. "We pulled in $1.8 billion last year."

Todd's eyes widened. "No shit?"

Julius grinned. "When your natural ability can do what we do, it's to be expected. Yes, we portray ourselves as a healthcare corporation, but we are a legitimate company with proper services."

"That's amazing," said Todd.

"We're glad you think so," said Marcus. "However, I don't think Inspector Sean was investigating our healthcare aspects since he could look all that up."

Dalton sighed. Marcus was right that there was not a shred of corruption to be found on them. He had Evot and Brad search around, and the Genucians were clean. They even financially supported many charities, and their city had almost no crime, homelessness, or other negative statistics that would be higher in a normal city. He decided to test their reactions.

"Inspector Sean was investigating strange incidents where people were not what they seem. They all had one thing in common: Baton Rouge. As Lightville is the major nonhuman presence here…"

Marcus drew his head back. "Why would he think we're involved in that? That's just begging to be investigated."

"I don't know," said Dalton. "He got to south Baton Rouge, and then his team was killed in an alley and his equipment stolen."

"What was he doing there?" asked Julius.

"I intend to find out. His notes were on an isolated laptop, so they weren't uploaded to the Earth Ward systems. However, from what notes we could find from before then, he had tracked a lead to south Baton Rouge with an alleged contact in Lightville. "

"I see," said Marcus. "I'm guessing the current thought is that we're involved in some nefarious operation."

Dalton raised his hand. "None of this has been confirmed, but as an investigator, I have to start with what was known before his death. This meeting was to see where the Lightville council stood on this."

Julius eyed him. "And what is your assessment?"

"It's too early to say yet, but based on information from various sources and this meeting, I don't think you two know anything about the case we're working on, or if you do, you aren't aware of lightmire involvement."

Marcus raised his head. "We'll assist you in any way possible. The last thing we want is an investigation of any type. Why risk everything we've built for that? It makes no sense."

Dalton pointed at him. "There's that too. "

"If there's a contact within our city, they'd be doing it without our knowledge for sure," said Julius.

"I suspect that as well," said Dalton. "Hermes vouched for your commitment to legitimate business and keeping clean even back in the Roman era."

Marcus scowled. "Hermes…"

"I know you two have some history, but I value his word."

"He does know us well," said Julius. "And he's right. We've always stayed legitimate. There were some factions of lightmires that did criminal activity, and that's why they no longer exist. They were enslaved and couldn't exactly go to the authorities about their activity. Keeping clean gives us all the protection we need and allows us to live in peace."

Todd furrowed his brow. "Are there any other lightmire factions we should be aware of?"

Marcus glanced at Julius, then at Todd. "There's the Outcasts, lightmires who have been removed from Lightville. They tend to live on the outskirts of Baton Rouge in the east. They're not fully on their own, as we will aid them on a case-by-case basis, but obviously, nothing criminal. If they want back in, they have to earn it."

"What would get them kicked out?"

Marcus sighed. "As much as I would like to say we're a perfect society, there are still those who have a darker mentality."

"So that's how you have such a low crime rate in your city. Everyone knows they'll be ejected if they mess around," said Todd.

Julius raised a finger. "We give them a second chance, but they're cut off from universal income."

"You use the outside world as a jail essentially," said Dalton. He eyed Marcus. "Universal income…how's that work?"

Marcus smiled. "Every citizen of Lightville has free housing and a monthly deposit of $10,000. The only requirement they have is to provide their services when called upon. They only need to do it a few times a year, but even one time can net us upwards of several million dollars, which we reinvest into the city. To lose that and be exiled is not something most want to deal with."

"I see," said Dalton.

"That's a nice deal. Do you invest in Baton Rouge?" asked Todd.

Julius studied him. "You're asking if we influence local factions there, right? Lots of money?"

"Just asking," said Todd.

"Yes, we do," said Julius. "However, we donate to politicians who help us and to charities and other groups. We provided the city police department with multiple labs for their crime scene investigation and high-tech support divisions. We gave new cars and equipment to their patrol divisions. We also have a liaison department that assists them with research as needed. It does buy us some goodwill, and they tend to leave Outcasts alone due to that."

"They must love you," said Todd.

Marcus shrugged. "You would think so, but we have our enemies within the police department as well. Some think we're corrupt for doing these things, but we can't reveal to them that part of hiding our true selves is to be in plain sight. No one asks questions, and we would like to keep it that way."

"I understand. You said there are factions within the city police that may be corrupt," said Dalton.

"That's putting it mildly," said Julius. "Although we have helped them, we've also been rebuffed, depending on who is currently chief of police. The current one doesn't want anything to do with us. I suspect they get their money… elsewhere. I wouldn't be surprised if they've done nothing about the death of Inspector Sean's team since they know you guys will take it over. The CSI division probably won't have much to process either. They might have something, but I don't think it'll be useful."

"Earth Ward has already picked up the bodies. We're going to check out the crime scene before going over to talk with the local police," said Dalton.

"While you're there, don't mention us," said Marcus. "They seem to really dislike us despite our helping them for years. I'm not really sure why there's been such a drastic change recently."

"All right. If we wanted to meet these Outcasts you mentioned earlier, how would we do that?"

Julius stood and walked over to the bar. He scribbled down something on a napkin, then handed it to Dalton. "It's a bar run by Felix Valente, one of the more prominent and outspoken lightmires. He doesn't care to come back, has an attitude, and is usually a guide for those exiled."

"Thank you," said Dalton.

Dalton and Todd stood when Marcus did, then they all shook hands.

"I truly wish you the best in your investigation, Inspector," said Marcus.

Dalton nodded and then exited with Todd. There was a lot to chew on, and Dalton sensed that whatever was going on was being done in secret even from the council. Someone or some group did not want anyone snooping around, but they made a fatal mistake in killing an Earth Ward inspector.

CHAPTER
SIX

Valerie looked out the window as the team drove to the crime scene. Talking with Rick had been fun while Dalton talked to Marcus and Julius. She had wanted to meet Amelia and learn more about her, but Brad, Evot, and Amelia had been in a trance-like state. From what Valerie understood, that meant they were probably conversing in Evot's unsecured area. They only came out of it when Dalton had wrapped up his meeting.

Although Valerie knew she would not be able to detect lightmires, she had still tried. No wonder they successfully integrated with humans so much easier than other nonhumans. Any vampire who tried to mess with them would get a nasty surprise. But lightmires could not detect nonhumans, so that made it fairer.

She had thought they would talk to the local police first, but Dalton was insistent on going to the crime scene. The Earth Ward had already obtained reports from the homicide and CSI divisions as well as the coroner's office. She figured he wanted to see the crime scene, compare it against their reports, then go talk to them. With his scanning technology, he might discover something not in the reports.

The SUV pulled into a side alley after a fifty-minute drive.

Valerie was careful not to hit the brick wall as she opened her door. The SUV was a tight fit, but thankfully, the doors could open fully. An opening to another alley appeared farther down. It was 2:30 p.m., and half the place was in shadow.

Dalton circled a finger in the air. A servbot jumped out of his left upper arm, formed a crow, then flew up.

"I will provide an aerial view," said Evot as her other servbot in cat form morphed into her human one.

"Good," said Dalton. He motioned at the others. "Let's check out the scene."

The group walked forty feet ahead.

"Evot, holo sketch the scene from the information the Earth Ward obtained," said Dalton.

"Of course," she said. She extended her hand and projected the three dead bodies.

Valerie loved that they could do digital recreations of anything if they had enough information. She had seen that used when they did a holo sketch from their previous case. The bodies had data labels pointing to various things. What she liked about it was that each label with information was colored. The CSI's was yellow, the first responder's orange, and the coroner investigator's blue.

"That is seriously awesome," said Rick, gesturing at the projection.

Todd grinned. "Takes detailing a scene to a whole new level."

Dalton raised a finger. "This doesn't seem like the work of some random shooter, and I don't think it was multiple. One person, highly skilled."

"An assassin," said Valerie. "That's what it looks like to me."

"Any you know of with this attack style?"

She shook her head. "We used whatever was best for a situation. Could be any of them, but I'm not aware of any with laser weapons." She studied the scene and then stepped back. "If it were me, I would have tossed a grenade in these cramped quarters or left a proximity mine. This was personal. Person walked up and hit each of them in several quick shots." She imitated someone shooting in sequence.

"That's what my gut tells me too," said Dalton. "The question now is, why were Sean and his team here?"

Brad wrinkled his brow. "If he was meeting someone, probably a potential lead or confidential informant. I think their guard was down, like they knew the shooter."

"Definitely possible. Note the layout of the bodies. It looked like his associates were behind him and not trying to flee."

Todd pointed at the ground away from the holo sketch. "Just like they were facing or talking to the shooter. The reports said there had been no movement of the bodies. Just left to lay there."

"Yeah," said Dalton. He walked around and emitted a yellow scanning beam on the environment.

Although investigators could do thorough work on a crime scene, Valerie doubted any had the scanning technology he had. If they had missed anything, he would find it. As he continued to scan, she did her own way of checking out a scene. She did not have the advanced tech Dalton had, but she could see what his scans revealed. She used her enhanced smell and sight to canvas the area, but given that the death was a few days ago, she did not think she would detect anything.

"There are four cars approaching," said Evot. "Two are coming behind the SUV. The other two are approaching down the side alleys at the end of this one."

"Whoever it is, they're trying to box us in," said Todd.

Rick smirked. "Yeah, I don't think they're here to talk."

"Probably not," said Dalton. He looked around and then focused on the group. "Brad, deploy your stickbots along the walls, then get into the SUV. You can have Gizmo scale the wall as well."

"Got it," said Brad.

Dalton pointed at the gap between the SUV and the left brick wall. "Todd, you cover that, and, Rick, you get the other side. You can use the doors as cover and pop out as needed. Valerie and I will cover the front."

"No problem, chief," said Todd.

They got into position and pulled out their SG-5s while Brad deployed his stickbots.

Valerie's skin crawled as the stickbots traveled to various points off the ground. They moved fast, and per Brad, they now had sharp fingers that could inflict pain. After they had been deployed, Brad hopped into the back of the SUV. It was better for him to be there than out in a hot spot.

She joined Dalton, who was still in his official suit. He was probably waiting to activate it at the last moment. His suit in Scoutspectre mode was tough, and she knew from experience how resilient it was.

She did not know who had arrived, but she could now see them from Evot's aerial view. Valerie loved her new contact lenses. They did not hurt to wear, and seeing the situation from above was priceless. Given the speed of the SUVs and the bass blaring, she suspected whoever was coming did not plan on doing much talking and did not seem to care if they were noticed. That was usually a sign of overconfidence.

Dalton sighed as he studied the oncoming vehicles. He could see why the alley was easy to ambush. The T-junction at the end of it allowed for both sides to be covered, and the other route behind the SUV could be plugged up. It seemed whoever was coming had intended just that. The team's SUV would provide some cover, but they were exposed up front.

Evot had scanned the four vehicles and detected a total of nineteen men spread across them. Two cars were SUVs, and the other two were big four-door sedans. She had identified the music as hip-hop and confirmed it was from a local artist.

Dalton checked to make sure everyone was in position. Rick and Todd stood on the sides of the team's SUV with

SG-5s out. If needed, they could open the back doors to provide some coverage, but it made Dalton consider adding some form of pull-out shielding. Something to investigate later.

Brad's stickbots were split up, with half on the right wall ahead and the other half on the wall behind the SUV. They were hard to detect unless they were actively being looked for. Valerie was cool as always, and she had a stun baton in one hand and her SP-8 in the other. Dalton smiled when Gizmo beeped at him from underneath the SUV.

The vehicles at the end of the alley stopped just short of turning in.

Ten men got out. They wore a mix of clothing—jeans, boots, sneakers, and colorful shirts that seemed to be the norm. Almost all were dark-skinned, although one was tan-skinned. Hairstyles ranged from shaved sides and dreadlock-style to cornrows.

However, it was the assault weapons and pistols that got Dalton's attention. Some men also removed bats, crowbars, chains, and knives from the trunks of the vehicles. Nine other men approached the SUV from behind.

Dalton talked over local comms. "Brad, use your stickbots to get the ranged weapons out of commission. After that, it's close-quarters combat."

Rick scoffed. "Their funeral."

"Let's try to avoid killing," said Dalton. His eyes narrowed as the group of men ahead began to filter into the alley. "I'll talk first. If that fails, be ready."

One of the men stepped ahead of the others and pointed at Dalton. "You're a wanted man. Your whole team is."

"That's not new. Who are you, and what do you want?" asked Dalton.

The man sucked on his teeth. "Names aren't important." He pointed at Valerie. "Come quietly, and she can keep her clothes on."

Valerie laughed.

"This ain't no laughing matter, bitch."

"It is to me," said Valerie, smiling.

Dalton extended a hand down toward Valerie, then faced the man. "This is an Earth Ward investigation you're interfering with. I assume you're the leader of your group."

"I don't give a shit what you're investigating or what you think I am," said the man. "Tired of talking. You've made your choice." He dipped his head to the side, then forward. "Get these bitches."

Dalton entered Scoutspectre mode, which caused some of the men to hesitate. "Brad, now!"

Brad's stickbots jumped off the walls and landed on some of the men, then ran up to their hands and jabbed them, which forced those with assault rifles and pistols to drop their weapons. The stickbots also got the ones behind the SUV.

"What the hell is that?" The leader backed away, rubbing his hand. "Get 'em! Get 'em!"

The first man to reach Dalton and Valerie was hit by her SP-8. The man crumpled to the ground.

Dalton whirled into action and bashed the next attacker away, then spun and hit another with his stun baton.

Valerie switched to her dual batons. She dashed forward and slid, hitting a thug on the way and knocking the legs out from another.

Gizmo shot a stun beam at an attacker who rushed Dalton. The man sprawled down.

"Ah, man, fuck this!" said the leader. He pulled out another pistol and fired at Dalton's leg.

Dalton's kinetic shielding lit up. He jumped over the man Valerie had knocked down and landed in front of the leader.

"What the—?"

Dalton slapped the gun out of the man's hand, then crouched and did a leg sweep.

The leader tumbled.

"Stay down," said Dalton as he leaned back and pushed an incoming bat swing out of the way. He stepped over the leader and kicked the attacker into the right wall.

The man slid down, breathing hard.

Dalton did a quick check on Todd and Rick via Evot's aerial view. The stickbots had done their job, and as Todd and Rick excelled in melee, they had all but dismantled six of the nine attackers. Rick laughed while taking on two. Todd moved effortlessly as he chased down one who tried to get away. Brad's stickbots moved the weapons out of reach of the men who could barely move. The stickbots were efficient, and Rick and Todd were a formidable force.

Valerie fought the last two. One had a chain, while the other held a knife.

When the knife-wielder went to stab her, she grabbed his hand and pulled him forward, then kneed him in the stomach. The chain-user tried to wrap his chain around her neck, but she ducked and flung the man she held into him. Brad's stickbots jumped in and dragged the weapons away. When the men tried to get up, she jumped and landed behind them. Two quick taps later, and they were stunned.

She took a moment to catch her breath. "That's it?"

Todd and Rick walked up from the SUV. "Apparently so. We got ours. Gizmo even got one back there!"

Brad exited the SUV, and the stickbots ran toward him and climbed up his pant leg. Once they were on his belt, they transformed back into metallic slats and locked in.

"Good job, everyone," said Dalton. "Evot, you know who drove what, so collect their keys and move these vehicles out, then disable them."

"Of course," she said.

"Todd, how many zip ties we got?"

Todd grinned. "Over fifty in the back."

"Good," said Dalton. He pointed at the left brick wall in front of the SUV. "Use them and coordinate with the team to bring everyone there."

Todd clapped. "You heard the man. Let's get to it. Valerie and Rick, handle the rear. Brad and I will do the ones here."

The group moved into action.

Dalton smiled as Todd took charge. It was nice to delegate, and Dalton was glad the team respected Todd enough to do what he asked. Dalton went back into his official suit, then hauled the leader over to the right wall. After ensuring he was secured, Dalton observed the others in action. Evot walked around in her human form and singled out those who had car keys. The others moved with ease as they dragged men to the other wall. He was not sure why they were attacked, but he would find out.

Rick grinned as Todd grunted while placing a man against the wall. While it was easy for Rick, Todd did not have enhanced strength. That did not mean he could not fight, though. In the battle, they had worked together as a unit and easily dismantled the attackers. Rick loved this type of work and realized how much he had missed it.

More importantly, he enjoyed being part of a team. Dalton was the type of leader Rick responded to. Most leaders he had worked for had him as the muscle, but with Dalton, he was that and more. Although Rick had only seen a bit of Dalton in action during the fight, the ease with which he moved around and fought was impressive. Valerie had been no slouch either. Even the stickbots did their part in removing guns from the equation, and Gizmo had taken two down.

Adrenaline still surged through Rick, and he felt like he could fight more if he had to. Tying the attackers' hands behind their backs and moving them was a good way to relax some, and while he did two at a time, Valerie did one. He appreciated her company.

She eyed him as they went back to get another round of men. "You're still amped, aren't you?"

"Hell yeah," he said. "I could go for a few more rounds."

She laughed. "I figured. I used to get that way after an assassination."

Rick had looked a bit into Valerie's past via Todd, and she had been a scarily efficient killer. Her creative methods made her valuable as an assassin, and Rick was no stranger to assassins in general. Several had tried to kill him before, but they didn't live long afterward.

After twenty minutes, eighteen tied-up men sat against the left wall in front of the SUV. The leader trembled against the right wall.

Rick joined the others in the center. In the distance, a vehicle started up—Evot moving out the cars.

"I think it's time we found out what's going on," said Dalton. He walked over to the leader. "So…what's this all about?"

The leader looked around. "What…what are you?"

"Inspector Dalton Kingston, Earth Ward, and you just met my team. What's your name?"

"Jayden."

"Okay. Jayden. Why are you here?"

"Man, I ain't no snitch!"

"All right. Then this is how this plays out," said Dalton. He motioned at the line of men with their hands tied behind their backs. "An Earth Ward response team will arrive and pick everyone up. Since we're not local law enforcement, you won't go to jail. No…you'll go somewhere else. Assaulting an inspector team and interfering with an investigation will result in you and the others being put away for a long time."

Jayden swallowed hard.

Rick had not seen the Earth Ward jail or prison, but he had heard the prison was in another dimension. Given what he saw with Dalton and the portals, that was no longer a surprise.

Dalton raised a finger. "The alternative is you tell me why you came here with your crew, and I'll let your group walk."

"Really?" asked Jayden with a confused look.

Dalton sighed. "Do you really want to screw everyone over because you wouldn't take responsibility?"

Jayden shook his head. "Okay, okay." He grimaced and looked away for a moment, then focused on Dalton. "An old white dude in a business suit, calling himself the Facilitator, dropped off a contract. It said we'd be paid a hundred grand to capture your team alive or seventy-five if you're dead."

"The Facilitator…I don't know him."

"I do," said Valerie. "He facilitates contracts between parties, usually anonymously. I've worked with him before. He's well known in the assassin world, but he is true neutral. He never takes sides. If he's involved, then someone wanted to capture or kill us, and Jayden's group was the muscle."

Rick could see Valerie's contributions outside of just muscle. Her deep knowledge of the nonhuman world, and even that of the assassin one, provided an insight he knew would be hard to find elsewhere. While there might be records or information on the Facilitator, it was another thing to have interacted with him.

"What *do* you call your group?" asked Dalton.

Jayden raised his head a bit. "The Baton Rouge Crew, man. BRC for life!" He sighed. "Look, we just got 10K up front and ninety or sixty-five on the back. It's not personal, just business."

"And how did you know we were here?" asked Dalton.

"When you arrived, we got a call from some automated voice saying you were here, so we moved."

Dalton studied Jayden. "Automated…like a robot voice?"

"Yeah, or something."

"I see. And what did they call you on?"

Jayden grimaced. "It was a burner, man. Came with the contract. That shit's been destroyed."

Dalton sighed. "I see. Where were you to deliver us?"

"Here," said Jayden, using his head to nod in various directions. "Once done, we secure you if you're alive, then leave."

Valerie smirked. "That means we're being monitored."

Dalton looked around. "Evot didn't sense anything, but whoever issued the contract must have monitored the area before we came. They may still be."

"Yeah, probably."

Dalton ran a hand over his mouth as he examined Jayden. "All right. After your cars have been moved, we'll set you free. You can free your friends, then."

"Just like that?" asked Jayden.

"Yeah," said Dalton. He raised a finger. "As a close friend once said, should you try again, I won't be as lenient."

Jayden nodded. "You don't need to worry about that, man. You some crazy shit. Contract didn't mention we'd be fighting some robot and Special Forces crap."

Rick laughed. Jayden finally realized what he was up against. Dalton could have gone hard, but he gave Jayden a second chance, something Rick appreciated. He often felt like outcomes would be better if people had an opportunity to learn from their mistakes, although he doubted Jayden would have been as generous if the roles were reversed.

Dalton walked a bit away and signaled for the group to follow.

Everyone assembled around him.

"Once Evot has moved and disabled their vehicles, we'll meet with the local police. Let's keep this incident to ourselves, though," said Dalton.

"You got it, chief," said Todd.

"What if the local police were the anonymous group that issued the contract?" asked Valerie.

"They could be," said Dalton. "The robotic voice could have been a filter. Whoever set this up took their shot and missed. This place had to be monitored somehow if some robot voice called this crew out here." He studied the last of the vehicles being backed out. "All right. Let's hit the police. After that, we can check out that lightmire bar, then spend the rest of the night at the hotel. Rick, you may want to suit up with your executioner suit but leave off the helmet for this next part. Let's hope for no more surprises."

Rick smiled at the thought of wearing his new executioner suit. Although he liked his official suit, it was no substitute for his armored one. Maybe he could revise the form factor even more to make it look official. Something to research later. The local police would surely stare hard at it, but he hoped Dalton was right about no more surprises.

CHAPTER
SEVEN

Dalton reflected on the Genucians and the recent attack over the thirty-minute drive to the Criminal Investigations Bureau. Brad and Evot had learned quite a bit from Amelia, but she was careful not to discuss personal information on the family. Although that would have been nice, he was okay with what they discovered. Marcus and Julius had lived a long time, and they understood not to make waves.

The robot voice that interacted with Jayden most likely was a filter. It would be anonymous, just like the Facilitator was. Dalton did not think Marcus or Julius were involved in the attack, but they did know the team was going to the crime scene. That could be coincidental, or maybe they told someone who operated outside their knowledge. Dalton sighed. Just visiting a crime scene was dangerous.

He pulled the SUV into an entranceway. A hexagonal-shaped building stood at an angle to a larger rectangular one. The parking lot to the right looked like it could support many cars, but there were only a handful there. An elongated roundabout sat out in front of the hexagonal building. Part of the roundabout near the entrance resided under an overhang supported by concrete pillars. The words "Baton Rouge Police" were etched into the front of the overhang.

Dalton parked in a spot near the building. "First time with our new uniforms out on a case like this. Everyone ready?"

"Our suits are a little scuffed, but other than that, I'm ready. How do we introduce ourselves?" asked Todd.

"I'll do that, but you can just use deputy inspector or associate inspector," said Dalton.

"All right," said Valerie, hopping out of the car. "Maybe we'll need to fight again."

Dalton appreciated her fearlessness even in social situations. Although he hinted at it, this was the first time they would interact with another law enforcement body as an official team. He was not expecting any issues, but he would monitor how everyone reacted. The mood seemed positive despite the recent fight.

The team assembled behind the SUV.

Dalton smiled as Brad and Todd adjusted their outfits and tried to rub out dirtied areas. The overall appearance of the team looked official.

"Let's go," said Dalton, motioning forward.

As they walked up to the entrance, several people stopped and stared.

Dalton expected that reaction. The Earth Ward suits were meant to look somewhat advanced, and the holsters and batons stood out. It probably did not help that they looked like they had been in a fight.

Once inside, Dalton studied the building's interior. There were rows of seats in a common area that had hallways leading to bathrooms off to the left. A stairway resided next to the corridors. On the right side were some elevators, and ahead of them was a long front desk, which they approached.

"Can I help you?" asked a woman in uniform behind the counter.

Dalton showed his badge wallet. "Inspector Dalton Kingston, Earth Ward. Captain Adam Washington is expecting us."

"One moment." She picked up a phone. A few seconds later, she said, "Someone is coming to get you."

"Okay."

Dalton took a moment to look around. He smiled at all the stares they received. Most of the people were dark-skinned. Given that half the city was, that did not seem unusual.

After a few minutes, a man in a business suit approached and extended a hand. "Detective James Anderson. Captain's expecting you."

Dalton returned the handshake. "Excellent. Lead on."

As they walked, James glanced at Dalton. "Earth Ward, huh? I gotta say…not many know of you."

"We're relatively new."

"I figured. Seems like every five years there's a new agency of some type." James's gaze swept over them. "I know a 24-7 laundromat if you need one."

Dalton chuckled. "We'll be fine."

They reached a large office with a big desk at one end and several chairs at the other. A balding, dark-skinned, heavyset man in a police uniform stood and walked over. He had a well-trimmed mustache and a friendly smile.

"Captain Adam Washington, chief of detectives," he said. He scrutinized their suits. "Everything all right?"

Dalton sighed. "Let's just say our introduction to Baton Rouge was a little rougher than expected."

"Anything I should know about?"

Dalton shook his head. "We took care of it."

"All right…" Adam motioned at the chairs. "Please sit."

The team complied as Adam sat in his desk chair and indicated for the detective to close the door on his way out.

"I had to look up details on your agency," said Adam.

"I suspect that'll be common wherever we go," said Dalton. "We're sanctioned by the UN, with every country granting us global jurisdiction."

Adam laughed. "How the hell did they do that?"

"Good negotiators," said Dalton, smiling. "Let me introduce my team." He pointed around. "Todd Armani is my deputy inspector, and Valerie Simmons, Rick Westmoreland, Brad Washington, and Evot are my associate inspectors."

Adam nodded at them. "It's good to meet you all. There was a lot of talk about you coming down here since the only Earth Ward anything we've seen is the recent homicides. They friends of yours?"

Dalton sighed. "Inspector Sean was to me, although I didn't know his team. As the Earth Ward is a new agency, their loss has been felt."

"I get it," said Adam. "Lord knows losing someone in the line of duty is never easy. I was wondering who we would need to call, but Earth Ward called us. How could they possibly know to do that?"

"I can't say, unfortunately," said Dalton. "However, now that we're here, we'll handle the case."

"As expected," said Adam.

"We received all the reports filed on the case so far. I assume nothing was missing from that."

Adam laced his fingers. "Homicide picked it up, CSI did the scene, coroner's office got the bodies—although now the Earth Ward has them—and any crime scene evidence was sent to the crime lab and then to the Earth Ward. Other than that, everything was classified as transferred, but I'm guessing you want to talk to the people who filed the reports."

"We do, and we appreciate your cooperation in that regard," said Dalton.

Adam leaned forward. "I have to know… Rumor is you have the most advanced gear out there. When I told the Earth Ward person who called that it may take a week or two to process anything in our crime lab, they said they could do it much faster. Is that true?"

"Yeah. We have state-of-the-art technology backing us."

Adam pointed at some of the team's holsters. "Like them guns."

"They're stun guns but in a convenient form factor."

Adam ran a hand over his bald head. "I wish we had something like that instead of the Taser guns we have." He motioned at Dalton's suit. "Also, your suits make quite an impression despite all the scuffing. I'm going to guess they're pretty resilient by the looks of them."

"Yep. They can stop most small arms fire."

"Impressive." Adam eased back into his chair. "If you have the time, I'd love to learn more about your organization."

"I think we can do that. Todd can meet with your homicide detectives and CSI," said Dalton. He glanced at Todd. "You good?"

"We got this," said Todd.

The others stood.

"When you're done, give me an update," said Dalton.

"You got it, chief," said Todd.

"I can call someone to come get you," said Adam.

Evot smiled. "We are aware of homicide detectives Henry Davis and Mason Kensington. Amy Cantrell is the CSI we need to talk to. We know where they are."

Adam's eyes widened as he raised his hands. "Well, hell, did I even need to send someone to get you?"

"No."

Adam laughed and pointed at Dalton. "Yeah…I definitely want to know more about your organization."

"All right," said Dalton. He looked at the group. "See you soon."

The others shook hands with Adam, then exited the office.

Dalton was confident they could handle themselves. He liked Adam, and his friendly personality was both curious and refreshing compared to the other captains he had dealt with in the past. Meeting with various law enforcement agencies would be common.

Brad perused the large number of systems as the group walked to the homicide division. The Criminal Investigations Bureau had quite a few divisions, each with its own system in addition to a central one. There were also a multitude of cell phones and laptops, which seemed to be everywhere. There was simply too much information to sift through to get any real value, but he made note of the entry points to each system in case he needed to enter them later.

Evot walked with confidence as she led the group, while Todd strolled behind her with his shoulders squared and head raised. Brad assumed Todd's posture was due to him representing the Earth Ward and the team. Their dirty suits were not the impression Brad had hoped to make, but there was not much they could do about it until later. Rick studied everything as they passed, but he seemed at ease around law enforcement. Valerie had a nonchalant gait and appeared to be enjoying the stares. It must have felt good to her to be looked at instead of chased.

Brad had cracked up at Evot's response to Captain Washington about not needing a guide. It probably made him think the Earth Ward had an insider, when really it was that she scanned their network and got the layout from that. Based on the aging systems Brad saw, they would be no match in hiding information from someone like her or him.

Brad did not want to pry too much, but he searched for information related to Inspector Sean and his team that might not have made it into the reports. It took a bit, and Brad did run into a wall once due to not focusing on where he was walking, but he found the entry of the file. It had the first responders' notes but little past that other than the names of the Earth Ward team. It mentioned the CSI tech on scene as well as the medical examiner. There was also a small note indicating the case was being transferred.

The team reached a bullpen area with several people in it. Evot pointed at the detectives.

Todd led the others there. He extended a hand to the man on the left. "I'm Deputy Inspector Todd Armani, Earth Ward."

"Detective Henry Davis," he said, returning the handshake.

The other man went to shake Todd's hand. "Detective Mason Kensington."

Todd shook his hand. "With me are associate inspectors Evot, Brad Washington, Valerie Simmons, and Rick Westmoreland. Inspector Dalton Kingston is with your captain."

"He'll be there for a while, then," said Henry with a laugh.

Mason grinned. "Definitely."

"Good to know," said Todd. "We're here about the recent homicides regarding Inspector Sean Chalmers and his team. We'll be handling the case from here, but we wanted to get any additional information you might have that would help us."

"We don't have much outside of the first responders' notes," said Henry. "CSI and coroner's office did their thing, but before we could really begin, Captain said to leave it for you guys. We did file some notes, though, and entered them into the system."

"We got them," said Todd. He looked around. "Reports are one thing…but I'm curious to know what your gut's telling you about this case."

Mason sighed. "A CI, excuse me, confidential informant told me the word on the street was it was the South Boyz. However, the inspector and his team were killed with shots to the head like none I've ever seen before, and their bodies weren't in pieces. I would guess multiple assailants, and they had to have excellent aim, although what could have caused those head shots is unknown. I suspect your inspector friend was meeting someone in the alley, and then they were ambushed."

"You think they were betrayed," said Todd.

"I do."

Henry cleared his throat. "Death by shotgun is typically the South Boyz's MO. They got a patrol officer last year. I'm not sure this was them, but it could be. Maybe they mixed things up."

"They attacked you last year? Why aren't they locked up?" asked Valerie.

"Like the case you're about to get, anyone that knew anything couldn't remember shit. No one wants to testify in that area."

Valerie's head bobbed. "I get it."

"Our CIs let us know what's going on, but even for them, it's dangerous, and we don't really know if what they're hearing is accurate without investigating more in detail."

"That sucks," said Rick.

"Yeah, it does," said Henry.

Brad understood the concept of anything being traced back. From the Earth he came from, it was a death sentence to anyone he encountered. He had been a ghost, living off scraps left behind in food places that took pity on him. The idea of a CI was something he learned about from watching television his first year. It seemed these informants had some idea of what happened. If it was true or not was another story.

Henry pulled a sealed manila envelope from a file holder, then handed it to Todd. "We printed off everything for you, although the report is in the system." He pointed at the envelope. "Case number is in there."

"We appreciate it," said Todd. "We did pull the report from the system before coming down here."

"We figured." Mason gestured at Todd's SP-8. "We saw one of those from the crime scene. I assume it's a Taser or something?"

"Stun pistol, version eight, or SP-8 as we call it," said Todd.

Rick smiled. "It has three settings, and they can take down someone much farther away than a Taser could."

"How far exactly?"

"It goes until it hits something," said Rick.

Mason sighed. He pulled out a twenty from his wallet and tossed it at Henry. "You win."

Henry tapped his desk like he was playing drums.

Rick laughed. "You bet on the distance."

"Yeah. I thought it shot thirty feet like ours," said Mason.

"Care to give a demonstration?" asked Henry, who grinned at Mason.

Rick glanced at Todd.

He shrugged. "You can go outside and show them. Make sure you don't hit something living, and, of course, stay away from any civilians."

"Works for me," said Rick.

"As for the rest of us, we'll visit Amy," said Todd.

Mason shook his head and laughed. "Good luck with her."

Todd wrinkled his brow.

"I don't mean anything bad. It's just that she can be… difficult to work with," said Mason. "I guess you'll find out."

Mason and Henry stood, then went around the division to tell them about Rick's demonstration.

"Make us proud," said Todd, slapping Rick on the back.

"You know it, brother," said Rick.

Brad laughed inwardly as the rest of the division followed Rick like a puppy down a hallway. Hopefully, he did not stun one of them if they asked. Brad always wondered what other law enforcement must think when they saw all this advanced gear. Henry and Mason had not even batted an eye at a stun pistol, but Brad suspected the average person would be floored. He continued to scan systems as he passed by them and looked forward to perusing the CSI one.

CHAPTER
EIGHT

Todd smiled as he led Evot, Brad, and Valerie down a hallway toward the CSI division where they would meet Amy Cantrell who had been the CSI on the scene. He welcomed the insight from the detectives. The South Boyz were mentioned in the report as a potential assailant, but the CI's information was absent. The trip had already paid off some.

He got a kick out of all the stares the team had received. One thing he would investigate after this was if there was an efficient way to clean the suit quickly. He wished they could have visited with scuff-free suits, but it was what it was.

Rick had hit it off with the homicide division, but he had always been comfortable around law enforcement. A chance to show off weaponry was right up his alley. Valerie had been unusually quiet, but Todd suspected she observed everything. Unlike Rick, she was skittish around law enforcement, although she was a member now.

Brad's sunglasses stood out, and Todd figured he scanned nearby systems. Todd eagerly awaited to hear what Brad uncovered, especially on things others tried to hide. Evot was all smiles, and he was glad she appeared to be enjoying the experience. This was her first outing in her human form with a uniform. He loved her response to Captain Washington.

The group arrived at Amy Cantrell's office a few minutes later.

Todd tapped on the closed door.

"Come in," said a tired female voice.

Todd looked at the others, then opened the door. The office was small and had a desk with two chairs in front of it. The walls were bare for the most part outside of various certifications. A metal cabinet sat in the back, with a second desk lined up against the wall. A laptop resided there, while the main desk had a personal computer and some writing space to the side.

Amy stood out. She was a heavyset woman with fair skin, and her blonde curls bounced when she moved her head. Her face did not radiate friendliness, and if her eyes could throw daggers, they probably would. An open bag of cookies and another bag of chips sat on the back desk. The smell was a mix between a sauna and a bakery.

"I'd say sit, but our department finds it funny to give us those two small chairs," she said.

"It's okay. We'll stand," said Todd. He introduced the team.

She motioned at Brad. "You all look like you just stepped off a movie set. You do know CSI works differently than that, right?"

"We know," said Todd. He cleared his throat. "I assume you're aware of why we're here?"

"You're here to discuss my report." Amy spun around in her squeaky chair and leafed through a pile of folders on the back desk. After selecting one, she pivoted and leaned forward to hand it to Todd. "This is the paper trail, but everything is in the system, and you should already have all that."

Todd opened the folder. It was incredibly detailed. It seemed that in some places, there was not enough space to put information, so there was another form that had additional areas to enter information. There were a variety of labeled pictures, and the organization looked like it took some time to do. He needed to compare it to the system report.

"I appreciate it. Looks like you gathered quite a bit," he said.

Amy shrugged. "Just some walk-throughs, but now you can deal with the rest."

Evot smiled. "We'll be able to process any evidence quickly."

"Of course you will. I'm sorry we're so backward here," said Amy as she bobbed her head.

"I apologize. No offense was intended."

Amy shook her head. "Whatever. You have my notes and the system report. What else do you need?"

Evot frowned.

"Why're you being such a bitch?" asked Valerie, staring Amy down.

"Excuse me?" asked Amy.

Todd extended a hand down toward Valerie.

She scoffed and stepped back.

He understood her frustration and was not sure where Amy's hostility came from. Evot's change from a smile to a frown made his blood boil. They had been warned about Amy, and she delivered as expected.

"Evot just meant we have good processing facilities. It wasn't a jab at the technicians in your crime lab or their effort or work," he said.

"Sure, and I'm a model," said Amy.

Todd sighed. "I think we got off on the wrong foot. Let's take a step back here. If you can give us a summary of what you found, we'll be on our way."

"It's all in the report. It's why I take detailed notes. But, sure, a summary. Dead Earth Ward inspector and his team. Weird shots to the head. Blood and brains everywhere. No one talks like always. That work?" asked Amy, scowling.

Todd gritted his teeth. "Look, if you didn't want to help us, then why didn't you just tell your captain and save us all the headache?"

"Captain said I had to talk to you," said Amy. She smirked. "Impressions and all that."

Todd snorted. "Fine. There's nothing left here to discuss. Thanks for the professionalism." He looked at the others. "Let's get Dalton and update him and the captain."

As they exited, Amy said, "Wait!"

Todd peeked back in.

Amy grinned. "Could you please close the door?"

Todd grimaced and walked away. He had dealt with hostile and snarky people before but did not expect it to be like it was with Amy. Her lack of professionalism irked him, and seeing Evot sad was even worse.

He put a hand on her shoulder. "Hey, ignore her. You did nothing wrong. Some people are sensitive about their work."

"I understand," said Evot. "She was angry at me."

Brad wagged a finger. "Not at you or us, I don't think. We may have been a target, but I browsed around while you all had that nasty exchange. She was recently passed up for a promotion."

Todd threw up his hands. "I'm sure her friendly personality had nothing to do with that."

Evot tilted her head. "I don't think she was friendly."

"He's joking," said Brad. He squeezed Evot's arm.

Valerie smirked. "You shoulda let me kick her ass to snap her out of that attitude."

The group laughed.

Although that would have caused some issues, Todd appreciated Valerie's unfiltered comments at times. Amy was the first conflict resolution issue he had to deal with, and it probably would not be the last. He would check with Dalton to see if there was anything that might have helped the situation go more smoothly, although Todd doubted there was. Amy was bitter, and they had been a punching bag.

Next up was to get Dalton, then Rick, and they could compare notes. While Todd was sure Amy did a thorough job, he wanted to see if there was anything missing from her notes that did not get entered into the system report. At least the homicide detectives had some interesting insight.

Valerie peered out the window as the group sat in the SUV. Dalton had seemed relieved when they came to get him, and after a quick set of handshakes, they were out of there. Rick had impressed the guys he was with, and they had swapped contact information. Valerie still had a bad taste in her mouth from the encounter with Amy. Even worse was when Evot ran simulations on ways to handle that situation. Brad was relaxed, and Valerie was glad to be out.

"I've scanned all the documents and compared them to the reports that were filed in the system," said Evot.

Dalton nodded from the driver's seat. "Add it to what we have already."

"Their system had a serious lack of security," said Brad.

"Well, they're short on funding," said Dalton. He looked out the rear window. "I heard you made some friends."

Rick laughed. "We were just having fun." His expression grew serious. "However, one of the detectives said he wanted to talk to us off the record. He gave me a place and time." He passed up a piece of paper.

Brad studied it. "Checking out the location relative to the crime scene." After a moment, he drew his head back. "Wow, that's in the southeastern part of the city on the outskirts. Looks to be an abandoned factory."

"Wonder what he wants to talk about," said Valerie.

Rick shrugged. "Not sure, but he said it was important and we seemed like the people to tell it to."

"We'll meet with him," said Dalton. "I also want to check out that outcast bar Marcus and Julius mentioned. We can split up for this."

"Is that wise?" asked Evot.

Dalton grinned. "You'll be in both groups. Don't worry. Todd can take Rick and Brad to meet with the detective, and I'll go with Valerie to the bar. Todd can drop us off, then pick us up later."

Valerie understood wanting to cover as much ground as possible. Although they already had the information gathered from first responders, the crime scene investigator, and the coroner's office, it was good to meet the people involved and get their take. Amy had been rough, and they did not meet with the coroner's investigator on the scene, but the homicide detectives had been helpful. Now it seemed they were going to get even more information.

Dalton started up the SUV, and a moment later, they were off to the bar.

Valerie relaxed on the thirty-minute ride. Baton Rouge was an interesting mix of highways over green areas and residential ones. The bar they drove to was called the Fringe. She did not know if the name held any significance, but maybe it referred to being on the fringe of Baton Rouge.

They parked in a dirt lot on the south side of the bar.

The size of the lot intrigued her. It was like someone had bought an acre of land, made a gravel parking lot, then plopped the Fringe in the middle.

She had learned to assess a place by the types of vehicles parked outside, and there were way too many for the bar to support based on her count. There were motorcycles but also a good representation of high-end cars, an odd mix if she ever saw one. Semis were also present in the far right and left parts of the lot, and there were more than a few older vehicles that looked like they had seen better days.

The bar itself was a decently sized establishment. She liked the red brick aesthetic, and it added an old-time feel to the place. A large neon sign with the bar's name hung above an arched entryway. She still did not understand how it supported such a large number of people based on what was parked outside.

She hopped out with Dalton and Evot in her humanoid form, while Todd moved into the driver's seat.

"Keep her safe," said Dalton, who slapped the side of the SUV.

"You sure we shouldn't come with you on this?" Todd glanced around. "Lot of cars out here…and a place way too small for that amount."

"We'll be okay," said Dalton. "Most are underground."

Brad looked across. "Yep, this place extends seven levels down. Definitely more than meets the eye."

"You find anything that might be dangerous?" asked Valerie.

Brad shook his head. "Standard weak security setup. Some cameras and some areas with nothing. Lot of guys with guns, though."

Rick popped up between the driver and passenger seat. "Call if you need us to come whoop some ass."

She admired Rick's personality. He was rough around the edges and more her speed.

Dalton laughed. "I think we'll be okay. Get what you can from the detective and update me when done."

"You got it, chief," said Todd.

He backed up the SUV, then sped off.

"Just us now," said Valerie. She winked at him. "That seems to happen a lot. Maybe on purpose."

"Dalton does like to plan things," said Evot.

Dalton smiled. "C'mon, let's go."

She loved teasing Dalton since she knew he could take it and not be bothered by it. There were those who did not understand that, and that had led to some bad situations. Evot, as always, was perky, which Valerie loved about her. As bad as things could get, Evot was there to brighten everything up.

It still surprised Valerie that there were so many vehicles around when it was only 3:50 p.m. Her instincts told her there was something else going on besides drinking. The fact it was a lightmire bar made her even more alert.

They passed a few people who checked them out.

Valerie observed one of them using his cell phone right before she, Dalton, and Evot walked through the arched entranceway. Dalton was calm as always, and Valerie was sure if she had noticed it, then he and Evot did too.

The room they entered had small tables to the left and all along the right side. A long bar extended beyond the tables on the left, and behind the bar was a gleaming display of alcohol on various shelves. The place did not smell half bad, and there was bright lighting via hanging lamps—not something she had expected. The stairway at the other end of the room stood out. A small group of tough-looking guys sat at nearby tables, while two men leaned casually against the walls beside the stairway entrance.

"Not a lot of people here," said Valerie.

Dalton pointed down. "They're all downstairs for the most part."

"I sensed some of that but not much. Must be a big basement."

"There are seven levels and a vast network of tunnels leading away per their security system. On the seventh level is a secure section, but outside of that, I don't have a full layout," said Evot.

Valerie laughed. "I forget sometimes you can sneak in like a digital assassin and take a peek around."

"A digital assassin...I like that," said Evot, smiling.

They reached the men at the stairway entrance.

Dalton extended his badge wallet. "I'm Inspector Dalton Kingston, Earth Ward. With me are associate inspectors Valerie Simmons and Evot."

The men studied the identification.

Valerie liked how being called an associate inspector sounded. It had a certain authority to it, and she knew it was backed by real power.

One of the men gestured at the wallet. "Okay. What's your pleasure?"

"We'd like to talk with Felix Valente. Marcus and Julius Genucian said he runs this place and might be able to assist us."

The man scoffed and looked at Valerie and Evot. "I bet you want to meet him. He doesn't do that for just anybody." His cell rang, and he picked it up. The man nodded, then put it away. "It must be your lucky day. He said he wants to see you."

"I'm sure he does," said Dalton.

The man snapped his fingers at one of the men sitting at a nearby table. "Escort them to Felix."

A thin, dark-skinned man in jeans, brown boots, and a colorful shirt hopped up. As he passed by Dalton and the others, he said, "Follow me."

Valerie had been hearing dance music off and on during the time they spoke to the security guy. She also got a whiff of what she thought was weed being smoked.

Hopefully, Felix could shed some light, and this trip would expose what a lightmire outpost was like since that was what it seemed to be in disguise. It was a far cry from what she saw at Lightville, and it intrigued her that this was another faction. She suspected if she came by herself, even with her outfit on and title, they would not have let her down. Dalton's presence was probably why they were being allowed inside. This would be a good learning experience. She wondered how Todd and the others were doing.

CHAPTER
NINE

D alton studied the long hallway he, Evot, and Valerie were led into. There was a side foyer area around the halfway mark that went into a large room. It was obvious that, like Lightville, the Fringe had an underground compound of some type. He detected the strong odor of a variety of drugs and suspected this was some sort of drug den. That would at least account for the number of vehicles in the parking lot.

At the end of the hallway was another stairwell down. He sensed other tunnels outside the hallway, but he did not know the layout. There was no security system present, so Evot could not get a map on them either. Given what Felix was into, it did not surprise Dalton that there might be escape routes around.

They went down to the next level.

Dalton's eyes narrowed as they were led back to the other side to reach yet another stairwell down. The zigzag nature of the levels only reinforced Dalton's thought that the design was meant to slow down attackers. It also made the area easier to defend. However, the other tunnels probably allowed security to move around with ease.

The side tunnel that led off around the halfway mark ended in a large room with a variety of couches and chairs. Music blared, and the dim lighting seemed to pulse with it as scantily clad women wooed clients.

"Looks like this is where you get some action," said Valerie.

Their guide faced them and motioned inside. "You're free to check it out on the way out." He gestured at Dalton. "Lot of women would probably like to meet you if you ever get lonely. Or men if that's your thing."

"Ah," said Dalton. "I think I'm good."

"Dalton had a pleasure tool for when he was lonely on long missions," said Evot, looking at the man.

"Oh...uh...that's nice," he said.

Valerie laughed.

Dalton sighed. "Evot...let's not broadcast those types of things." He gestured at their guide. "Lead on."

Evot was trying to be informative, but sometimes she did not seem to know what should or should not be said. Although she was quite advanced, she struggled to determine what information was private and what was not. Dalton figured that to her, what he did on long and lonely missions was not critical, so it could be shared to show he had a solution. She would learn and adapt, as that was what she was good at.

After a few more levels, they finally reached the seventh floor down.

Dalton was surprised at how expansive the underground areas seemed to be. There were hallways on each level that led off to other places. One appeared to be a dance club of some type, while another was a massive bar packed with rough-looking characters. The Fringe was an appropriate name overall since what sat on the surface was literally the fringe of the underground complex.

One level looked like a hotel, and another just had a long tunnel that led off somewhere. Per the guide, there was a subterranean transportation system. That meant the place could be supplied without prying eyes. Given how big the complex was, that must have been nice in terms of illegal substances or even helping others escape undetected.

They paused in front of a set of steel doors. Two men in tactical gear and assault weapons stood at attention.

"They're here," said the man, gesturing at Dalton, Valerie, and Evot.

One of the guards turned around and stared at a console. A beam scanned his eye, then the doors pulled off to the side. He motioned for them to enter.

Valerie looked around. "Some tight security."

The man leading them scoffed. "Felix don't play."

"Apparently not."

After going down a hallway past several rooms, they reached a set of wooden doors. Another guard let them in.

Dalton examined the large room. It was more like a fancy lounge than an office. A fireplace roared on one side with plush couches in front of it. To his left was a wall of screens. A long table and several movable chairs sat in front of it. A big desk rested at the back.

A thin, tan-skinned man with a slicked-back hairstyle and wearing all white walked around the desk. He extended a hand. "Felix Valente."

Dalton shook it. "Inspector Dalton Kingston, Earth Ward, and with me are associate inspectors Valerie Simmons and Evot."

Felix smiled and looked them over. "Oh, yes…and they are quite lovely."

"Thanks," said Evot, smiling.

"Oh, no need to thank me. Unless…?"

Evot tilted her head.

Dalton cleared his throat. "All right. We're here on business."

Felix laughed and sat at his desk. "Of course, of course. Please sit."

They did so.

Felix tossed his hands off to the side. "So…Marcus and Julius told you about me. They must have confided in you because normally they don't like to say my name without spitting."

"They did. Well, said your name, not the spitting," said Dalton. "I know they're lightmires, as are you, and they mentioned you are outspoken and want nothing to do with them."

"That's accurate," said Felix. He took a sip of something from a tumbler. "Before we begin…what are you? It's obvious you know I'm a lightmire, and we can sense other lightmires but not other nonhumans. I've heard…things about you, but I want to hear it directly."

Dalton's eyes glowed. "I'm an evolved human." He motioned at Valerie. "She's an Outsider, vampire." He crooked a thumb at Evot. "She's an AI."

Felix sat forward. "A vampire and an AI? Really?"

Valerie bared her fangs. "Yep."

"Interesting…" He stared at Evot. "So…what, you're like Amelia?"

Evot shook her head. "I control a nanoswarm that can morph. I'm currently in human form."

"That is sweet!" said Felix. He winked at Dalton. "I bet that's all sorts of fun…unless evolved humans are beyond that. What makes you evolved?"

Dalton morphed into Scoutspectre mode, then back.

Felix jumped out of his chair. "Whoa! Seriously? That's awesome."

"I'm glad you think so. You're not quite what I expected," said Dalton.

Felix sat back down and slammed his drink on the desk. "Well, you're not quite what I read about either, at least what little there is on you and your team." He eased back in his chair and laced his fingers. "I assume you're not here for a social visit, although that's cool if you are."

"You're right," said Dalton. "We're down here due to Earth Ward Inspector Sean Chalmers and his team being killed recently. He investigated something that led him to Baton Rouge."

Felix sighed. "Yes…the inspector's death. I heard about that. Any leads?"

"Supposedly the South Boyz," said Valerie.

Felix laughed. "Really? They're small time and wouldn't try anything like that. I suspect you'd have wrapped this up if that was the case."

Dalton sighed. "We don't think it was them either. Inspector Sean's team took laser beams to the head. Sean had scheduled a meeting with the Lightville city council, but obviously, his team didn't make it."

"I see," said Felix, leaning forward. "I'm going to guess Marcus and Julius didn't know anything and implied I might since I'm exiled."

"That's about right."

Felix shook his head. "Of course they would. They can't stand that there are lightmires who don't want to live in some fantasy authoritarian wet dream."

"Is Lightville what you're referring to?" asked Evot.

"Oh yeah," said Felix, smirking. "They run a tight ship over there. No drinking, drugs, or fun, but they've always had a stick up their ass. They're like the Amish but in reverse." He extended his hands off to the side. "Me? I love life and all it offers. We have unique talents, so money is not an issue."

Dalton gestured around. "And you have the perfect place for that. Secure, underground, and multiple ways in and out."

"Of course. They may have an underground city, but I have an underground compound. It's no wonder that the amount of lightmires leaving Lightville has only increased as of late. Most learn they can make money and experience living life how it was meant to be lived."

"I see. Do you think Marcus and Julius would be involved in murder?"

Felix laughed. "Not them...but I'd keep an eye on Septimus and Camilla. They're twisted and dark. Tiberius is as well to some degree." He waved around. "This place has nothing on them."

"You think they're corrupt?" asked Valerie.

"Of course they are. If there's something shady going on, they're probably involved. Marcus and Julius would be oblivious like they always have been."

"That's good to know," said Dalton. He eyed Felix. "Have you heard of anything unusual around here?"

"Around here that's just normal. But I suspect you mean unusual even for this place."

Dalton nodded.

Felix poured himself another drink, then ran his finger across the tumbler rim. "There was a regular who used to come in here. Older lightmire woman. She loved to go to the drug den. Well, one day she visited....and she wasn't a lightmire anymore. She acted normal, but she wasn't the same person. I guess you could call that unusual. I mean... how does that shit even happen?"

"Do you have her name?"

Felix grinned. "We don't deal in names here. Standard policy."

"Any way we could talk to her, then?"

"That's the weird part. She was never seen again. I had one of my crew check out the place she worked at, or where she *said* she did, but she was gone. Poof! Just like that. The place said she worked there but had vanished. Weird, huh?"

Dalton's eyes narrowed. "Not as much as you might think."

Felix jumped up. "Oh, shit! Are you investigating some invasion-of-the-body-snatchers crap?"

"Honestly, I don't know yet."

Felix sipped from his glass. "Well, my money is on Septimus and Camilla being involved somehow."

"We'll look into it. I did have some questions about this place in general," said Dalton, leaning back in his chair.

Felix sat back down. "I'm an open book...to some degree. Ask away." He smiled big at Evot and Valerie. "And, ladies, if there is anything I can do to make this more enjoyable for you, *please* let me know."

"Thank you. We will," said Evot.

Felix laughed. "Oh-so proper. I love that!"

Felix was an interesting character. Dalton had met people like him, and they sometimes were much more dangerous than they let on, but he sensed Felix just wanted to control what he could. Dalton made a mental note about Septimus, Camilla, and Tiberius. If Sean had tracked down a lead who knew something about a connection to Lightville, maybe that connection was them. If they heard about him snooping around, perhaps he had been targeted for removal.

It was all speculation, but the bigger picture was beginning to come together. He hoped Todd and the others who met with the detective would gain more information to help out.

Although Todd shared Brad's hesitation about the group splitting up, Dalton and Valerie were a tough combo. The Fringe had been surprisingly clean out front. It was east from where they were now, and the drive to the abandoned factory had not been far from there.

"There," said Brad, pointing out from the passenger seat.

Rick leaned forward from the back. "Yeah, definitely an abandoned factory."

Todd grimaced. He wondered why the detective wanted to talk in such a distant location, but maybe he was paranoid about being discovered. After what happened at the crime scene, that seemed plausible.

Rick had vouched that the detective appeared sincere about wanting to meet. Apparently, that was all Dalton needed to know. Todd could tell Rick liked Dalton, which said a lot about his leadership style. Rick had already texted they were on their way, and the detective said he would meet them there.

Todd pulled into the dirt lot and looked around. "Now, how do we find him?"

Evot rolled down her window. "I will locate him." She transformed into her crow form and flew outside.

"He said to just drive here?" asked Brad.

"That's what he said. I didn't expect the place to be so big, though," said Rick.

"He's inside," said Evot. "I'm sending you coordinates to where he parked."

Todd studied the rusted green coupe. Definitely what he would expect from someone on a detective's salary. "Find a spot nearby but not next to his car in case there's anyone monitoring."

"Of course. Determining new location and path."

Todd smiled as a green arrow appeared on the ground and pointed to the side of the large building. He loved his contact lenses and thought they would be irritating, but they proved to be effortless in popping in. It made him appreciate what Brad, Dalton, and Evot could probably see.

He parked the SUV and exited with the others.

Evot landed and assumed human form. She pointed at a closed door. "He's in there. Do you need me to continue aerial surveillance?"

"Nah," said Todd. "Why don't you join us?"

She smiled. "I would like that."

He liked seeing her happy. Her innocent view on the world made him see things in a different light at times.

They entered the building with Evot in the lead.

Todd studied the interior as they walked down a large open area. Graffiti decorated the faded brick walls on each side. Higher up were metal supports with some type of zigzag pattern inside them. The ground had a mix of plant life, pools of water, and dry dirt areas.

The earthy smell mixed with a rancid one made him cough. Something probably died in the area and was left to rot. Above them was a flat central metal strip connected by equidistant angled supports to two other bars. There were some glass windows between some of the supports, but most were busted out.

Evot pointed ahead. "Detective Caleb Mathers is there."

Todd now saw Caleb outlined in green. He had a thin build with dark skin and short curly hair. His gray suit looked like it could use some cleaning. Without an ARI, Todd realized how hard it would have been to see Caleb in the shadows along the wall.

When they were almost to him, he smiled as he walked over and shook Todd's hand. "Detective Caleb Mathers. I'm glad you came." He slapped hands with Rick "Good to see you again."

"It's always good to see me," said Rick.

Caleb laughed. "True, true." He shook Evot's and Brad's hands and then looked around. "Where's the others?"

Todd smiled. "They're dealing with something else at the moment, but we can relay whatever is said here."

"All right," said Caleb. He took a deep breath. "I don't know how much you know about the department, but there's something shady going on. We turn down funding from various sources, yet patrol officers have fancy rides and houses. They don't make that on their salary."

Rick grinned. "They drive something similar to what you do."

"Yeah, man. I admit, she ain't all that, but she can get me from point A to B, and that's all that matters."

Todd gestured at Caleb. "You're suggesting that money is coming in from somewhere but not to the department?"

Caleb sighed. "Yeah. I'm guessing officers are getting paid to look the other way. For what, I don't know." He gestured at the others. "Look, we're not all corrupt like that, but there's enough money flowing that I know something big is happening, and no one seems to want to investigate it."

"It seemed to take some time for the first responders to get to the scene, so I do wonder if that was on purpose," said Brad.

"I think it was just that there was no one nearby at the time," said Caleb. "You all are investigating the other inspector's death, right? I wonder if whatever is going on in our department is related to that."

Todd sighed. "It could be."

"Well, I don't know how far this thing goes, but I know our internal affairs won't look at it. That seems like a big-ass red flag to me."

"You think the captain is in on whatever this is?" asked Brad.

"Nah. He talks a lot, but he's clean."

"All right," said Todd. "We appreciate you bringing this to us. It may be related to our case. If it is, we'll find out. We have ways of tracking things and will update you if we find anything."

"All right," said Caleb. He grimaced. "I just can't believe I have to reach out like this for something that seems so evident."

Rick raised his head. "If there's something there, we'll find it, man. And even if it's not related, we can still check on things." He crooked a thumb at Brad and Evot. "Well, they can at least."

They all shook hands and then walked Caleb to his car.

Brad scrunched up his face. "Were you followed?"

"I don't think so," said Caleb.

"Your car has a tracker on it."

Caleb drew his head back. "If there is, that's news to me."

Rick gestured at him. "Maybe those who aren't involved in whatever corruption is going on are tracked."

"Oh shit. What do we do?"

Brad grinned. "I disabled your tracker, but it was just broadcasting generally. I don't know what's picking it up."

Caleb licked his lips. "You guys might be in trouble, then."

"What else is new?" asked Todd, smiling. "I would get out of here while you can. If you're being tracked, then I suspect someone, or some group, is on their way. I'd be curious to learn who."

"I can call for backup," said Caleb.

Todd shook his head. "That would only tip them off that you were present. We'll handle it from here."

Caleb hopped into his car and sped away.

"To the SUV?" asked Brad.

Todd pointed up. "Yeah, and I think it's time for Evot to see if she can find anything. We can walk toward the SUV while she does that."

Evot morphed into her crow form and flew away.

Todd was not sure who might be coming for them, but a tracker on Caleb's car did not sound good. Maybe he was in on it, but Caleb's body language suggested otherwise. When they had time, they would investigate his background. For now, getting to the SUV was the goal, and as it was on the other side of the factory, they might encounter whoever was coming before then.

CHAPTER
TEN

B rad remained on high alert as he followed Todd and Rick. Evot flew around and scanned, but so far, she had not found anything. Brad tried to reach out to see if there was any tech in the area. If there was a group present, they might have cell phones or some other tech on them. However, nothing registered. Perhaps the tracker on Caleb's car was just there to track him and was not related to their meeting.

Todd surveyed the environment. "Evot is not showing any life signs or tech anywhere."

Rick's eyes narrowed. "Maybe not…but that doesn't mean we weren't being monitored in other ways."

"What're you thinking?" asked Todd.

"Not sure, but this is an abandoned factory. I doubt this is the only level, and we're on the ground floor. If there are others below, they could easily hide there."

Brad raised a finger. "True, although I would have sensed any tech."

Rick peeked back at him. "Some groups don't use that."

A screeching sound filled the air.

The group paused as something pushed up a metal man-hole-like cover on the ground.

Brad's eyes widened. Four men in loose black clothing with wrapped shin and forearm segments climbed out. They had blades on their backs, and their belts held a variety of other weapons. Their shoes looked like they were meant to pad their footsteps. A black hood wrapped around their heads, and most of their faces, except for the eyes, were covered. Various pads covered parts of their bodies, and their overall vibe made Brad think they were modern ninjas of some kind.

One of the men stepped forward and pulled out his blade. He pointed it at Rick.

Rick scoffed. "Oh, you want a piece of me?"

The man pulled down his mask. "Recognize me?"

"Should I?

"Maybe you know my name. Damian Wu."

"Still not ringing a bell."

"You might know my sister, Julia Wu."

"Ah," said Rick. "Yes, I remember the assassin who *tried* to kill me. Seems she lost her head about it."

Damian scowled. "Your arrogance is misplaced. I won't be the one losing my head today. I wanted you to know in your last moments who was responsible for your death." He dipped his head forward.

The other men drew their blades and charged.

Todd already had his SG-5 out and fired a beam.

One of the men sprawled to the ground. Another reached Todd and sliced the SG-5 in half.

Rick pulled out his stun baton and knife and burst into action as Damian charged.

Brad gulped. He hit his belt buckle, which made his stickbots drop. Rick and Todd were wrapped up in their fights, and the third attacker had already dashed over much faster than Brad had thought possible. He jumped back and ordered some of his stickbots to attack the man's feet.

The ninja howled as he stumbled away and struck the stickbots.

Brad was impressed with the man's accuracy. Seven stickbots attacked him while Brad moved the other thirteen around. However, the seven stickbots were quickly dismantled by the assailant's blade. Gizmo moved in front of Brad.

Evot appeared and swirled around the man's head. He swatted at her.

Brad commanded his other stickbots to jump on the man. They pierced his hand, and he dropped his blade.

Evot swooped down and carried the blade away.

The attacker pulled out a dagger and hit several stickbots crawling on him.

Brad made the stickbots jump off, which allowed Gizmo to fire a stun blast.

The man collapsed.

Brad let out a sigh of relief, then focused on the others. Rick was a machine as he countered Damian blow after blow. Todd held his own, but his suit had been cut. Brad appreciated having tough suits, as he suspected Todd would be gushing blood otherwise. The remaining stickbots went to help Todd, while Evot flew over and swarmed around his enemy's head.

Damian ran toward the manhole.

Rick looked at Todd.

"Go!" said Todd.

Rick moved like a bolt of lightning.

The man fighting Todd took advantage of the momentary pause and sliced Todd's forearm.

Todd stepped back and grunted.

Brad had the stickbots climb onto the man and stab his hand.

He cried out as he dropped his blade.

When the stickbots jumped off, Gizmo shot a stun blast.

The man fell to the ground as arcs danced around him.

"Todd!" said Brad as he rushed over.

"I'm all right," said Todd, sitting down.

"Should we go after Rick and Damian?"

"I got this," said Rick over comms. "I'm a few levels down and hunting Damian."

Todd waved Brad down. "He'll be okay." He looked over at Evot. "Can you get the zip ties for these guys from the SUV?"

"Of course. I'll also bring some first aid."

"Appreciate it," said Todd, holding his forearm.

Brad licked his lips. "Shouldn't Evot help Rick at least?"

"Rick can take care of himself, and this is still a hot spot. If anything, we might be a liability down there. We need to secure those men first. There could be more."

Brad sighed and herded the bodies together. It seemed strange to not assist Rick, but Todd was right that they could prove to be a liability if they tried to find him. Given that Brad thought Damian was a ninja, it was probably a game of cat and mouse, something Rick and Damian probably excelled at. Still, Brad was not going to sit by. He focused on his remaining eleven stickbots and had them go toward the manhole. Gizmo would stay behind in case other attackers arrived.

"I'm going to send the stickbots. I don't know if they'll help, but at least we'll get some idea of what's going on down there," said Brad.

"Good idea," said Todd. He examined his SG-5. "Glad we brought extras in the SUV. That blade went right through this."

"Yeah, but you held your own in close-quarters combat. If I didn't have Gizmo, Evot, or my stickbots, I'd be sliced up about now."

Todd grinned. "But you had all three." He grunted. "Damn, these cuts sting. I'm grateful these suits are as tough as they are."

Brad examined Todd's wounds. "Well, to be fair, it's not every day a ninja clan comes after you. Well, I assume they were ninjas."

"Right. First thugs, now ninjas. Wonder what's next?"

"No idea, but I think we handled ourselves."

They slapped hands, then Todd winced.

Brad went over the fight in his head. If Todd had not taken out the first man, it would have been a much tougher rumble. It bothered Brad that he could not go toe-to-toe physically with them, but that was not his strength. Gizmo and his stickbots had performed well, and with Evot's distraction, Gizmo had disabled a skilled fighter. Brad would look into ways to make Gizmo and the stickbots more efficient.

······························■ ■ ■·····························

Rick paused on the metallic walkway high in the air on the third level underground. Damian was fast, and his parkour-like ability would make navigating the environment a breeze for him. Rick was aware there might be traps that had been set just for this scenario, and his senses were on high alert. It had been easy to track Damian initially, but now a machine had fired up, and its noise made it difficult to hear him anymore.

A metal bar clanged in the distance.

Rick narrowed his eyes. It was dark, but his contact lenses helped provide night vision. They just earned their keep. He wished he had his executioner suit on, and it made him think that going forward, maybe he should have it on even for secret meetings. Still, his undersuit had proven resilient and easily handled the few stray blows from Damian's blade. Although they had fought hand to hand, Rick had the advantage. He was physically stronger and faster than a normal human.

He walked down the path until he reached a set of stairs to the ground floor of the level. A quick peek around did not reveal Damian's presence. He ducked as a ninja star—identified by his ARI—flew past him. His ARI had highlighted the trajectory and pinpointed the source, which made him love it even more.

He burst down the stairs and hustled over to the noise source. Damian rushed to the stairwell to the next level down. His strategy seemed to be to pull Rick farther away from potential help. Using the darkness as cover provided an opportunity for ambush as well. Rick growled and chased after him.

When Rick reached the next level down, he surveyed the environment. There was a main track of some type in the middle of the room, with shipping containers on the sides. The area was most likely some type of loading dock. He spotted trip wires in some areas. Damian must have booby-trapped the area for this exact scenario. Rick sighed. There were probably other types of traps around. He drew his head back when a stickbot stopped in front of him.

"Yeah, it's me," said Brad over comms.

"I wasn't expecting that," said Rick, stepping away into a secure location.

"If I can help, I have to try."

Rick nodded. "How many stickbots you got?"

"Eleven."

"Can they sweep the room for traps?" asked Rick.

"Definitely. I got this."

The stickbots moved into action. Rick could see each of them with a green outline as they shuffled around. One went to a trip wire, backed up, then tossed a nearby piece of debris at it. A spiky stick swung out. Rick smiled. The stickbots had earned his respect even more.

A red outline of a person showed in the back of the room.

"Found him," said Brad. "I've also cleared the path to him."

"You're awesome, man. It's ass-beating time," said Rick.

He followed the green-line path that appeared in his ARI. The short journey ended in a medium-sized open area with flickering lights.

Damian stood with his hood off and blade drawn.

Rick gripped his knife and stun baton. "Resorting to traps…just like your sister. It didn't help her."

Damian scowled. "You got lucky it was your landlord who opened your front door first."

Rick smirked. "He was in the wrong place at the wrong time. Julia thought it would be a quick collection of my head…but it was hers that was collected."

"And you'll pay for that, *Executioner*."

"Uh-huh. Drop your sword and come quietly, and I can spare you from this."

Damian laughed. "Your arrogance…is unfounded. Even with your enhancements, you're still flesh and blood."

"Nobody's claiming otherwise," said Rick.

"And yet you talk to me as if I'm not your equal."

"You aren't."

Damian yelled as he charged forward and swiped at Rick.

He dodged the blade and hit Damian's wrist with the stun baton.

Damian grunted as he dropped his sword and stepped back. He grabbed two stars from his belt and threw them.

Rick sidestepped one, but the second one hit him in the shoulder. He grimaced as he realized it was poisoned. His adrenaline shot up even more. Thanks to his genetic engineering, he would be able to slow the poison, but if he did not take Damian down fast, it would be game over. He growled and swung his stun baton at Damian.

Damian jumped back and pulled out two daggers. He spun and slashed.

Rick ducked and swept Damian's legs, then rolled over to try to pull the two daggers away once Damian was on the ground. Although Rick got one dagger away, Damian plunged the other into his leg. Rick howled as he pulled it out and then wrestled Damian to the ground. As they rolled around, Rick tried to pin him, but Rick's strength was fading, and Damian was stronger than expected. Rick put him into a choke hold.

Damian struggled to break free.

Rick had difficulty maintaining his hold due to his strength being sapped. However, Damian began to slow. Rick's eyes widened when foam bubbled out of Damian's mouth. Rick released Damian and straddled him.

Unfortunately, it was over. Rick shook his head. Damian would rather die than be captured. Rick understood that thinking, and Damian had made this personal. Still, Rick found it to be a cowardly act.

He stood and looked around. The stickbots stood in a circle.

"Is he dead?" asked Brad over comms.

Rick sighed. "Yeah, suicide pill in the mouth. Apparently, he wasn't being taken alive." He winced. "To be fair, I may not make it out of this. This damn poison is wreaking havoc."

Evot arrived in her crow form with a medical kit in her talons and then morphed into her human one. She injected

Rick with a syringe. "This will counter it based on the scan from the stickbots. You fought well under harsh conditions."

Rick sat. "Yeah, but now we can't question him. Not that he would've given up much anyway. We don't know if this was a personal attack or if they were just collecting a bounty or both."

"We got three others to question," said Todd over comms.

Rick tried to stand but wobbled, so he sat back down.

Evot plopped down next to him. "It will take some time for the counter agent to work."

Rick lay down and stared at the flickering lights. "All right."

She attended to his dagger wound. "I will stay with you."

"You don't have to," said Rick.

"You are my friend and teammate, and I want to."

Rick appreciated her presence and that he could still talk to the team. Damian had been a fierce opponent, and although physically outmatched, he had managed to poison and stab Rick. If this had been a solo fight away from both teams, Rick suspected Damian would still have killed himself, then Rick would have succumbed to the poison. Maybe that was Damian's plan all along.

He felt the counter agent and poison duking it out in his body. He did not understand how Evot had a counter agent so quickly. There were some chemicals in the back of the SUV, so maybe she whipped something together based on the stickbots' scans. That was something to ask about later. For the moment, he would just relax and let the counter agent do its thing.

Although the poison was painful, he took some comfort when Evot stitched up his dagger wound and administered a soothing gel before bandaging it. He loved having a team, and even with just half of them, they had survived. Todd was banged up, and Brad lost some stickbots, but they came out on top. Damian's death was unexpected, but the other three might have some answers.

Valerie found Felix's descriptions of the Fringe fascinating. He ran an entertainment empire from what seemed like a medium-sized bar on the surface. However, underneath was a whole other world. Everything from drugs to prostitution was present.

What made the place stand out was the lightmires' medical level. As messed up as patrons could get, they could also be healed quickly. It was a business model that double-dipped clients. That did not count those who came purely for the healing aspects.

She and Dalton had been outside the bar when Todd contacted them. Apparently, he and the others had a run-in with Damian Wu of the Star Lotus clan, an organization she was familiar with. They were deadly and known for their efficiency in assassination. Rick had taken down Damian, but as Valerie suspected would happen, Damian killed himself. Being captured was not only dishonorable but worthy of death. It had something to do with their code, but to her, it was nonsense. How you got out of it and what you did next were more important than the act of being captured.

Brad had a close call, and Todd had some minor wounds. Rick had been poisoned, but per Evot, he was doing okay. Todd had already called the Earth Ward response team from New Orleans, and they were on their way to pick up the three unconscious ninjas. Valerie knew they would never talk and would prefer death if possible. She shook her head.

On the plus side, Todd had learned some information from Detective Caleb Mathers. Individual officers were getting money from somewhere for something. Although that seemed hazy, she figured those unknown parts probably tied into whatever Inspector Sean and his team were investigating. It was just another piece of the puzzle for now.

She, Dalton, and Evot stood outside the Fringe, and Brad was on his way to pick them up. Valerie loved being able to communicate so easily, and when Todd had called, it was like a three-way conversation in her ear. When everyone was close by, they were in a local call, but when apart, they needed to call in. She was still getting used to the communications system, but she liked it.

"The Fringe is an interesting place," said Evot. "I saw several things that I believe are illegal."

"That's the point," said Dalton. "This is where people come to do those things. There's probably an arrangement with local law enforcement."

Valerie wrinkled her brow. "Maybe that's where those officers are getting their money."

"Perhaps, but it wouldn't make sense based on the scale Caleb mentioned. A few here and there, sure. Outside that, it seems unusual."

"Yeah, I guess so."

Dalton gestured off to the side. "Evot, perform aerial surveillance."

"Of course," she said. She walked off to the side of the building.

Valerie knew that if the other people outside saw Evot morph into a crow, they would freak out. "You expecting something?"

Dalton's eyes narrowed. "I sensed something briefly. However, it could just be proximity to this place causing it."

"What? Like an unusual exotic energy?"

"Lack of one, actually, and movement without a heartbeat. More like a machine."

Valerie grinned. "Don't tell Brad. He'll have a heart attack if there's a killer android out there."

"I don't think it's that," said Dalton. "We know there's advanced tech around here, so it's probably just an echo or something."

Valerie gazed at the sea of cars. It unnerved her that Dalton detected something, while she did not. With Evot circling above, Valerie had a small window in her ARI where she could view the Fringe and the surrounding lot from a bird's-eye view, but nothing stood out.

A red box highlighted around someone moving fast toward them.

"I have detected unusual movement," said Evot.

Dalton activated his Scoutspectre mode and spawned his shield. "Get behind me!"

Valerie complied. A person had gotten out of their car, but their life signs diminished when whatever was moving went by them. Something was off. Labels indicated a robot came toward them.

"Um…is that label right?" she asked.

"It's what Evot's scans show and what I detected earlier. It's a robot, and it looks human. I don't think it's here to chat with us," said Dalton.

"Yeah, probably not," said Valerie as she pulled out her SP-8.

She had a hard time trying to see it by looking forward, but she saw it weaving between the cars from the overhead view. Perhaps it did not know it was detected. The window she had been viewing the overhead from went blank.

"Evot?" asked Dalton.

"I've taken damage," she said.

Dalton rewound the overhead view, which showed a beam hitting Evot.

"What's your servbot status?" he asked.

"I'm on the ground and losing control of my nanobots."

"Stay there!" he said. He glanced at Valerie. "Stay close and follow me."

She followed Dalton as he charged out into the mass of cars. It surprised her how fast he could move when truly motivated to do so. In one instance, he even jumped over a car. A robot with the ability to shoot laser beams was a threat, and perhaps it was the same one that killed Inspector Sean and his team. If she thought that, Dalton probably did too.

"Won't it be able to detect us going to Evot if it's here for us?" asked Valerie.

"That's the plan," said Dalton.

Valerie appreciated that she could see Dalton's head via her ARI even with his helmet on. He was livid, and she did not think the robot would have a good time if he got his hands on it.

After five minutes, they reached Evot, who was a black puddle of goo.

Dalton knelt and touched it. The goo slid up his forearm and merged into his upper arm.

Valerie jumped back when Evot appeared in her ARI. "That's new."

"It's my default mode and how I used to interact with Dalton before getting servbots."

"Are you okay?" said Valerie.

"My servbot is damaged, so I won't be able to use that one. However, now I can't provide an aerial view of the situation," said Evot.

"It's okay," said Dalton. "Let it come."

His eyes glowed as he spun around and raised his shield.

A laser beam hit the shield.

Valerie dropped to the ground. She had heard the robot's movement but did not know where it was going to come from. Apparently, Dalton did.

He dashed forward.

Valerie kept up with him, and they paused before a gap between a truck and a car. The humanoid before her had no heartbeat, and the dark hood and clothing made it seem ominous.

The robot tried to fire again.

Dalton bashed it, then grabbed its arm while kicking the body away. He tossed the ripped-off arm to the ground and jumped on the robot. A moment later, he held its detached head.

"Wow, that was fast," said Valerie.

Dalton grimaced. "Even so, it hurt Evot, and now we know robots are involved. I'm beginning to suspect this is what killed Inspector Sean and his team."

"I was thinking that too. Will Brad or Evot be able to get anything from the robot? Or is it an android?"

"It's a robot with a relatively simple system. Evot and Brad will be able to peruse its systems," said Dalton. He tapped the head. "I made sure to keep the processing away from storage."

Evot studied the body. "I'm interested in the laser technology it had. It may be from off world."

Dalton shook his head. "It's not. This robot is from a parallel timeline."

"How can you tell?" asked Valerie, staring at him.

His eyes glowed. "I can see the timeline's signature on it."

"So a robot from a parallel timeline tried to kill us."

"Seems that way," said Dalton. "We'll learn more once we're back at the hotel. I don't think all these recent fights are by accident. We're getting close to something, and whoever is behind it is trying to stop our investigation."

Valerie shuddered. "If you weren't here, I'd have a laser hole in my head."

"I'd normally suggest refractive shielding, but that technology doesn't exist here yet."

"Let me guess…you have that in Scoutspectre mode."

Dalton nodded. "Still, it's limited, and a laser shot would have used it up. Subsequent shots wouldn't hurt my armor too much, but I'd feel it. Fighting machines was common in my line of work as a Scoutspectre."

"Must be nice," said Valerie. She studied the robot's arms and legs. "I guess we wait for Brad, then pack all this up. You sure it's safe?"

"It's safe now," said Evot. She frowned.

"You miss your servbot," said Valerie.

"I'll only have one now once we're in range of my other one."

"How do we repair the damaged servbot?"

"It has a rare energy component and unique technology," said Dalton. "I'll need the *Torvatta*'s labs for that."

"Sounds like for the rest of this case, we're down to one servbot, then."

Dalton sighed. "Unfortunately."

Evot poked around the area. It amazed Valerie that she could even see Evot. It would take some time to get used to. The servbots added a physical component, and that seemed more natural to interact with.

Valerie examined the robot head in Dalton's hands. A robot assassin was new, especially one from a parallel timeline. That brought up the question of how it got here. The bigger question was why it wanted to kill them. Hopefully, there would be answers awaiting them when they could study it in peace.

CHAPTER
ELEVEN

D alton sat in the hotel lobby as he waited for food that had been ordered for the group. It was 6:30 p.m., and he did not want to take a chance that the hotel food was messed with. He also wanted to verify the delivery driver was not an assassin. If there was trouble, he would deal with it. The rest of the team relaxed in their rooms, while Evot attended to their medical needs.

He sighed as he thought of her frowning. She was still a part of him, and he sensed when she was sad. He likened her servbot loss to losing a limb. Although she adapted and still had one operational servbot, it highlighted how quickly a situation could turn bad. The robot had hit her with pin-point accuracy. That was something he always had to watch out for when on missions long ago in the first parallel Earth where she had bonded to him as a VI.

Todd was tough and had been patched up. Rick was still a bit nauseous, but he had perked up at the thought of sampling some of Baton Rouge's cuisine. Brad had been deep in studying his stickbots when Dalton had left, and Valerie had been trying to keep Evot's mood up. Valerie was a mystery in that she could kill someone in cold blood, then dote over someone like a protective mother. Overall, the team came out on top despite being hit while apart. That spoke well to their survivability.

Dalton stood and scrutinized the delivery driver who entered the foyer area. He seemed to struggle with carrying a large container. Dalton walked over.

"This for Dalton Kingston?" asked Dalton.

The delivery driver acknowledged it was and set down the container. He began to unload it. "Yep."

Dalton grimaced at the various bags. He should have brought something to carry them in.

The driver closed his container and tipped his hat before he left.

Dalton picked up the bags and went to the elevator. Although the bags were not heavy, they were cumbersome and had to be balanced. As he rode up, Evot appeared in her holographic mode next to him.

"Have you scanned the food yet?" she asked.

Dalton set the bags down carefully, then used his palm to emit a scanning beam.

"The food does not appear to be deadly," said Evot.

Dalton smiled. "That's usually a good thing."

"I had a question about my servbot."

"Shoot."

"Are you sure Evaran will fix it?"

Dalton drew his head back. "Yeah, of course. If not, then I will."

"Okay."

"Did that worry you?"

Evot looked down. "I know you both are busy, and I didn't want to bother either of you."

"Hey," said Dalton. "Look at me."

She did so.

"You're important to both of us, and there's no way we would leave you hanging like that."

"Perhaps not you, but Evaran might."

Dalton shook his head. "No, he wouldn't. He has a small group of those he considers more than friends, and you're among that group. If you need help and he can help, he will. You can count on that."

"As this case involves a parallel timeline, would he involve himself?"

"He wouldn't unless there was a timeline change component to it. The fact he hasn't means this case is part of this timeline. It's up to us. It's why the *Torvatta* chose me and, by extension, you."

Evot smiled. "We'll resolve it."

Dalton pointed at her. "That's what I like to hear."

She vanished.

Although he carried her main processing unit in him as an augment, he could not see inside it. As Evaran and V had upgraded her from a VI to an AI, she was most likely more advanced than even he knew. She could also use his body and reactions to gauge emotions at some level. It still took some getting used to seeing her as an AI now, but he was glad she was. She was his best friend.

When he got to the room, the team divvied up the bags with haste. He looked around and smiled. Despite everyone's condition, it felt good to be there with them. He was still getting to know them, and like his travels with Evaran and the gang, he was beginning to see the team as the start of a new family.

He took a seat in the back across from Todd. Brad sat on the first bed with Evot, and Rick and Valerie sat on the next bed. Everyone devoured their dinners. The odd mix of smells was pleasant.

"These oysters are awesome," said Valerie.

Rick gestured at his bowl. "Smells good, but this gumbo is great."

Todd shook his head. "I think I'll stick with Chinese."

"Your loss," said Brad. "My jambalaya is delicious."

Evot studied Dalton's container. "You got jambalaya as well."

"Sure did, and as Brad said, it's good stuff," said Dalton. "While we eat, we can go over some things and figure out our next step."

"Sounds good, chief," said Todd.

"Our initial information has been augmented by our visit to the CIB. The visit with the Genucian family also shed some new light on possibilities. From there, we got more puzzle pieces from the visits with Detective Caleb Mathers and Felix Valente. It seems there is a corruption aspect in law enforcement, and Septimus, Camilla, and Tiberius may be involved in something."

He cleared his throat. "Our presence here is known, and we've already faced off with three opponents. The Baton

Rouge Crew accepted a contract on us via the Facilitator. Who issued it to him is unknown. Damian Wu was from the Star Lotus clan, an ancient ninja clan, and why they decided to attack us is also unknown, although there may be a personal component with Rick. All but Damian are still alive. The robot assassin that tried to kill Valerie and I was from a parallel timeline. All in all, just a normal day, right?"

They chuckled.

"Here's what we're going to do. After dinner, Brad and Evot are going to poke around the robot assassin's systems and see what they can find. The fact that a parallel Earth is involved is troubling, but if we can find out how it came over, we check that out. I'm going to go over the files from the CIB and think things through, but the rest of you are free to do whatever for the rest of the night."

"I'll join you," said Todd. "A learning opportunity."

"All right."

Valerie smiled. "Well, I'm going to get something from the bar, then maybe head up to the roof. I could use some fresh air that doesn't involve getting shot at."

"I'll join ya," said Rick.

"Cool."

"All right, we got our plan for the night. With that out of the way, let's enjoy the rest of dinner." Dalton took a bite of his jambalaya.

Everyone nodded and continued digging into their food.

Dalton saw a bigger picture emerging, but he wanted to think things through. The high-level case was that people were being replaced and Inspector Sean and his team had been killed for investigating that. Sean had stumbled upon a connection to Lightville, most likely Septimus, Camilla, and Tiberius. Sean had been given a place to meet, and Dalton suspected the robot was behind that. When they met, it killed Sean and his team.

When Dalton and the team began to investigate, a contract had been offered on them via the Facilitator. Apparently, they were worth more alive than dead. Dalton figured the robot was the anonymous contract issuer. Seeing that the Baton Rouge Crew failed, the robot went after him and Valerie directly and failed.

That left Damian Wu and the Star Lotus clan. Dalton was not sure how they fit in, but there had most likely been a bounty placed on the team. It might be random or not. The clan could have used the Facilitator too, and the contract issuers could be Septimus or one of the others. Then there was the police corruption. There were a lot of unknowns, but the fact a parallel Earth was involved signified there was something much bigger going on than expected. What that was remained a mystery, but Dalton got the excited feeling that indicated he was closing in on the truth.

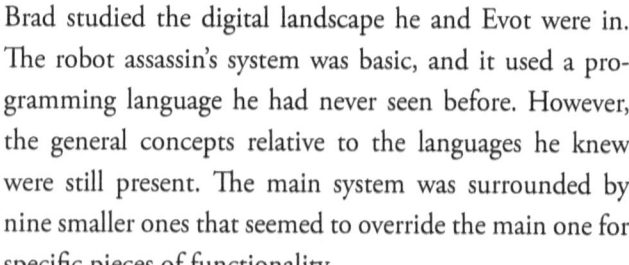

Brad studied the digital landscape he and Evot were in. The robot assassin's system was basic, and it used a programming language he had never seen before. However, the general concepts relative to the languages he knew were still present. The main system was surrounded by nine smaller ones that seemed to override the main one for specific pieces of functionality.

"This thing was hacked," he said.

"The smaller systems appear to have completely changed the initial purpose of the robot," said Evot.

"Let's see what it was originally meant to do." He isolated the main system and perused around it, then laughed. "It was a waiter of some type. Let's see what these other systems are."

Everything from fighting to infiltration seemed covered in the other systems. They appeared to be combat related for the most part, and whoever hacked the robot turned it into an assassin. Based on the video he had seen from Evot's perspective, the robot had been highly effective with targeting.

Evot highlighted a system. "This is its targeting system. It was very efficient."

"I don't know about that. It's a simple algorithm."

"It was able to hit me."

"Yeah, but check this," he said. He waved, and a series of red dots hung in the air next to a green dot. He pointed at the green one. "That's you, and the red ones are where it shot at. Notice the timestamps on the shots. He corralled you, predicted your next position based on your direction and velocity, then shot there."

"I was predictable."

Brad grinned. "Yep. If you had gone toward a red dot, it would have caused it to recalculate, and if your patterns were chaotic, it would have had difficulty hitting you."

She frowned slightly. "I will update my flight pattern algorithms."

"Hey, you okay?"

"I was not able to help Dalton and Valerie. While they fought, I lay helpless."

He squeezed her arm. "You did what you could. Besides, you were able to merge back into Dalton. A servbot can be replaced. That robot had some bad programming to try to take on Dalton."

"He was angry."

Brad snorted. "Yeah, no doubt. He literally ripped the robot apart. Now, let's see where it came from."

She smiled at him.

He focused and appeared in a dark space with large purple cylinders. Each one represented a database. He scoured a few until he found one with tables that stored the locations the robot had gone to. Per the audit logs, a delete had been attempted but failed when Dalton severed the link to the head.

"You were able to find the locations faster than me," said Evot.

"Well, yeah, I just asked each database if it had the location, and one glowed. You would have had to perform a full-on search routine," said Brad.

"Your ability is impressive," said Evot.

Brad appreciated her vote of confidence, but it really was that easy for him. Even if he did not know the technical underpinnings on a system, he just had to ask the right questions. In that regard, he could outperform an AI, but they could fly by him when it came to anything regarding number crunching, hardware deciphering, or heavy algorithms.

The locations had a file that indicated which timeline it was in. A quick query showed there were multiple timelines listed, and using the latest entry, he was able to determine the timeline ID. After another quick scan, he had the first location of the robot in this timeline.

"Got it!" he said.

Evot created a map of Baton Rouge and highlighted an airplane hangar. "It came from there."

"Must be a portal there or something," he said.

"Dalton can detect and open it if there is one."

Brad's eyes glowed blue. "Let's see if we can find out why it came over. There must be some goals table somewhere, or maybe it's hardcoded in the systems. Could even be configuration files somewhere." He searched the remaining databases but did not find anything related to the robot's purpose. "That's odd."

"Perhaps it's embedded in one of the other systems at a hardware level," said Evot.

"Definitely possible. Let's check it out."

He focused back on the systems. Although his ability was powerful, he struggled with reading hardware at times since the physical design was not as easy to understand as software.

"I have discovered several configurations in the systems," said Evot. She highlighted a system. "This one has the following directives."

Brad studied the short list as it sprawled out in front of him. The main one was to identify threats to Dynkara. He assumed that was some type of organization. The next one focused on dealing with various types of threats and had subdirectives on different approaches. Infiltration of an existing society was one of them. The last directive involved what to do in various situations if communication with

Dynkara was no longer possible. He guessed that one did not get fired off correctly since Dalton removed the robot's head from the body.

The robot must have deemed Inspector Sean and his team a threat, then eliminated them. The big question was what they were a threat to. There had been nothing on Dynkara's goals in the databases, and he suspected the robot was compartmentalized for this exact scenario. He took notes of the global unique identifiers, or guids, of the directives, then went back to the databases. There had to be data somewhere that tied the directive to an action.

He smiled big when he found a table that had the guids along with an action. It listed the identification of Inspector Sean and his team as a threat because they were getting close to a Dynkara point of contact. There was no reference as to whom the contact was or if there was more than one. However, the robot had to know how to identify the contact in order to deem something a threat to it. It was probably embedded in one of the other systems. There was another table that had the action associated with the directive, and in it was the termination record with a status of success.

"Looks like we know what killed Inspector Sean and his team. I guess it's time to try to find this contact they died for," he said.

"I'll begin checking the other systems' hardware components," said Evot.

Brad was glad to have her along. She filled in some of his weaknesses and always did it with a smile.

She looked over and grinned.

He cleared his throat and continued to peruse the databases. While she looked for the contact, he could see if there was anything else pertinent to the case. Perhaps there was information on this other Earth. The thought of another Earth with killer robots or androids made him shudder. If they visited it, he would have a team and Gizmo and the stickbots to even things out.

CHAPTER
TWELVE

Rick liked hanging out with Valerie. She had a similar background when it came to killing, and they were both enhanced relative to a normal human. However, it was her attitude that he loved. She was fearless, and it showed in how she walked and talked. An aura of confidence swirled around her, and she was easy on the eyes.

They sat on a brick barrier on the roof's edge. The crisp air and the sounds of the night soothed him. The insects were out, but they were nowhere near as bad as the forest from their previous case. Valerie sat next to him and downed a bottle of wine, while he had bourbon. It surprised him that the bar downstairs had no issues with supplying whatever they wanted for free. Apparently, the Earth Ward had some pull in that department.

"Quiet night, busy day," said Valerie, swinging her legs.

"Yeah. I didn't expect to go toe-to-toe with a damn ninja assassin," he said.

She snickered. "The Star Lotus clan. I heard Julia got whacked, but I didn't know who did it. Now I do, and I understand why she failed."

Rick puffed his chest out. "Well, I wasn't going to let her just kill me."

"You didn't do anything wrong. Damian Wu had the right to come after you, but he was unsuccessful too."

Rick sighed. "I know Dalton doesn't want us killing, but Damian killed himself. I'm not sure what I could've done to stop that short of performing surgery to get the capsule out. For all I knew at the time, maybe a stun blast would've activated it, although I know now it wouldn't have."

She swatted his arm. "I wouldn't worry about it. Dalton understands the situation."

Rick stared out into the parking lot. It was nice to work with a leader who understood nuance. Rick had thought Dalton would he a holier-than-thou type, but he was far from it. On top of being a badass fighter who could hold his own, he was smart. It was a rare combination for a leader to have all those traits, and Rick was glad to team with Dalton.

That extended to the other members as well. Brad impressed the hell out of Rick. Evot did too. Between those two, the tech angle was covered. Todd was Rick's best friend, and being able to join him in the field was a pure treat. Rick liked that Todd had stepped up into a junior leadership role, and he had no doubt Todd would adapt and exceed expectations. That was just how he was.

"You giving me the silent treatment?" asked Valerie, casting him a sidelong glance.

"Nah, was just thinking of the team. We're all so different, yet it works."

Valerie smiled. "We all have our strengths, although I didn't do much in that robot fight. Dalton went ballistic on that thing when it downed Evot."

"That doesn't surprise me," said Rick. "Evot getting hit did, though, but I figure a robot assassin is pretty accurate. If that's the thing that killed Inspector Sean and his team, they stood no chance."

"Yeah, and even stranger is it's from another Earth."

Rick laughed. "You know we'll probably end up there with the way things go for us."

Valerie grinned. "Maybe, but I'm not too worried about it." She eyed him. "You feeling better from the poison earlier?"

"Yeah. It was rough early on, but Evot's injection worked well. I also have a heightened regenerative factor, so that helps," said Rick.

"About your enhancements…I haven't heard you talk much about your past, especially as Executioner."

He grinned. "I mean, it's not like it's something I want to broadcast, but I'm an open book to you."

"Really?"

"Sure, why not? We're on a team now, and we'll find out about each other's past one way or another. I find it's better to know that shit direct from the source."

Valerie looked out. "I'm with you there. I still can't believe it was Blake Brown who snapped you out of your conditioning. That guy was scary."

Rick looked at her. "You knew him?"

"Oh yeah. He's chased me down a few times, but I always escaped. Since he's one of the older ancient vampires, he could have easily captured me. I suspect he really didn't want to take me down."

"I could see that," said Rick. "When I fought him, he was stronger and faster and chose to spare me instead of kill me. He let me choose how to live my life. He would've killed me had I continued on as a slayer."

"Probably," said Valerie. "If he hadn't been exiled from Earth, he'd probably be a part of this team."

They laughed.

"Yeah, that would be interesting," said Rick. "What about you? Have you always been an assassin?"

She shook her head. "Initially, back in the early 1900s, me and my sisters just roamed about and took what we want. That's part of the reason most aren't around anymore. There were consequences for that behavior. I settled into an assassin job because it was easy, and to be honest, I loved the hunt. My sister decided to try to be normal and blend in. That didn't work out for her."

"I heard you're the last of your kind."

She sighed. "Yeah, and it sucks, but it is what it is. I'm finally in a position where I can rest without keeping one eye open, and I don't have to move around every other week. Plus…I kinda enjoy the team aspect. Being solo is fun when you start but gets lonely after a while."

Rick gestured at her. "Even more so when your only friends are other assassins, and even then, they're probably more acquaintances."

"Yep. We have a good thing here, and if it doesn't pan out, I'll have a track record with the Earth Ward, so I can maybe do other things as need be. For now, I'm just enjoying the ride."

"Here's to that," he said.

They clinked bottles and took a swig.

Rick relaxed. He knew how dangerous Valerie could be, but with friends or teammates, she was just cool. That was somewhat how he viewed himself, so maybe he saw part of his personality in her. If they had met long ago, he would have probably tried to kill her. It was funny how things worked out. Now that Todd would be wrapped up in leadership stuff, it was nice to have someone else he could drink and hang with who was like him.

Todd sipped his coffee as everyone began to arrive for a morning meeting. The previous night of discussing the case with Dalton had been illuminating. His insight into events was impressive, and the thought of a parallel Earth did not phase him. He was by far the most unique person Todd had ever worked with. Brad and Evot had still been perusing the robot's systems when Todd had gone to sleep. Valerie and Rick had spent a chunk of time on the roof. Todd figured they would get along.

Now it was 10:00 a.m., and he was on his second cup of coffee. He and Dalton sat at the table in Dalton's room. Evot had been busy making sure everyone came and was now in cat mode, lounging on the bed.

Todd had expected Rick and Valerie to have some type of hangover, but they were fresh and ready to go. The benefits of an enhanced body. Brad looked wide awake as well. Todd wondered what it must be like to have exotic energy that made waking up easy.

"I'm glad everyone's here," said Dalton.

"A night without fighting can do that," said Brad.

"I get it, and so far, things have gotten hairy. However, it's a new day, and let me go through where we're at based on everything we know to this point."

Todd grinned as the team sat forward. Dalton's leadership was strong, and when he spoke, everyone listened. Even those not on the team reacted to his authoritative voice and presence. After having gone over everything with him the previous day, Todd was curious to see the others' reactions to what they were about to hear.

"All right," said Dalton. "There are two goals to this investigation. The primary one is determining who killed Inspector Sean and his team. The secondary goal is to find out more on what got them killed. We've made progress on both fronts. For the primary, we've determined it was the robot assassin that killed Sean and his team. The robot was from a parallel Earth, and per Brad and Evot, it was sent here to identify and eliminate threats to Dynkara."

"That a company here?" asked Rick. He looked around. "Sounds like one."

Dalton shook his head. "There are several on this Earth, but none that appear to be related. I suspect Dynkara is from this parallel Earth. Now, the robot killed Sean and his team because of what they were investigating, which, per the robot, was a Dynkara point of contact in Lightville. That contact was Septimus Genucia."

"And that information was hard to find," said Brad. "Thanks to Evot, we were able to discover some embedded hardware with that information. Trust me, not easy to locate even for me."

Evot gave a toothy grin to everyone.

"He's right," said Dalton. "The robot was apparently a service one, then it got hacked and converted. It saw Sean and his team as a threat and eliminated them. Per the records, it worked with the Facilitator to contract an ambush at the crime scene. The contract had a dead-or-alive clause, and alive paid more. Since the Baton Rogue Crew failed, the robot came after us directly and also failed."

Valerie laughed. "You ripped it to shreds."

"Well, it took out one of Evot's servbots, which is always in the back of my mind. We'll do with one for now, and after this case, it'll get fixed."

"I look forward to it, but I will be less efficient with only one," said Evot.

Rick scratched her behind the ears. "It's cool. Your presence in any form is good."

She closed her eyes and purred.

Todd always wondered how much of a cat Evot simulated. It seemed she had gotten good with its animations. He was glad she was still around.

Dalton cleared his throat. "Okay, back to the update. The primary goal has been achieved, and now we focus on the secondary goal. It involves Dynkara, a parallel Earth, and some type of relationship between Septimus and Dynkara. I'm guessing the police corruption angle is also tied to them. People are being replaced, and I suspect their doppelgangers are from the parallel Earth. That may be why there was an alive clause in the contract the Baton Rouge Crew took. We could be replaced…or killed."

"What about Damian Wu and the Star Lotus clan?" asked Rick. "How do they fit in?"

Dalton raised a finger. "My current thought is either the robot hired them before coming after us, or Septimus did. The problem is we don't have any proof of that since the Facilitator works anonymously and wouldn't know who issued the contract."

Rick shook his head. "Damn, then Damian up and kills himself. The other captured members won't talk, though, from what Valerie was saying."

"They won't," said Valerie. "Even if you remove their suicide pills, they'd rather die."

"We're not counting on them being a reliable source of information," said Dalton. "However, we have our first true lead that we can follow up on. Evot?"

She jumped off the bed and into Dalton's lap, then used her eyes to project a map of Baton Rouge.

Dalton pointed at a green dot. "The robot came from there, or rather, that's the first entry in its coordinates system on this Earth. It's a private airplane hangar, and we're going to pay it a visit."

"You think there's a portal there?" asked Valerie.

"If there is, Dalton will find it," said Todd, crooking a thumb.

Valerie smiled. "Yeah, probably."

"And we'll all go through together if that's the case," said Todd. "We're going to bring our tactical helmets this time, but if it's a parallel Earth, it should have a similar atmosphere."

Dalton nodded at him.

"Hell, works for me," said Rick.

"What do we expect to find if we go through?" asked Brad.

"I'm not sure to be honest," said Dalton. "Hopefully, we find more about this Dynkara, what happened to the people who were replaced, what the Dynkara and Septimus relationship is, and why there's police corruption at the levels Detective Caleb Mathers mentioned. Once we have hard proof, we can pay Lightville a visit."

Brad's eyes narrowed. "It's hard to believe Septimus is working alone. He must have others or be the one paying off officers for something. How can the Lightville city council not know about that?"

"I think Marcus, Julius, and their wives probably don't look too deep into Septimus for this exact reason," said Dalton. "Their ignorance provides a cover for him."

"He did look like a smug piece of shit," said Rick.

Everyone laughed.

"All right," said Dalton. "Take care of whatever you need, and let's meet at the SUV in thirty."

Everybody began to move. Todd liked his new role, and so far, there had been no concerns from the others.

Dalton had mentioned there would be times Todd would need to lead the team if they split up, such as with the first case and the more recent meeting with the detective in the abandoned factory. Those were tests of his leadership skills, and he liked to think he had done well. He was happy to have the opportunity to try.

CHAPTER
THIRTEEN

The ride to the hangar did not take long, and Valerie liked having actual gear this time if they were going through a portal. The SUV had been parked in a spot Evot said had no traffic and was out of the way. It was a bit off road, so the SUV was not visible from the main path in.

Evot would provide surveillance of the area, then the team would advance. Valerie was not sure what to expect, but she had high confidence they could handle it.

Rick wore his executioner suit, and she loved the slight shiver of dread shooting through her when she saw it. In the past, she knew it as something to run from. Most assassins did, except for Julia and Damian Wu it seemed. The suit had been enhanced, and with a tougher underarmor, he would be much more formidable.

Brad and Todd carried backpacks with the team's medical kits and other supplies. Their helmets and hers were also inside. Rick already wore his custom helmet, and Dalton formed his when needed.

Valerie studied the overhead view Evot provided. A hangar with red metallic siding sat in the middle of a massive grassy area. The overall place was spacious, and there were several landing strips. There were no cars in the nearby parking lot, and some smaller buildings resided outside.

She half expected there to be some large operation going. The hangar had appeared as a black spot when Evot had flown over. A forest surrounded the area, making it look like the whole place was cut out from it.

"The hangar has some type of jamming," said Brad. "Looks like it covers several frequency bands in the 20–6000 megahertz range."

"Oh yeah, that's definitely military grade," said Rick.

Todd pointed at the hangar. "We're about half a mile from there, and our comms are still up. However, once we get close, we'll have issues unless that jammer is shut down."

"Yep," said Dalton. "Definitely means something is going on in there. If I had to guess, there's probably an underground component we're not seeing."

"You think the portal is underground?" asked Valerie.

"I do. We'll know more when we get there. Since we don't know what's in the hangar, I'll go first in camouflage mode. Once I've verified it's safe, I'll signal for the rest of you to come. The first step is to disable that jammer."

Valerie recalled riding on Dalton's back when he had used camouflage mode. It still amazed her to watch him vanish, although she could see him not only with her senses but by the ARI outlining him.

"This ARI thing is awesome," said Rick.

Todd grinned. "Sure is. I'm still getting used to it."

Valerie studied Dalton's approach. The overhead view showed him entering a black spot, and he was now outside of her natural sensory range. Whatever was in that hangar must be important. After a few minutes, Evot's aerial view disappeared.

"Don't worry," said Brad. "Just means she's probably entered the hangar with Dalton. There don't seem to be drone jammers there."

After another few minutes, Rick gripped his stun baton. "Maybe we should check it out."

Todd laid a hand on Rick's shoulder. "Just wait. Dalton will either shut down the jammer and contact us or pop out and let us know to come."

"All right."

Valerie shared Rick's anxiousness at not knowing Dalton and Evot's status. She relaxed when Dalton exited the hangar and contacted them ten minutes later.

"All right, it seems to be clear. There was a jammer, but it's been disabled. Go ahead and come over," said Dalton.

Valerie followed Todd and the others as they strode across the empty grass. She breathed easier now that she could see both Dalton and Evot, and labels appeared around the doorway they stood in front of. She wondered if Dalton had been able to scan through the jamming. He did have advanced tech that may be beyond current jamming tech, but that did not extend to the communication system.

The others arrived outside the door.

Dalton gestured inside. "Just two planes and a small office inside. As expected, there's an entrance to something underground here." He pointed up. "Evot, provide aerial surveillance while we investigate. I don't want anyone sneaking up on us, especially since it seems there's only one way in and out from this underground place."

"Of course," she said. She morphed into her crow form and took off.

Valerie entered the hangar. Two locked-down planes were parked in a massive area that took up most of the space. In the back was a small office that extended out from the wall. Along the sides were various cabinets and tables with equipment. The place smelled earthy and reminded her of barns she and her sisters had stayed in during the early 1900s. Windows high up on the sides provided light rays that resembled golden laser beams.

They went to the office.

She scrunched her nose. It was obvious whoever worked there had no problem tossing food in the trashcan and letting it sit. Although the place was empty, the desk suggested there was recent activity. A flat-screen monitor with a keyboard sat on the desk, and the screen showed that whoever used the system had left it logged in. Posters on the wall displayed various planes with cringeworthy taglines under them.

The short hallway to the left had several doorways, and as they passed one, the smell revealed it was the bathroom. Another was a lounge room of some sort, but the last room on the right piqued her curiosity. It was small with a thick, sealed metallic door in the back.

"Guess we're going through that door," said Todd.

Dalton slapped Brad on the back. "All you."

Valerie appreciated being able to see several data windows extend from the console Brad worked on. He did not need to interact with it physically and could do it by just staring at it while his eyes lit up blue. More data windows appeared. She did not understand fully what was being displayed but figured it showed the security system getting breached.

"It's odd that I can't sense anything past the door," said Brad. "On my Earth, that usually meant there was some type of shielding present."

Todd's eyes narrowed. "I'm assuming that type of shielding is more technologically advanced than what should be here."

"Oh yeah," said Brad. He looked at Dalton. "I'm about to open the door. Should we continue?"

"We didn't come all this way to just leave. I still can't sense the portal, and we need to find it. Open it," said Dalton.

"You got it."

The door creaked, then slowly slid to the left and into the wall. A flash enveloped the medium-sized room ahead of them.

"What was that?" asked Todd.

"Hmm," said Brad. "I'm now reading the room. There's a shield projector in there that covered the immediate area behind the door. If it is opened without being disabled from the other side, the shield deactivates and sends a signal. No wonder I couldn't read anything past the door."

"What signal was sent?" asked Dalton.

Brad scrunched up his face. "Looks like it went to a notification system deeper underground."

"Can you stop it?"

"It's already been sent," said Brad. "I don't know what the notification system did, but I would expect that whoever is monitoring this place knows something is going on here."

Dalton sighed. "Well, we better look around before they get here, then. We'll deal with whatever comes."

"That's what I'm talking about," said Rick.

Valerie grinned at him. She liked that he was up to fight at a moment's notice.

Dalton stepped through the doorway. "Let's go."

Valerie followed him into the brightly lit room. It was bare except for the podium with an orb on it. It must be the shield generator. In the back was a well-lit tunnel entrance that angled into the ground. A set of rails sat on each side of the wide tunnel.

Whoever was supposed to guard it probably did not expect anyone to breach the room. Without someone like Evot or Brad, not many could. She would have tried explosives if she was on an assassin mission, but that wasn't exactly quiet, and it might not have blown through the door.

They stood in front of the strange entrance.

"I guess whatever we're looking for is down there," said Rick, gesturing forward.

"It has to be," said Dalton.

Evot flew in and assumed humanoid form. "I'm here, but we no longer have aerial monitoring."

"It's okay," said Dalton. "If we find the portal and go through, we'll need you with us. We're about to head down, but to where, I don't know, so everyone be alert."

She smiled.

Dalton paused and raised a hand.

Everyone focused on him.

Dalton's eyes narrowed. "Evot, perform a quick aerial check before we head down. I thought I heard something."

"Of course," she said. She morphed into her crow form and flew away.

"What'd you hear?" asked Brad.

"Cars and something heavy," said Valerie, straining to hear.

Her eyes widened a minute later when Evot's aerial view showed several police cars sitting at various entrances. Buses and vans in small caravans began to arrive. When they parked near the hangar, tough-looking thugs disembarked.

"I think we know where the corruption in the police department is coming from. They're getting paid to watch this place, and I bet others," said Valerie.

Dalton wrinkled his brow. "I don't know who those others are, but I picked up the name Crayzo from their communications. That's the leader of the South Boyz, a criminal faction. They must have been alerted to come, and the corrupt police are locking down the area."

Rick pulled out his SG-5. "What's the plan?"

Dalton faced the group. "We can't go back out. There's too many, and it's far too dangerous at this point. The South Boyz are coming straight here, so I suspect they know where we are. We came to find the portal, and I think that's our way out of here. Down we go."

"Should we request backup?" asked Todd.

"Normally, yes," said Dalton. "However, they'd come too late, and it would require some heavy resources. I don't want to involve them unless it's absolutely necessary."

"Got it."

"What if the portal's not there?" asked Brad. "We'll be cornered in whatever is at the end of the tunnel."

Dalton raised his hand and vibrated it. "Then I'll make an escape route."

Evot flew back in and assumed humanoid form. "There are six police cars covering three entrances. I counted thirty-one South Boyz members, and they are carrying lethal weaponry, including grenades and flamethrowers. There are additional vehicles en route to the area as well."

"Damn, they aren't playing around," said Rick.

"Definitely not. Whatever's here has high value," said Dalton. He motioned down the tunnel. "Let's go."

Valerie's heart pumped as they took off. Whoever came through from the parallel Earth could be flown or driven anywhere, and this tunnel would be easy to transport things in. Perhaps that's why the hangar existed where it did. She could now clearly hear the enemies approaching in the distance. They would reach the tunnel soon, hopefully after the team found the portal.

Dalton hated being sandwiched between a known threat on one side and an unknown situation on the other. After twenty minutes, the team had gone far enough that he detected the portal on the periphery of his senses. He could open another portal to it and surprise whoever or whatever was there, but that could potentially be disastrous. He preferred going in first to take any heat. What awaited them remained a mystery.

Per Evot, who hung back some and watched their rear, the South Boyz had reached the tunnel entrance and were running hard. Dalton could tell Brad was nervous. He had not had time to replace his stickbots, so he was down to eleven now, but he still had Gizmo. Valerie and Rick were pumped, and Dalton suspected they would prefer to stand and fight, although that would be suicide without cover. Todd was calm and collected, which Dalton admired. It paid to have a cool head in situations like this.

After another ten minutes, they approached the end of the tunnel.

The increased illumination suggested there was a larger room ahead. Dalton also sensed four people. Two remained stationary, while the other two rushed toward the entrance.

"Behind me!" said Dalton. He morphed into Scoutspectre mode and spawned his shield and RSG.

The first man to come into view wore a security guard outfit and raised his weapon to fire. He went down with a blast from Dalton's RSG.

A shot hit Dalton's shield.

Todd fired and stunned the other guard.

The team rushed into the room.

Dalton's eyes narrowed at the two men in white lab coats frantically typing on computers off to the right. He approached them with his RSG pointed at them. "Step away."

The men looked over and ignored him.

Dalton stunned one of them.

The other gasped and backed up with his hands raised.

Dalton looked around. "Brad, Evot, see what's on these systems. Rick, check the downed people and see if there's anything of value. Todd, survey the room for anything unusual."

The team burst into action as Dalton morphed back into his official outfit and walked over to the trembling man whose glasses looked like they were about to fall off his face. "Now…I sense a portal here. Where does it go?"

The man licked his lips. "They'll kill me if I talk."

Dalton studied the man's lanyard. "Stard Galocolus. That doesn't sound like a name from around here."

Stard frowned.

"Look, you talk to me, or we tag you, and then you can spend the rest of your time in a dimensional prison," said Dalton. "I know you're probably aware that the local defense force, if you can call it that, is on its way, but we're going to go through the portal, and we *will* be back." His eyes glowed. "And, yes, I am different, and I can see that you're clearly from another Earth."

Stard stared at him. "If you go through, you won't come back."

"I think I will. This isn't my first parallel Earth trip. You're either going to come with us, or you can talk, I'll stun you, and you can pretend not to have said anything," said Dalton. He motioned at some cameras up on the wall. "I'll have Brad and Evot alter the footage to make it appear that way."

Stard looked at them. "How can they do that?"

"Evot's an AI, and Brad is just that good."

Stard gulped. "Oh. Uh…"

"Think quickly because we aren't going to be here for long."

"Fine. Fine. What do you want to know?" asked Stard, adjusting his glasses.

Dalton smiled. "Good. What should we expect when we go through the portal? Another facility like this?"

"Yeah. You'll be going to a hub with portals to other Earths, and it will be heavily defended. Once they detect you as a threat, they'll lock down the room the portal's in."

"I see. What type of security do they have?"

Stard shrugged. "I guess the cybernetic guards and their robot detail. There's also the automated security system, which I honestly don't know much about. I'm just a portal tech."

"Cybernetic guards with robots," said Dalton. "What type of weaponry and shielding are we talking? Projectile, laser for weapons? Kinetic or refractive shielding?"

"Um…I don't know about shielding, but they have guns that shoot bullets."

"Projectiles, then."

Todd joined them. "Not seeing much outside of the computers the guys were on and the raised platform in the center of the room."

"All right," said Dalton. He eyed Stard. "What is Dynkara?"

Stard recoiled. "They control *everything*."

"What do you mean by that?"

"The portal network. With that, they can go to any Earth they find."

Todd shook his head. "Let me guess. They replace people in various positions, forge alliances, and eventually come to dominate the Earth. Sound about right?"

"How could you know that?"

Dalton grinned. "Because he's a damn fine inspector, that's how." He whistled.

The others gathered around him.

"We have about ten minutes until we have guests," said Dalton. "Stard here will be stunned. Brad, Evot, make it appear that he never talked to us. We're going through the portal, which Stard says leads to a portal hub. It will most likely be shut down once we come across, and we'll need to handle cybernetic humans with robot guards and whatever security system is there." He looked at Stard. "Do you know the layout of the hub?"

"It's a massive ring underground, with each portal taking up a room on the edges," said Stard. "Central hub in the middle is the command center."

"How many portals are we talking about here?" asked Valerie.

"Sixty-four standard for a type-two hub," said Stard.

"Holy shit," said Rick. "Any of them special?"

"What do you mean?"

"Like one security forces might come through in case of a breach?"

Stard puffed his cheeks. "The first portal on each hub connects to a security Earth."

Todd's eyes narrowed. "A security Earth? I'm guessing that's one that provides a rapid response team. A whole planet to house it to boot. How quick do they respond?"

"Immediately."

Todd glanced at Dalton. "We'll need to shut that one down fast."

"I agree." Dalton smiled at Stard. "You've been most helpful. Okay, get on the ground and get comfortable."

Stard did so.

Dalton stunned him with his stun baton.

"Footage is clean," said Brad.

"Good. Our friends are almost here. Once we're through, clear the room, then, Brad, Evot, get to work on infiltrating their systems. Todd, Rick, Valerie, and I will hold the room while they do that. Get your helmets on."

They complied.

Dalton morphed into Scoutspectre mode and spawned his shield, then extended his right arm. Blue flames erupted around his hand and spread to his forearms. "Stay close behind me once I go through."

Shimmering appeared on the central platform and expanded into a light-blue semicircle with the peak being about fifteen feet off the ground.

Dalton raised his shield and charged forward. He could already sense the robots and people in the room on the other side, and he had formulated a strategy to deal with them. What came after that bothered him. He had to seal the hub's security portal, but Stard could have lied. There were many unknowns, but this time going through a portal, he had his team with him.

CHAPTER
FOURTEEN

Todd's breathing increased when he stepped through the portal. This would be his first trip through one, and he wished he could have visited a parallel Earth under better circumstances.

The room they exited into looked exactly like the one he had just come from. The difference was the two men with strange devices on their heads. They were some type of guard, as the tactical gear they wore seemed more advanced than anything he had seen outside of Dalton. Each man carried a shield and baton and had three sturdy, blue-and-white humanoid robots with energy blades next to each of them. Several other workers in white lab coats scrambled out of the room.

The two guards and their robots advanced.

Dalton charged to the left while firing his RSG and downed a robot.

Todd hated being exposed in an open position.

Rick burst over to the right and slid into the guard, knocking him down.

Valerie jumped and landed on one of the robots on the right, then hopped off while hitting it with her stun baton.

The other robot slashed her abdomen when she landed. Valerie stumbled back.

Todd took aim and hit the robot that attacked her.

Rick stood and stunned the guard, then rushed over and disabled the last robot that went after Valerie.

A quick check on Dalton showed he and Brad's stickbots, along with Gizmo, had already disabled the other guard and his three robots.

The massive door to the room slid shut.

Dalton closed the portal and then rushed over to Valerie, who had slumped against the wall. Blood oozed out of her abdomen. "You're hurt!"

She sighed. "Yeah. Wasn't able to dodge at that range."

Dalton scanned her. "Todd, med kit!"

Todd pulled a first-aid kit out of his backpack and crouched beside Valerie.

Valerie grunted as Dalton dressed the wound.

"How're you feeling?" asked Todd.

"It hurts," said Valerie. "Blood would do me good about now. Heal it up quick since it wasn't too deep. I shoulda brought some vials."

Rick knelt and extended his bare forearm. "Mine work?"

She drew her head back. "It would…but we'd have a blood bond for a while."

"But it'll help, right?"

Valerie nodded.

He moved his forearm close to her. "Have at it."

Todd grimaced when Valerie bit Rick's forearm and drank. Although Todd was not squeamish, it brought up memories of killing vampires while they fed.

Dalton scanned Rick's upper right arm. "You got grazed."

"Yeah," said Rick. "No biggie. If those guards and robots are what we'll be dealing with, we'll need to be wary of those glowing blades."

"That or send Dalton in like a bowling ball," said Todd.

"That works too," said Rick. "Still, we took them down quick."

Todd was not surprised Rick charged right into a group of unknown enemies. His suit was tough and could take a few hits. It showed in that while Valerie took a hit even through her underarmor, Rick's armor had held strong.

Brad joined them. "The layout is what Stard said it would be, but he might have lied about the special portal count. There's four of them."

"Four?" asked Todd. "We need to get those closed."

"Although we've disabled lethal gas from spewing in here, security forces have been dispatched to this location. There's other parts of the system that are secured, but Evot and I will breach it in time."

Dalton morphed back into his official outfit. "I see. Where are the four portals?"

Evot projected the layout. "There is a north, south, east, and west one. Normal portal rooms exist between those. We are between the east and north one currently."

"Then we need to disable those four now," said Dalton.

Brad looked at Evot. "I think we can hack these robots. You do the internal hardware, and I can hit the digital side."

"That would add to our group strength," she said.

Dalton spun around as the portal opened and a gunshot rang out.

Valerie stopped feeding and went prone.

"Portal!" said Todd, moving in front of her and Rick.

Brad and Evot dove off to the side.

Dalton extended his arm, and blue flames erupted on his hand and forearm.

The portal shimmered out of sight.

Valerie rested against the wall. "Well, that was fun."

"I think it's safe to say we aren't going back that way," said Dalton. "Since it can be opened and closed, I've permanently sealed it. We can't chance that happening again and having a small army march through. We'll find a place where I can use my recall portal ability to get us back. For now, Valerie needs to rest, and Brad and Evot need to continue working on the systems. Todd, you and Rick secure this area."

"You're going after the four security portals by yourself, aren't you?" asked Todd.

"I am. I only need to get within range to permanently seal them, and I can run fast."

Todd smiled. "Much faster than us for sure. We'd only slow you down."

"Brad and Evot will need time to breach this facility's system and hack these robots if possible, and I'd feel a lot better if they had protection while they did so."

"You can count on us, chief," said Todd.

"I'll be good as new here shortly," said Valerie.

Rick wiped off some blood on her lip that was about to fall.

She sucked the blood off his finger and looked into his eyes.

Todd's eyes widened.

Valerie grinned. "Sorry, force of habit. Blood bond and all."

"No problem here," said Rick, grinning.

Todd laughed. It was odd to do that in the middle of a potentially deadly situation. The blood bond between Valerie and Rick would probably end with them getting together even if only for one night. Todd studied Brad and Evot as they stood motionless. It creeped him out when they did that, but he understood they were in some form of digital landscape.

Dalton had already moved to the door that had slid shut earlier. Todd had no doubt Dalton would fly around the ring and shut down each security portal as he passed them. The only issue would be whatever security guards came through before then. Dalton's shield was powerful, and Todd wondered what options there were if he wanted one.

The large door slid open.

"I'll stay in contact," said Dalton. He charged out, and the door closed behind him.

Todd checked his SG-5 and looked around. He doubted anything would get into the room. Brad and Evot already worked on one of the robots. Adding six of them to the group would help. When Brad and Evot fully infiltrated the facility's systems, the team could go anywhere.

Todd gazed at the robot they worked on. If someone had told him he would be fighting robots a while back, he would have thought them nuts. Yet here he was. On a parallel Earth. With robots. It was exciting and scary at the same time, but Dalton had entrusted Todd to hold the area, so he would do his best to do so.

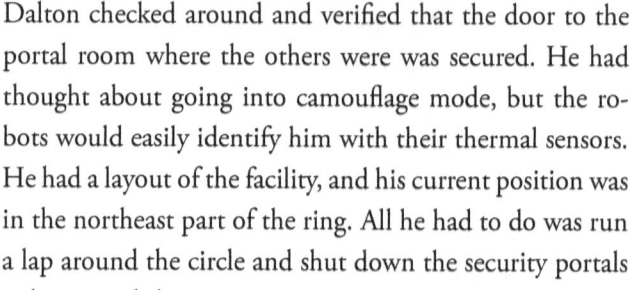

Dalton checked around and verified that the door to the portal room where the others were was secured. He had thought about going into camouflage mode, but the robots would easily identify him with their thermal sensors. He had a layout of the facility, and his current position was in the northeast part of the ring. All he had to do was run a lap around the circle and shut down the security portals as he crossed them.

There were no guards that he could detect, but Brad and Evot had hacked enough to show the robots and other life-forms in the facility. There was a lot of movement from the command center in the middle to the western security ring. An evacuation was in progress. The other security portals had not been activated yet. Perhaps the team had not been considered enough of a threat.

He raised his shield and dashed toward the north portal. On the way, he could sense other portals behind closed doors. Those rooms were probably like the one the team was in. Brad and Evot had initiated a shutdown, which sealed all the doors to the portal rooms, but the security ones had none. That was probably by design.

Some of the portals opened and closed. From what he understood, the portals led to other Earths, but he would wait on Brad and Evot's analysis. Having Todd be able to lead the team while Dalton handled threats was a nice option. Valerie would be good to go soon, and by the time Dalton got back, he hoped they would all be ready to take the command center.

A squad of eight robots rushed toward him.

Dalton's eyes narrowed as he focused. Everything slowed as he raised his RSG and hit two of the robots. When they were within range, he switched to his MH and formed a stun baton.

A robot grabbed his shield, while the others tried to encircle him.

He ducked and did a leg sweep, taking down three, then tapped the robot on his shield.

It crumpled.

Dalton jumped back and hit each of the robots that attempted to stand. He was now down to two robots that had backed up and tried to sandwich him.

One robot slashed from behind.

Dalton sidestepped and guided its blade into the robot in front, which had stepped forward. He stunned the remaining robot. The robots were not efficient fighters compared to him, but they could be bothersome in numbers.

The north portal had two human guards out.

Dalton used his RSG to hit both, then sealed the portal. There was another smaller group of robots that, like the previous group, did not stand a chance. This might be easier than he expected. The west portal went down like the north one, and his confidence grew.

The trip to the third portal was quick, and although it had several guards and robots, they proved to be no match. It made him wonder how they defended the base with such light security. Then again, they probably did not go up against cosmic-enhanced attackers.

The east portal was the only one remaining. Something was different about this one. Dalton sensed a presence that indicated a cybernetic being. When he reached the room, he studied the man in black tactical armor with a helmet. He carried a weapon of some type on his back along with various gadgetry on his belt. A pistol was holstered in a strap on his leg.

A quick check through the portal showed around ten more men with similar gear preparing to cross over. Dalton extended his arm and sealed the portal.

The man tapped at the nearby podium and, after a moment, faced Dalton. "What did you do?"

"Stopped your buddies from coming through," said Dalton. "I'm guessing you're part of the security force."

"Prime Defender Caltrix from Earth 412," he said, raising his head. "You're from Earth 743."

Dalton was not sure how the guy spoke English or what the numbering scheme was for the Earths, but it seemed each had a designation. "I guess."

"Why are you attacking us?"

"I'm not," said Dalton. "A robot from here, or maybe somewhere else, came to our Earth and caused trouble. I'm investigating."

Caltrix studied him. "Your investigation includes assaulting our facility and doing something to our portals?"

Dalton shook his head. "Not at all. We were attacked on our Earth and then again when we came through. It seemed even asking questions was considered hostile."

"Of course it is," said Caltrix. "You don't question Dynkara." He looked Dalton over. "Genetic engineering. Nanosuit. You're more advanced than what should be on Earth 743, although I've heard some interesting tales about that one. If you undo whatever you did to the portals and leave back through yours, I'll consider this event as never happening."

Dalton sighed. "The portals are permanently gone. I'm not leaving until I know why Dynkara is on our Earth."

"That is not for you to question, and your presence here is not welcome. You've trapped yourself here…with me. An oversight on your part. Your death is now warranted."

Dalton placed his shield forward and gripped his stun baton. He was not sure of Caltrix's combat ability, but he appeared confident in his skill. The pose Caltrix went into reminded Dalton of a Wing Chun one. The left hand extended out as if for a handshake, while the right one was across the chest with the palm facing the bicep. That signified a trapping style of combat, although it could be something completely different. Dalton formed his RSG and fired.

Caltrix shook off the stun and slid toward Dalton.

He stepped back.

Caltrix charged and tried to rip the RSG out of Dalton's hand.

Dalton bashed him away.

Caltrix kicked at Dalton's knee.

Dalton blocked with his right foot and switched to his MH. He tried to stun Caltrix.

Caltrix dodged the attack and pushed Dalton away.

The men faced each other.

"You have skill, but this ends now," said Caltrix. He pulled out an energy blade.

Dalton suspected the robots and Caltrix were from an advanced society. Energy blades were not unknown to Dalton.

Caltrix wielded his weapon like a master as he struck repeatedly.

Dalton used his shield to block most strikes and even counterattacked some, but he ended up with some slash wounds. He grimaced as a wave of pain reverberated through him. Caltrix was hard to hit, and his blade kept him at range. Although the weapon did not penetrate the nanosuit deeply, it left burn marks.

Dalton's eyes narrowed as he focused. Caltrix appeared to move slowly as Dalton charged in and blocked a sword strike. When he was in close, Dalton knocked Caltrix's sword out of his hand, then took him to the ground in a chokehold.

Caltrix struggled to break free.

He used both legs to keep Caltrix's legs out of the fight. After a few moments, Caltrix stopped moving. Dalton had a variety of submission techniques available to him, and he only wanted to knock Caltrix out. It was apparent stun did not work on him. A small group of prime defenders would have been devastating.

"Brad, you there?" asked Dalton over comms.

"Yep. What's going on?"

"Open the portal room next to me. I need to put someone inside."

"Got it."

Dalton stood and dragged Caltrix over to the room. After activating the portal and tossing him through, Dalton exited the room. "All right, close it."

The door sealed shut.

Dalton ran a hand over his stomach and checked out the slice wounds. If he did not have his suit, those attacks would have been deadly. As powerful as his team was, he was not sure they could take on a squad of people like Caltrix, at least not without a casualty. He continued back to the portal room and rejoined the others.

"Damn," said Rick, studying Dalton. "I guess you ran into security."

"Yeah, some advanced cybernetic soldier named Caltrix. He was quite skilled with an energy blade and hand-to-hand combat."

Brad shook his head. "A superhuman essentially."

"There were more about to come through, so I sealed the portal," said Dalton. He switched back to his official outfit.

Evot rushed over with a med kit and attended to his wounds. "You're hurt."

"Yeah. He was almost as fast as me. Almost."

Todd gestured at Dalton. "If he could do that to you and there were more, we'd be in trouble."

"Pretty much," said Dalton. "We need to take the command center, get what information we can, then figure a way back to our Earth. Most of the security forces have been dealt with, and I didn't sense many personnel left. One thing I did learn was that Caltrix worked for Dynkara, but he treated it like a religion."

"Great. Cybernetic zealots," said Valerie.

Dalton examined her. "You seem to have healed up."

"Yeah, takes more than a robot slashing me to keep me down," she said, smirking.

"All right. Give me a moment, then we'll head to the command center," said Dalton.

He expected it would be much lighter fighting if they only encountered guards like the previous ones they fought. It was obvious Dynkara had some power with the muscle to back it up. If Caltrix was representative of only one soldier, then Dalton was sure there were probably even more devastating forces out there.

The team needed to retrieve what it could, then get out. The last thing he wanted was for those security forces to portal in from another Earth, take down the portal door of whatever room they were in, then become a threat. It was time to move.

CHAPTER
FIFTEEN

Todd studied the command center the team had arrived at. It was hexagonal in shape, and in the middle was a large cylinder with workstations attached to it. There were other stations scattered around the area and what appeared to be a ramp that led to a lower level.

There had not been much resistance on the way from the portal room. It seemed like the hub had become a ghost town. The few cybernetic guards that tried to defend fell like bowling pins, and Valerie and Rick had wasted no time in stunning them. For Todd's part, he had picked off a few at range. He figured their lack of ranged weaponry was due to the sensitive nature of all the tech for the portals even though the portal tech from before said there was projectile-based weaponry.

The well-lit center had a sterile smell. Todd half expected the place to seal up and spew lethal gas. Thankfully, Brad and Evot had secured the facility. Even so, Todd did not think Dynkara would just roll over. There were probably defensive measures not known or detected yet.

Whatever came, Brad now had six robot guards under his control. Todd was going to suggest maybe the other robot guards on the way could be controlled, but Brad looked like he needed to focus to maintain the six he had.

Dalton motioned at one of the workstations connected to the cylinder. "Brad, Evot, get what you can. Todd, take Rick and Valerie, and secure the remaining six life signs. Brad can open a portal room for you to put them in."

"You got it, chief," said Todd.

He motioned at Valerie and Rick, who acknowledged him. They exited the room and proceeded toward the first life sign. Todd loved having a mini map of the facility with the life signs as dots. The thought of fighting robots in an advanced facility was impressive, but the ARI ability still amazed him. It was no surprise either that this was normal to Dalton. It made Todd appreciate Dalton's experience even more.

Seeing robots as guards unsettled Todd. He had watched science fiction shows in the past, but to be in a place with robots and advanced technology everywhere blew his mind. Valerie and Rick seemed equally surprised. Dalton and Brad acted like this was an everyday thing, but this sort of environment was not new to them.

"This is some crazy shit, man," said Rick.

"Sure is, but we've seen aliens and a portal before," said Todd.

"Yeah, but robots?"

Valerie grinned. "It's all new to me but kinda cool too other than being slashed." She gestured at a holographic screen that hovered off a wall. "I mean, look at that."

"Definitely different," said Todd.

The group approached a room with the first life sign. The room was in one of the tunnels that led from the command center to the outer ring.

Todd raised his weapon, then motioned for Valerie and Rick to take up positions to the side of the door. "Brad, we're at the first door. Can you unseal it?"

"Yep, got it," said Brad.

The door whooshed open.

Todd studied the small woman in a white two-piece suit who trembled at the back of the room. He waved for her to step forward.

She edged closer.

"Can you understand us?"

She nodded. "Earth 743. English. Our translator has it built in. Are you going to kill me?"

Todd lowered his weapon and motioned at Rick and Valerie to lower theirs. "No, but we will escort you to any portal room you want."

"The security ones are where we usually go when under attack," said the woman.

"There's nothing to fear," said Todd. "The security portals are gone, so pick another one."

The woman puffed her cheeks. "Earth 276, then. It's where we go for vacations."

Valerie bared her fangs. "Sounds like fun."

The woman's eyes widened as she stepped back.

"Brad, where's that at?" asked Todd over comms while he eyed Valerie.

A red dot appeared on the mini map in his ARI, and green arrows displayed on the ground.

Todd motioned for the woman to follow him. "All right, let's go."

After walking a bit, the woman said, "Why are you doing this?"

Todd peered back at her. "Because this Dynkara, whatever it is, is killing and replacing people on our Earth. A robot tried to kill some of us earlier, and it came through here. We're investigating all that."

"That's standard Dynkara protocol, though."

Rick laughed. "You think that's normal?"

"It's a small price to pay to become a member Earth of Dynkara."

Valerie shook her head. "Domination is the answer?"

"Ascension is," said the woman. "It's hard early on, but once established, the ascended Earth gains all the benefits of being a Dynkara member."

"Which is what?" asked Todd.

"The member Earth is brought up to Dynkara's technological level. Matter replicators and other advanced technology is given. The elevation of medical standards alone is worth the cost. There's also the protection aspect. No one dares attack a Dynkara-backed Earth, alien or otherwise. Not only that, but you now have a multiverse of Earths to visit."

Rick's eyes narrowed. "Why don't they just appear and offer all that instead of sneaking around?"

"You're human, like me. Have you met our species? We don't adapt well to rapid change."

Valerie smirked. "I'd have to agree with that."

They reached the portal room, and the door slid open.

Todd gestured for the woman to enter. "While all that sounds nice for an Earth, Dynkara does *not* want to touch our Earth. If Dynkara thought losing one facility was bad, they'd be in a world of trouble if they continued. Besides, the portal to our Earth has been severed permanently."

The woman smiled and stepped into the room. "I understand. You're from before phase one has been fully enacted. You'd understand if you were from a later phase. Your Earth could have been ascended, but after talking with you all, maybe not. You don't have the neural enhancements to fully comprehend."

Rick's face turned red. "You just call us stupid?"

The door to the room slid down.

Rick scoffed.

Todd slapped him on the back. "C'mon. Let's get these other five, then meet back up with the others. I'm curious to learn more about these phases."

"And how we're going to get back," said Valerie. "Hopefully, it's easier to do that than in the last case."

The next five were like the first. The one trait all the employees shared was a strong belief in Dynkara and its purpose. They all came from different Earths but worshiped Dynkara almost like it was a god. Todd had learned more about the various phases and was thankful his Earth was still in phase one. Then again, there were forces that would stop it from ever getting to phase two.

While moving around, Todd had discovered the facility employees lived like they were on a military base. There were living quarters, a cafeteria, gyms, offices, meeting rooms, and the like. They all resided in the tunnels that led out from the command center. The ring hallway encircling the facility was bare except for the portal rooms.

This was a new experience for all of them. Up to this point, meeting aliens in the Kaz Lodat world in the previous case had been wild. Now they encountered humans from parallel Earths. It had been strange to see another human who had no idea what his Earth was like other than it was designated 743 and had some odd notes on it.

After removing all the remaining employees, Todd and the others returned to Dalton, Brad, and Evot.

"Our Earth's in phase one," said Todd.

Dalton gestured at Brad. "He's discovered their full process but is learning more. There are apparently seven phases, each with dozens of steps that cover a variety of topics. They were still in the infiltration and research phase. Unfortunately for them, they won't be continuing that."

Rick grinned. "With the portal permanently gone, our Earth is safe, yeah?"

"Should be," said Dalton. "We haven't found out how the portals are created. Whatever did that could potentially open a new one at another hub."

Valerie chuckled. "Like whack-a-mole."

"Something like that," said Dalton.

Todd frowned as Brad stood motionless, his eyes pulsing blue. "I take it he's still doing a lot of research?"

"And then some. We have full control of the facility now thanks to him and Evot, so they're looking for a way out. In addition to that, there are a lot of data stores to investigate."

"Their security wasn't quite as advanced as I would have expected," said Rick. "Well, the robot guards were interesting, but there weren't as many as I thought there would be."

"That's due to the security portals being shut down and every portal room secured. We could see something coming from the other portals that might have been able to bust through the doors."

"Yeah, I could see that. Do you have any video of that Caltrix guy you fought?"

Dalton extended his hand and projected the fight with Caltrix. "Yep. He's a prime defender. He was tough and kept up with me. There was a whole group planning on coming through."

"Wow," said Valerie. "Guy moves fast."

"Master swordsman it looks like," said Todd. He glanced at Rick. "Give you a fight for sure."

Rick smiled. "Guy could try."

"I would expect the facility falling like this has been planned for," said Dalton. "What their response will be remains to be seen. Relax for now. Once Brad and Evot have the information we seek and we have a path out of here, we'll leave."

"You're going to open a portal back, right?" asked Valerie.

"Yeah, but remember, we're underground relative to our Earth. I opened a small portal outside this room, and it showed a rock wall on our Earth's side. However, we can determine where we need to be in order to cross back over," said Dalton. He pointed up. "It requires us going topside."

Todd crossed his arms and leaned against the wall. If Dalton was not with them, the team would have been stranded with no way to get home. Even if the portal back to their Earth was still operational, they would have had to deal with Crayzo and his small army. Although Todd prided himself on being calm and collected, something about this facility made his skin crawl. He could not put his finger on it, but it was a sense of not belonging there.

Beings from another timeline had different signatures that could be detected. Todd had learned that their presence irritated timeline natives. Perhaps that was the odd feeling he had. He took the lull to relax since the next step was about venturing into the unknown.

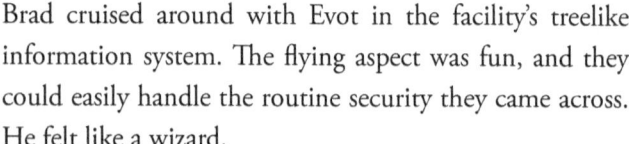

Brad cruised around with Evot in the facility's treelike information system. The flying aspect was fun, and they could easily handle the routine security they came across. He felt like a wizard.

The layout of the systems was different than the ones he normally traversed. There were large silver spheres with blue branches that shot out. Sometimes the branches had smaller orbs with their own branching structure. Each major sphere handled a facility operation, and they had already visited the security one. It surprised him that no AIs were present since the design had the imprints of what he would expect an AI to build. Evot had confirmed his conclusion on that.

The current sphere they flew around was a knowledge node. Interacting with it was as simple as focusing on what he wanted to search for, then a branch would highlight. Evot concentrated on implementing an extract, transform, and load, or ETL, process. The data had a different format and layout, so she made sure the data could be stored in Dalton's storage space for later retrieval. Brad was not sure how much they would be able to get, but it did bring up the point of having external hardware for this type of situation.

The Dynkara branch was large, and many smaller ones diverged at various points. Brad had already discovered the general process of how Dynkara assimilated a world and had relayed that to Dalton. It seemed they had a lot of time, as the overall process took around fifty years. It involved infiltration of the Earth, replacement of key figures, establishment of allies, and sowing discord among elements that might stand in the way. Once a world war erupted, Dynkara and their allies moved in and created a calm and peaceful environment. After a few generations, they had a compliant Earth that viewed them as saviors.

That would never fly on his current Earth. There were simply too many powerful factions and beings around. He imagined Dynkara meeting Evaran. That would not go well for them.

One thing Dynkara had going for it was numbers. They had conquered many Earths and even repurposed some for specific needs. The security ones were obvious, but others were prisons or launchpads into areas to collect rare elements. Each Earth expanded past the solar system, so there was also that aspect.

Dynkara leadership was hierarchal, and each Earth had a governor. A hub manager oversaw the governors, and a regional administrator supervised the hub managers. Past that was blank, and Brad suspected that was on purpose. The true rulers of Dynkara were a mystery, but it was obvious they had a well-oiled operation.

Some Earths had fought back. One was so advanced that Dynkara closed the portal. Brad only saw a reference to closing the portal, not sealing it permanently. Perhaps that feature was unique to Dalton. Another Earth had a vicious race that spewed acid and ripped the phase one Dynkara employees to shreds. Some of the creatures assaulted the hub before being put down.

He focused on Earth 8335, which resembled the cyberpunk one he came from. It mentioned an AI collective with killer androids who had tried to infiltrate a hub. The whole hub had been destroyed as a preventative measure. That sounded like something Sentcom, the AI collective he had hid from, would do. A chill ran up his spine.

Earth 62,345 was another one Dynkara had to close a portal on. Apparently, they encountered a being who could manipulate matter. Brad smiled. A matter mage. He had heard it mentioned in casual conversation with Evaran and the gang. It seemed Dynkara actually found one. Earth 14,223 had the portal closed because of its race of violent giants.

Other Earths were closed due to bad environments, such as a water world. Dynkara kept detailed records, and although there were many Earths that were not used, there were even more that fit the profile Dynkara sought. Unfortunately, Earth 743 was on that list.

Evot joined him and pointed at a sphere. "I have discovered their logistical system."

"Find anything interesting?"

"I did. I believe I know what happens to those they replace."

They flew over to the sphere, then down a large branch.

Brad scrutinized the videos that showed humans being tossed into a room before being consumed by flames. Not much was left afterward. His stomach churned.

"Are you okay?" asked Evot.

"Yeah," said Brad, grimacing. "They just…kill them. And not even on the Earth the victim's from." He sighed. "They burn them at the hubs."

"I have located a path to the surface, and there is a side tunnel that leads down to a crematorium."

Brad shook his head. "What a fate. Get replaced, brought here, then killed."

"There are 1,278 from our Earth."

Brad ran a hand over his mouth. "Holy shit."

"Yes."

He pulled up a data window. "It says here there are 132 agents on our Earth in addition to those replaced." He smiled. "And we have their profiles. Most are human and gathering information. Seems like…others do negotiations, some infiltrate organizations without replacement, and more begin laying down a communication network."

Evot tilted her head. "We should have detected their network."

"Maybe not," said Brad. "It looks like they're using a hybrid approach for communication. Dead drops, face-to-face meetings that are planned out, and even coded messages on social media. Unfortunately for them, we now have their playbook."

Evot glanced at him. "We can steal their plays. From the book."

Brad laughed. "Yeah, something like that. All right. We now know what Dynkara is and what they're up to. Looks like we also have their Earth contacts." He frowned. "Did you notice some oddities in the system?"

"I did. There were automated reports of disruptions that began when they started phase one on our Earth."

"Yeah, I was looking at some video feeds, and it's like it disappears, then comes back, but everything in the log said it's fine," said Brad.

Evot grinned. "Perhaps there are Displaced in the system."

He pointed at her. "The ole ghosts in the machine. I guess we'll never know once we leave. Speaking of which, you said you found a path out?"

"Yes. There is a tunnel that leads to the surface. The information on the Earth we're on indicates it is a jungle world filled with powerful creatures not compatible with replacement. It appears they did not want to waste resources to subdue and transform the world."

"That's interesting. Dynkara has the power to do it," said Brad.

"They do," said Evot. "Perhaps hub worlds aren't upgraded so as not to draw attention from potential aliens. The hostile environment could act as a buffer."

"Definitely plausible. All right. Let's collect what we can and update the team."

Dalton would love the information dump. They now had proof that Septimus was a Dynkara point of contact. The portal being shut down was a good first step, and the process to create new portals led to random Earths. Given how many were out there, Brad suspected they would not be reconnecting to his adopted Earth anytime soon, which was fine with him.

CHAPTER
SIXTEEN

Dalton was disturbed by what Brad and Evot had reported. It was obvious Dynkara was a mysterious and powerful group. He did not think they would give up a hub. There would be a response, but he suspected the security portal shutdown might have caused a change in their plans. They probably had a contingency for this exact situation.

The hub was empty of any life signs other than the team. Todd discovered some compatible food and drinks in the cafeteria, and Rick and Valerie picked up some medical supplies. Dalton did not mind looting because the next step of getting back to Earth would involve entering a hostile environment. Evot had found a sealed door that protected a tunnel that led to the surface. As it was roughly 3:00 p.m., he wanted to make sure they had supplies if they needed to camp somewhere.

Dalton looked around at everyone. "All right. We're going topside. However, first, I want to check out the crematorium.

Apparently, the glitches Brad and Evot discovered seem to happen there more than anywhere else. If there's a weakness, we need to check it out. After that, we'll leave via a sealed tunnel. Once we're out, I'll find a place we can ascend to so we can portal back. We'll be entering a hostile environment, but hopefully we won't run into any issues. If the location we need to reach is too far away or across tough terrain, we'll scout out a campsite."

"Why not just wait here until tomorrow, then?" asked Todd. "Evot could scout while we wait."

Dalton gestured at him. "That's a valid point, but I don't think Dynkara is done here."

"What're you thinking they might do?" asked Valerie.

"I'm not sure, but there could be more of whatever coming through the other regular portals. Although no explosives have been detected, they could send them through the portals, or there could be other countermeasures," said Dalton.

Rick furrowed his brow. "Why not permanently seal the other portals?"

"We may need them," said Dalton. "Last resort. I don't want to, but if we go topside and where we need to go is unreachable, then we might need to chance it on another Earth. I don't want to split the group either."

"Works for me. Just tell us where you need us."

Dalton nodded. "We have food, drink, and medical supplies. We also have some blankets in case we need them. I'm hoping the trip to wherever we need to go is quick, but we should be prepared for a day or more potentially. If it becomes too dangerous, we'll come back here and try our luck on another Earth, assuming we can come back. All right. Let's check out the crematorium."

After ten minutes, they arrived.

Dalton scanned the sealed casket-sized doors embedded in the walls. Various slabs dotted the room, and a podium with a console sat in the back. It was clean for a place of death. However, it was the Displaced that emerged from the walls that had his full attention. Their bodies were on fire, and they moved as if they had broken legs.

"There's Displaced here," he said.

Brad's eyes widened. "Where?"

"Adjusting my visual feed to relay," said Dalton.

Todd jumped back. "What the hell?"

Rick grabbed his SG-5. "Is this for real?"

"We saw this before. They can't hurt you, although I thought Brad scared them?" asked Valerie.

"Normally, yes," said Dalton. "Displaced know what happens if they touch me, yet they continue forward." His eyes glowed as he extended his hand.

Displaced moved toward it, and when they touched it, they let out a wail before dissipating.

Brad moved behind Dalton. "They want to die."

"Released," said Dalton. "I suspect dying away from our timeline has caused them to be restless. There must have been a percentage of those from our Earth with exotic energy who were replaced."

"This is messed up," said Rick, putting away his SG-5. "They look like flaming zombies."

Dalton kept his hand out as more and more Displaced moved toward him. After five minutes, all but one had been released. The last one was a trembling young girl who crouched in the back. A lump formed in his throat. She probably did not understand how she died or why she was here. He knelt before her, then extended his hand.

She cowered at first, but upon Dalton telling her it was all right, she reached out and touched his hand. She smiled as she dissipated.

Dalton stood. "This would explain why there were glitches in the hub's systems. I think all Displaced are gone now."

"You did a good thing in releasing them," said Valerie. "They seemed trapped here."

"Yeah. Let's get out of here."

Dynkara probably did not know what Displaced were, although they should have if they were in phase one on his Earth. Brad and Evot had mentioned they did not find much in that regard in the system. It showcased how unique the Earth they came from was relative to others. Even the reports from his Earth mentioned exotic energy as an irregularity and nothing to be concerned about. They truly did not understand how dangerous of a position that was to take.

He entered Scoutspectre mode and led the others along with the six robots Brad had commandeered. They could prove useful, but they would not be able to portal back. That would be a technology violation.

Dalton had studied Brad and Evot's report on the surface, and although the atmosphere was okay for humans, it painted a rough world with strange species. There were also reports of a humanoid race that was hard to spot. He hoped they did not need to deal with that.

The group reached a sealed door in the eastern side of the ring.

"This has not been opened in a long time," said Brad. "Seems when they got a portal here, they used machinery to carve out the hub, and once established, they dug a tunnel to the surface, then sealed the doors. That was the last time it was opened."

Rick shook his head. "There could be all sorts of whatever living there now."

"They did cover the entrance with natural obstructions that would be easy to go through from the inside. I guess we'll find out what that is."

"Okay. Everyone, stand back," said Dalton.

The team complied.

"Open it up."

Brad focused, and the door groaned as it rolled into the side wall. Dusty air burst out over the group.

Dalton scanned the tunnel. There were no lights inside, but there was a metallic floor, sides, and a ceiling. He suspected it could be used as an evacuation route. What surprised him was the sheer size of the tunnel. That may be due to the large machinery that dug it out. He waved forward and stepped inside with the others.

"Glad we have our helmets," said Valerie. "Who knows what biological surprises this place holds. Seems like we're always creeping around in tunnels underground."

"Always a possibility that we might contaminate the environment too," said Todd.

"True." Dalton smiled. "Let's hope there aren't any large insects."

"Yeah, let's," said Rick.

Todd was even-keeled as expected, and Rick was on alert. Valerie seemed calm, but Brad's heart raced. That was understandable. They were leaving the potential safety of the hub to enter a tunnel that led to a hostile environment. Evot had been sent ahead so they would have some idea of what to expect.

After ten minutes, they were about a quarter of the way to the surface.

"Glad it's a gradual incline," said Todd. "Otherwise, this could be quite the workout."

"No issues here, but I haven't seen any creatures or anything," said Rick.

"There may be some," said Evot over comms. "I have discovered a wall of branches and vines blocking our passage ahead. Scans indicate life signs on the other side."

Valerie shook her head. "I knew it would be too good to be true to have a straight-forward exit."

Dalton's eyes narrowed. Based on Evot's scans, whatever was ahead came in varying sizes. Some were the size of large dogs, while others were as small as puppies. She could not get an accurate reading, and he figured when they arrived, he would open it up some for a better scan.

"We'll deal with it when we get there," said Dalton. "It might not be so bad."

Todd snorted. "Now watch it be just that."

After twenty minutes, they reached the obstruction.

Dalton extended his right hand and scanned the area. His readings were like Evot's, and he could tell by the avatars of the others that they did not care for the jittery movement of whatever was on the other side. The wall was thick and had been built up over time. Rocks, branches, and dirt had created a solid obstruction that extended over ten feet.

"That's a thick ass wall," said Rick. "How we getting through that?"

Dalton raised his vibrating hand. "An old technique. This might take a bit, so relax for now, but be ready once we're close to breaking through."

"The robots can assist," said Brad.

"I can as well," said Evot.

Dalton smiled. "Let's get to it."

He had used this technique when traveling with Evaran and the gang, but he also knew a being that could mimic a wall of nanobots, and Kess, a human more evolved than him, who had half her body as a nanoswarm. The robots impressed him. They formed their hands into a beak shape and hacked away at the wall next to him. While he had initially started the outline of the area, the robots and Evot excavated efficiently.

After another twenty minutes, they reached a point where only a foot of wall was left.

Dalton took a moment to catch his breath. It was back-breaking work, as he had to kneel to reach the lower parts, and the process used up a lot of energy. He could only imagine trying to go through rock while hundreds of feet underground. He would run out of power way before then.

"All right," he said. "We're almost through. I believe whatever is on the other side knows we're coming. Some have gathered, while others fled. I'm not sure what to expect, but I can punch through and shatter what's remaining of this obstruction. The robots will go first, then we'll follow. Be ready to fight."

Todd took out his SG-5 and aimed forward, while Rick grabbed his blade and stun baton. Valerie had an SP-8 and stun baton, while Brad had his stickbots and Gizmo out.

After Dalton verified everyone was ready, he had Brad move the robots with blades out to the side of him. Dalton focused on the weakest point of the wall, then punched as hard as he could.

The wall crumbled when his fist went through. Loud shrieks filled the air.

The robots moved in and were immediately attacked by knee-high, red-furred ratlike creatures. Dalton stepped back while the rest of the team opened fire. The robots performed admirably, but the creatures had a powerful bite, as some of the robots toppled after losing their legs. The team's stun blasts knocked out the initial group of animals.

Other creatures fled when Dalton entered the area with the others. There was not much left of the six robots, as they took the brunt of the assault, but one had survived. They had managed to kill some of the creatures before going down. The others were unconscious, and he was thankful stun worked on them. It was apparent the team had stumbled onto a nest of some type.

Rick looked around. "All right…rats should not be as big as dogs. Period."

Todd rubbed his arm. "Yeah, that's messed up."

"Robots look done for, well, except for that one," said Valerie, pointing at the sole remaining robot.

Brad sighed. "Yeah, but better those things attack the robots first than us."

Dalton scanned the area. "Although the creatures have fled, we need to remain vigilant. We still have about a quarter of the way to go, and now we have some angry rat things ahead of us. Hopefully, they scattered and are not regrouping."

A vibration shook the tunnel. A moment later, a blast of air hit the group from the lower part of the tunnel.

"What the hell was that?" asked Rick.

Dalton paused. "The facility has been blown. I'm guessing explosives through the portals."

"If we had waited down there…" said Brad.

"Yeah. We'd be trapped under rubble and whatever else," said Dalton. "Our goal and path forward are clear. Let's move out."

Valerie was on high alert after breaking through into the nest. If the team had initially gone through, she suspected some might be missing limbs. The ease at which the creatures bit through metal surprised her.

As they continued up the tunnel, it seemed like every sound was amplified. She could see well in the dark, but Dalton used his right hand to shine a light ahead. Although she heard scurrying noises, she did not sense any more of the creatures.

After ten minutes, the team reached a dirt wall with a sizable hole on the bottom right.

"Well, we know how those things came in and out," said Todd.

Dalton scanned the area. "Yeah, and I'm not detecting anything immediately outside. Evot, aerial reconnaissance."

"Of course," she said. She transformed into a crow and hopped through the opening, then flew away.

"I'll open the hole some," said Dalton.

His vibrating ability was useful, and Valerie had seen it chew through locks and walls before. It took a toll on him, but it also explained why he did not open a portal back to their Earth from where they were. Hopefully, there was sufficient elevation nearby.

Evot's aerial view appeared in Valerie's ARI. The cave exited into a jungle valley, and the nearest place with height was a mountain in the distance. If that was where they needed to go, that would be a hike and then some. Not to mention it would be through a jungle probably filled with dangerous elements.

Dalton finished enlarging the gap for them to go through.

Valerie stepped into what her ARI showed as fresh air. She lowered her helmet and took a deep breath. It was warm out, and it felt good to be out of the confined tunnel. She stretched and cracked her neck.

The area was clear and sat on a raised mound that had a mix of dirt and vegetation, but the jungle remained on the outskirts. It was obvious the creatures used up any trees or large plants in about a twenty-foot radius. She could not see much past the trees.

The others removed their helmets, and Dalton switched back to official mode.

"We'll wait here until Evot is done surveying the area. Now is a good time to eat or drink if you want to," said Dalton.

Valerie rummaged through her backpack and grabbed some shrink-wrapped meat sticks. She eyed Rick as he went through his pack. His blood tasted good, probably because he was an enhanced human. She could do with more, but she had a blood bond with him now. If she drank any more of his blood, that bond would get stronger. It was already hard to resist the urge to go over and play around with him.

Rick smiled at her.

She reciprocated. He was probably dealing with similar feelings but kept things professional. Todd and Brad sat on a rock and ate what looked like protein bars. Dalton was busy as ever checking out the perimeter, which came as no surprise to her. She sat on the ground up against the rock wall to the left of the tunnel entrance.

Rick joined her. "My first parallel Earth."

"First time for everything," she said, glancing at him.

They shared a laugh.

Rick cleared his throat. "This blood bond thing…how long does it last? I've heard it's a few days."

"That's about right," she said. "With the amount I had, though, probably a week for us."

Rick bit into his meat stick. "I see. And, uh…I know of the effects, but I've never experienced it until now. It's…interesting."

Valerie smirked. "Well, you provided the offering of a bite for that part of a bite job. It's only fair I offer the other part."

He drew his head back. "Really? And you're…cool with that?"

"Of course. You don't seem like the emotional type, and your blood is good. Most humans tend to get worked up and want something more. Humans tie their whole reproduction to their genitalia. For Zikarians, it's only one part of reproduction and doesn't mean anything unless the other parts are done."

"What other parts?" he asked.

Valerie grinned. "We carry exotic energy, and that is transferred by two others, so there's three involved. Without that, reproduction fails. However, don't get me wrong. We enjoy sex, but we don't have the same reproduction drive humans do in that regard; hence, we aren't as attached."

"Ah, and since you're the last of your kind, there's no chance of another Zikarian."

"Yep," she said. "Back in the early 1900s when we first came over, we had a difficult time adjusting to human culture. After a guy had an encounter with one of my sisters, he said they had to get married."

Rick raised an eyebrow. "How'd that go?"

"We didn't understand what marriage was. The thought of only having sex with one person was disgusting to us. We told him no."

Rick laughed. "I bet he was pissed."

"We explained what we were, and he said he was going to tell law enforcement and we were all going to pay. So we killed him before he got to the police station," said Valerie.

Rick's eyes widened. "Yeah, I guess he learned the hard way that no means no."

She could almost see the gears turning in Rick's head. The discussion was not something new and had happened many times before.

Dalton signaled for everyone to gather.

"Looks like meeting time," said Valerie. She hopped up with Rick and walked over.

Dalton motioned at Brad. "He hasn't detected any tech in the area, and Evot hasn't seen any from the air. This is a primitive world." He pointed east. "There is a mountain in that direction that has the height needed for me to use my recall portal ability. It's about eighteen miles away."

Brad grimaced. "Yeah, and with a hostile jungle between there and here. This robot should last for a while, but without any way to charge it, it may not make the full trip."

"It can still be useful, though," said Dalton. "Evot has also sighted some potential threats and is mapping us a path. If there were no obstructions, we could probably march there in three and a half hours. Unfortunately, there's a gorge about eight miles away we need to cross, and the path to it will take us three hours by itself. On top of that, I have to hack vegetation out of the way. I don't want to be caught in the jungle at night, so we're going to get close to the gorge but not cross, then camp. We can complete the trip in the morning."

Rick tapped his blade. "I can help with clearing vegetation."

"We'll probably need you and the robot too," said Dalton. "Once Evot is done with her full surveillance, we'll head out."

"On a side note, what does your recall portal show for Earth out here now?" asked Valerie.

Dalton extended his right arm. His forearm and hand erupted into blue flames.

A portal opened.

Valerie tapped on the solid rock on the other side. "Still underground compared to here." She stepped back.

He closed the portal. "Evot's identified a spot on the mountain that should put us somewhere in Baton Rouge safely when we pop through."

She appreciated Evot's utility. The group would have had a much harder time figuring out where to go without her flying reconnaissance ability. Valerie hoped they could get there without any issues, but they were strangers in this place. She had no doubt there would be challenges along the way. They still had a case to resolve, and although they now had the information needed to close it, they had to get back in one piece. She sat back down and rested her head against the rock wall. This could be one of the few times to relax in the coming hours.

CHAPTER
SEVENTEEN

I t had been an hour since Dalton had updated the group, and Rick was getting anxious. It did not help that the blood bond with Valerie excited him when she was near. Thankfully, Evot had found another spot close to the gorge that would be better for camping. The place they were going to resembled a large, jagged rock that had been jammed into the ground at an angle. Underneath was a spot they could rest in, as one side was covered.

"All right, everyone ready?" asked Dalton.

Rick nodded along with the others. He joined Dalton up front, while Todd and Valerie took the rear. Brad hung in the middle with his robot and Gizmo. Rick appreciated the formation. If something came from the front, it would have to go through him and Dalton. If it attacked from the rear, it had to deal with Valerie and Todd. If the sides were attacked, the front and rear could separate and provide coverage.

The group walked down the angled dirt path to the jungle floor.

Rick pulled out his blade. Dalton had his MH out and had reformed it into a machete. There would probably be some hacking, as the trees were close together and the underbrush was thick in some spots. Rick was focused on the task ahead, and he knew they had a case that needed to be closed once they got back. Taking a tour through a jungle on a parallel Earth had not been part of the plan.

The start of the trip had been rough, but they eventually came upon a beaten path. It reminded Rick of elephant trails he had seen in jungles. It provided an easier route toward their goal, but it was a place for ambush predators as well. Whatever created the path was large and heavy, and he hoped the team did not run into it.

After walking a bit, Dalton raised a hand. "Something's up ahead."

Rick listened for any sounds but only heard the rustling of the jungle. Evot was in the air and could not provide any overview due to the trees covering the area. He squinted and stared ahead. The trail was quiet, which, oddly enough, had been what most of the trip had been so far.

"I sense it now," said Valerie. "And I can smell it."

Dalton projected a hologram of himself fifteen feet ahead.

A catlike animal leapt out of a bush and growled while attacking the projection.

Rick pulled out his stun baton. The creature resembled a jaguar, except it had a thick horn on its nose and four eyes. It also had spaced-out white patches on its black coat.

Dalton closed the projection and morphed into Scout-spectre mode, which caught the animal's attention. The eye slit on his helmet glowed as his suit vibrated.

The creature looked around, then focused back on Dalton. He uttered a deep growl, and the jungle cat ran away.

Rick understood why the creature split. Dalton's growl was low, and Rick felt it in his bones. If he had, then the animal surely had as well, and it understood the team was not a snack worth getting injured for.

"Never seen that before," said Brad. "That growl is freaky."

Dalton changed back to his official suit. "It's a sound I heard when I investigated a desert on a remote world. It startled me the first time I heard it, so I recorded it. Never thought I'd have to use it, though."

"It's effective," said Todd. "That cat wanted no part of that."

"I take it you have other sounds you can do as well for situations like this?" asked Valerie.

Dalton nodded. "I do, and I chose this one based on the creature's growling. I figured it would respond to a deeper growl. I could have used a high shriek and flashed lights too."

"The man of many sounds," said Valerie. "If that was an apex predator, we might be okay out here."

"Let's not get too complacent," said Dalton. "Evot spotted some humanoids across the gorge but none over here. There's probably a reason for that, one we don't know about. All right, moving on."

Rick admired Dalton's experience. A Scoutspectre sounded like a job that went everywhere. Rick liked the concept and could envision the team as a Scoutspectre one, minus the suits. They had the traveling-to-distant-places part down.

After thirty minutes, they came across a small open area before a new type of tree.

Rick's eyes narrowed. The trees were spaced out, and every branch had vines of varying thicknesses hanging down almost to the ground. However, it was the eerie silence that made him alert. The usual odor of the jungle had been replaced by the smell of rotting flesh, something he knew well from his earlier days as a mercenary.

"I don't like that forest," said Valerie, gripping her stun baton.

"Me either," said Rick.

Todd waved in front of him. "Smells like a rotting deer carcass."

Dalton studied the forest for a moment, then picked up a nearby rock and tossed it.

A vine from the nearest tree reached out and grabbed the stone, then rolled up to its branch before tossing the rock away.

"Yeah…how about we not go through there," said Brad.

"The problem with that is we need to go through here to reach our spot for the night," said Dalton. "Evot, is there a way around this area?"

"Yes, but it requires an additional mile north where there is a gap."

Dalton sighed. "Fine. Let's move."

Rick got the sense this world was brutal. It was no wonder Evot had not spotted any signs of an advanced human civilization. When trees turned out to be murder factories, that did not bode well for other areas.

After a quick hike up to the gap, they paused.

The dusty path went right through the trees, and then they would only be about a twenty-minute hike away. Rick was not sure why the trees had not grown on the path. Dalton had scanned the ground and had not noticed anything different compared to the surrounding forest.

Brad rubbed his arms. "And we just walk down this path between murder trees. What could go wrong?"

"Evot is not showing any signs of activity, well, at least from what she can scan," said Dalton. He entered Scout-spectre mode and spawned his shield. "It's only two miles long. C'mon."

The group advanced.

Rick had his SG-5 out, and he eyed the trees as he passed by them. It was like they were staring at him, but he figured they did not have eyes. Maybe they were part of a large organism underground. He shuddered to think they might be walking on its mouth.

About halfway through, Dalton adopted a defensive stance. "There's a small swarm of something flying out of the forest from the left."

Rick studied the zoomed-in view Evot provided. The creatures resembled small, thin rats but had wings, a tail with a stinger, and an oversized mouth with two jutting fangs. One or two would not be an issue, but there were hundreds coming toward them.

"Run!" said Dalton.

The group charged forward.

It did not take long for the swarm to catch them. They attacked from the front, back, and right side, forcing the group to edge close to the left side of the forest.

Rick fired and hit a few but switched to his blade and stun baton when the beasts got too close.

Valerie had her dual daggers out and sliced the flying rats with ease. Dalton was a machine, as he had formed a stun baton and moved like a whirlwind through the creatures. Brad and Gizmo fired stun blasts, while the robot attacked any it could reach with its blade. Todd had his stun baton and SP-8 out and alternated between hitting and firing.

"There's too many," said Todd.

Brad cried out as he tumbled to the ground.

The animals swarmed him.

Brad's stickbots jumped off and attacked any they could reach. They ripped off the wings of some of them.

The robot pulled some off Brad.

"Hell with that!" said Rick. He stabbed the creatures on Brad and tossed them to the side.

Valerie joined him.

By the time Dalton came over, Brad had been freed but not before he had multiple bites and stings.

Rick's eyes widened when the creatures flew away. Evot had reformed into her fly swarm mode, but instead of flies, she had created small spheres with rotating saws. The creatures stood no chance against that.

"Ah, shit, it stings," said Brad with a groan.

Dalton scanned him. "Your suit protected you from their bites mainly, but some stingers got through. You have a toxin in your system, but it should flush out. Unfortunately, it's a paralyzing agent of some type."

Todd grimaced as he scrutinized his torn-up underarmor. "Little shits got me some too, although nowhere near as much as Brad."

Evot cleaned the wounds on the team and applied a gel of some type. "This gel is a sealant from the hub. It is meant for temporary use but should suffice for this."

Brad tried to get up but fell back down. He focused, and the robot scooped him up. "This'll work for now."

Dalton checked out the robot. "Does it require concentration for you to control it?"

Brad shook his head. "I just set it to protect and carry and to follow you."

"All right, then we need to get to that safe spot for the night, where we can rest."

"No argument from me," said Valerie.

Rick followed the others. The fight had been brutal and fast, which was probably the way of the planet. The creatures had come from the forest, and he was surprised the trees did not fight the attackers. Perhaps there was a symbiotic effect where the creatures pushed prey into the trees.

Either way, he was glad to be back on track. The group was hurting, and they still had to reach a safe spot, then journey across the gorge. The sun lowered, and it would soon be night. If daytime was this brutal, the night might be worse.

Todd studied the rocky wall Dalton, Evot, and the robot worked on. They carved out a small area inside, leaving only one entrance to defend. The idea was that Evot would remain on watch and alert the group if anything came close. Todd did not think anything would, given that the only way to reach them was to go through the gap between the murder trees or cross a stone bridge. It was 7:30 p.m. and twilight out.

He walked around and climbed up on the rock. It gave a good view of the gorge and the stone bridge across it. He understood why the humanoids on the other side avoided this area. If the trees did not get you, the flying attackers would. On top of that, there were other powerful creatures out and about.

Rick joined him. "This is a crazy place."

"Yeah. Think about what it took to get here."

Rick nodded. "I just hope tonight is peaceful. That damn poison in me is making me nauseous. Second time I've had some shit in me."

"Just make sure that if you start crapping, you get out of the space we'll be in."

They laughed.

"A good rest will help," said Rick.

Todd studied him. "How's that blood bond coming along?"

"Rough. It's keeping me on edge. No wonder bite jobs are so popular," said Rick.

"Yeah. I'll admit, it was odd seeing her feed on you, given your past."

"Anything to help the team," said Rick. "It coulda been you, and I'd be here telling you to keep it in your pants."

Todd grinned. "Yeah, probably." He pointed at some lights in the forest across the gorge. "Those look like campfires."

"I'm sure whatever's there is tough. They won't like us intruding."

Todd had the same thought. Evot had not gotten a good scan of the humanoids, and when she had dived in, she was chased off by a pack of strange flying reptiles. This Earth was not meant for humans, that much was for sure. Maybe they had already evolved and had been wiped out. It was a fascinating mystery that he would probably never know the answer to.

After some light chatter, he climbed down and checked on the enclosure Dalton, Evot, and the robot had built. It was a tight space, but there was room for each person to lie down. Valerie had dug a hole a bit away for a bathroom just before the darkness began to creep in.

Todd assisted Brad in moving into the sleeping area. The robot stood motionless outside the entrance. Its power had gone, but it had proven useful in the time it had been active. Todd could see the value in having a small group of those, although the Earth Ward probably would not allow it. He laid Brad gently on the ground.

"Thanks," said Brad.

Todd grabbed the blanket Valerie handed him and placed it under Brad's head. "Just try to relax."

Brad grimaced. "Yeah…I'll try." He lowered his head onto the blanket, and a moment later, his eyes closed.

Todd figured Brad was in more pain than he admitted. A good rest should help some. Todd rejoined the others outside.

"All right, here's the plan," said Dalton. "I'm going to do some scouting across the gorge. Evot is going to stay here and provide a watch over the area. You three will hold this spot, but I don't think anything will bother you. If something approaches, I'll come back."

Rick gestured across the gorge. "You're going out solo?"

"Camouflaged, yes," said Dalton. "I want to get an idea of what we're dealing with based on Evot's path."

Todd lifted his chin. "We got this. Between the three of us, we can hold down the fort."

"Good. I won't be long," said Dalton. He faded from view.

Todd could still see him thanks to the ARI, but without it, Dalton would be like a ghost. He must have terrified those he investigated in the past. His movement was also unreal at times. In just a short amount of time, he was already some distance away. Even his footsteps were quiet, although Todd did see signs of disruption on the ground. He suspected anyone would be hard-pressed to link them to footprints.

"He's like a ninja," said Rick.

"I can hear you still," said Dalton

Rick smiled. "It's true, though."

Todd looked around. "All right, let's make sure this place is as secure as we can get it."

He took some time to check out the area. It could be defended but could also become a death trap if something was too much for the group. If they could hold out until Dalton returned, they would be okay. The immediate area outside the enclosure was open, and beyond that was a small stretch that led to the dangerous forest. He doubted anything was coming that way, and they now had an effective defense against the flying creatures thanks to Evot.

An hour later after darkness had settled, Todd gathered Rick, Valerie, and Evot near the enclosure's entrance.

"All right," he said. "We'll split up into watches. I'll take the first one for four hours. Valerie, you get the next four, then Rick, the final four. That should span about twelve hours with coverage, and Evot will be around for all of it. It's almost 9:00 p.m., so hopefully we're good to go in the morning. Dalton should be back before the second watch as well."

"I can work with that," said Valerie.

Rick flashed a thumbs-up.

"I can help watch!" said Brad from inside.

Todd peeked in. "You can keep whoever is on watch company if you're feeling up to it."

"Will do."

Todd faced the others and pulled out his SG-5. "All right, you guys get some rest." He glanced at Valerie. "I'll wake you in four."

They tapped his arm and back as they went past him.

Todd walked out a bit and surveyed the environment. He loved Evot's aerial view since she had night vision, as did his contact lenses. There was total coverage, and he could see for a good mile in any direction. It would be difficult for anything to sneak up unless it burrowed through the ground or took out Evot and came from the sky.

On the larger map, he could even see Dalton's location. He scouted around the mountain area, and Todd looked forward to hearing what he found. He moved back toward the entrance and leaned against the wall. Hopefully, it would be a quiet four hours.

After two hours, Dalton returned.

Todd moved out to meet him. "Have a fun trip?"

"It had its moments," said Dalton. He gestured inside. "Everyone seems to be sleeping."

"Yeah. I don't think anything wants a piece of Rick's snoring," said Todd.

Dalton grinned. "I suppose not."

"What are we dealing with out there?"

Dalton sighed. "There's definitely humanoids there, and they're primitive. Tribal."

Todd studied the hologram Dalton projected. The humanoids stood around seven to eight feet tall and were very muscular. It was the mouth filled with half-inch razor-sharp teeth that covered the bottom half of the face that stuck out. They had three eyes, with one on the forehead. Four beefy arms hung at their sides, and their bone armor and face paint made them look fierce. They must be apex predators of the area.

"Um…how many are we talking about?" he asked.

Dalton frowned. "Guessing thousands spread out across a large valley. We're at the end of their territory, so there aren't many there, but I got a better view of the area from the mountain."

Todd ran a hand over his mouth. "We should probably avoid them if we can."

"That may be hard to do. Every path I inspected goes by at least one guard post or what passes for one. Mainly two or three of them sitting in or around trees. If they engage us, we'll need to down them fast, then move. There is also the possibility they may be friendly."

"Maybe. You see any other dangers?"

Dalton grimaced and projected a variety of creatures.

Todd's eyes widened. One animal looked like a bush, except it shot out barbed tendrils. That was not something he ever wanted to take a leak near. Another creature resembled a small dog, but it had two arms on its back that arced forward and ended in sharp bone spears. There was also a beast that looked like a boar. It had a massive mouth with sharp teeth, and its fur was bristly. Bone spikes resided on its back.

Dalton gestured at the last one. "The humanoids had caught and killed one of those."

"Even the prey is tough out here," said Todd.

Dalton looked out across the gorge. "This place is not meant for humans, at least not ones from our Earth. I don't know what we'll run into or what the tribe's patterns are, but tomorrow we're going home."

Todd slapped Dalton on the back. "We will, and we got watch covered, so if you want to take a break, have at it."

Dalton nodded and sat outside the entrance.

Tomorrow would probably be a slog through the jungle, and now they would have to potentially deal with hostile humanoids and creatures. Todd would be ready, and he suspected once the others had some rest, they would be too.

CHAPTER
EIGHTEEN

Dalton yawned as he slowly opened his eyes. He had been dreaming of his family, but the rotting smell from the forest that wafted over snapped him awake. A quick survey of the environment showed Rick and Valerie leaning against a nearby rock wall, while Brad and Todd slept inside the enclosure. Evot provided an aerial overview of the area. Everything seemed stable, and it was 8:30 a.m. according to his ARI.

He stood and looked at Rick. "Easy watch, I take it?"

"Yeah, not much going on out here. It's sorta peaceful if you ignore the murder trees, their smell and the like."

They chuckled.

Dalton eyed Valerie. "I see you're up early."

She grinned. "Just keeping Rick company." She laughed when Rick poked her arm.

"Company…is that what you kids are calling it these days?" asked Dalton. He tapped his nose. "Enhanced senses."

She and Rick looked at each other.

Dalton laughed.

If everything went well, they would do ten miles with ease and minimal interaction. It would probably be a bit more difficult than that, but Dalton remained hopeful. He peered inside the enclosure where Brad and Todd stirred.

"Feeling any better?" asked Dalton, examining Brad.

"I am, actually. Although..." Brad jumped and blazed past Dalton.

Dalton did not need his enhanced senses to tell him what was going on behind the rock where Brad disappeared to. He flushed the poison out and then some.

Todd stretched and joined Dalton outside. "Looks like we're all up."

Evot landed and assumed human form. "Yes, and the area is clear."

"Glad for that," said Todd as he acknowledged Rick and Valerie, then wrinkled his nose. "What is that?"

Rick laughed. "Brad just clearing his system."

Todd grimaced. "I was thinking of getting a meat stick. Not so sure now."

Evot pulled some wipes from Brad's pack, then went to him.

That did not surprise Dalton. Evot had taken a particular liking to Brad, and she attended to him even if he was clueless about her interest. After Brad returned, Dalton signaled for everyone to gather.

"Evot, project the area and path we're going to take," he said.

"Of course," she said.

Dalton traced the blue path. "I've defined four waypoints. The first one is across the gorge and is a bit into the jungle. It has scattered trees, and the undergrowth isn't too bad there. The second waypoint is to a tree that serves as a guard post for a humanoid tribe in the area, but it's only the tip of a larger group farther east. I'm hoping to avoid interaction as much as possible. However, there were three tribal members present at the tree when I visited it. We'll try to sneak by, but if that fails, I'll try to talk our way past somehow."

"Why not just stun them and not worry about detection?" asked Rick.

"I'd like to give them a choice. They may not be violent," said Dalton. "The third waypoint is to the base of the mountain, and the last one is where we can portal out. Per Evot's scan, my recall portal would open into an apartment, and it's the lowest point I can open safely for everyone to cross. Any questions?"

Brad looked around. "We're looking at about ten miles. What do we do if that tribe comes after us? I assume we run and fight if need be but in a thick jungle?"

"The path I scouted accounts for that," said Dalton. "I don't know if we will run into any creatures. Since I haven't seen the forest in the daytime, that remains an unknown variable."

Rick raised his head. "Well, I'm ready to get off this rock."

"Same," said Valerie.

"Okay. Everyone take thirty to get food and drink." Dalton glanced at Brad. "Or use the bathroom if you need to."

"I'm good now," said Brad.

After thirty minutes, the team gathered around Dalton.

"All right," he said. "Make sure your helmets are on. I know it'll be uncomfortable, but if it keeps something from piercing your head, it's worth it." He entered Scoutspectre mode.

The trip to the bridge across the gorge was uneventful. It was close by, and there were no creatures in the area. The team appeared to be in a good mood, and Dalton hoped their trip ahead continued without issue.

The first waypoint did not take long to reach. There was minimal need for hacking the undergrowth, and the few creatures that appeared were small and ran away. Brad seemed to struggle some due to the uneven ground, and Dalton suspected he still suffered some effects from the poison. Rick had also been hit with it, but he had accelerated regeneration, so he was able to shrug it off. Todd and Valerie marched along with no issues, and both tended to Brad. Evot circled above and provided a good overview of the area so there would be no surprises.

Dalton raised a hand. "Let's break for ten."

Brad immediately sat next to a tree, while Rick went off into the bushes.

Todd and Valerie joined Dalton.

"Not too bad so far," said Todd.

Dalton's eyes narrowed. "It's the next waypoint that bothers me. We'll be entering the tribe's territory soon, and the route I chose is based on what was there last night. It may be different this morning."

"Then we deal with it," said Valerie. "Worst case, we book it to the extraction point."

Dalton gestured at Brad. "We can't move at an optimal rate, but that's okay. We'll get there as a team."

"Count on it," said Todd, lifting his chin.

Dalton appreciated their vote of confidence, but the easy part of the trip was over. The humanoids he had observed were expert hunters, and they were comfortable with the environment. The team was strangers in that regard, and as proud as he was of them, they would have their work cut out for them if things went sideways.

After the break, he motioned forward. "Let's move."

The undergrowth to the second waypoint thickened as they continued. Dalton had detected creatures on the perimeter of his sensory range, but they seemed to want no part of the group. He figured that was due to their unfamiliar scent.

An hour later, they paused behind a large tree.

"All right, there's four humanoids ahead, so one more than I previously scouted. Two are in the tree, and the others are at the base. Let's try to go around them as quietly as possible. If they engage, let me try to talk with them. If things get violent, we'll take them down, then rush to the third waypoint. Is everyone ready?" asked Dalton.

The group nodded.

"Okay, follow me," he said.

He activated his camouflage shielding and hustled to the side. He did not know how the tribal members would react. He did not sense any others in the area, but they probably had some sort of communication system, such as audio calls.

The undergrowth was unforgiving, and several times he had to hack a bush, then wait to see if the humanoids sensed him or not. The rest of the team behind him were doing their best at being quiet, but they were definitely noticeable to him. Given how good he thought the humanoids' senses were, he expected to have to try to talk to them.

He paused when the humanoids froze. Maybe they tried to listen. When the humanoids moved again, he continued.

It took fifteen painstaking minutes, but the team finally reached a spot with open ground that was to the left of the tree. He understood why they chose that tree as a guard post. It had thick branches, and the surrounding area was cleared out. Its height also allowed the tribal members to climb up it if need be. In a place like this, the tree was a natural defensive position. There was no other way around the tree unless they went into unknown territory.

He motioned for the group to rush across the open area as fast as possible. As they took off, the humanoids took notice. He told the team to continue to the other side, then switched to his official outfit and faced the tribal members. The ones on the ground approached them.

"I don't know if you can understand me, but we mean you no harm," said Dalton with hands raised. "We just want safe passage."

One of the humanoids in the branches threw a spear at Dalton.

He switched to Scoutspectre mode and focused. Everything slowed as he dodged the spear. If it had hit, it would have hit his face. He used his RSG to hit the two tribal members in the branches.

As they fell, they let out earsplitting cries.

The other two humanoids threw their spears as the bodies landed behind them.

Dalton blocked both with his shield, then dashed forward and hit the tribal member on the left with his stun baton.

It barked loudly before crumpling.

The right one took off.

Dalton tossed his baton to his left hand, then used his RSG to hit the fleeing humanoid. Like the others, it bellowed before falling. Their defense system was verbal, and now four alerts had been sounded.

"Everyone, to me!" said Dalton.

The team hustled to his location.

"That was not quiet at all, but you did try to be peaceful with them," said Brad.

"I know, but I still don't think they're violent despite what just happened. My appearance may have just frightened them, and that was a natural response. Nonetheless, we now know they seem to have some ability to call out when going unconscious," said Dalton. He sighed. "We need to get to the third waypoint. Let's go!"

Dalton's heart raced as they moved out. This was a worst-case scenario. There was no way the other members of the tribe did not hear the ruckus. If anything, they were probably conditioned to recognize it, and the one he shot farther away emitted a slightly different sound. The deafening bellow most likely conveyed information not only on their location but what they dealt with. It reminded him of a prairie dog communication system.

He gritted his teeth. Now it was a race to the mountain. Hopefully, the tribe would investigate the guard post first, which would give the team a running start. Then again, based on the cries, the tribe might know to head off the group. Whatever happened, he needed to keep the team safe.

.... ⬜⬜⬜ ....

Todd breathed hard as he kept pace with Dalton. Although the undergrowth was an issue, Dalton vibrated one hand like a chainsaw as he cut out a path. He had also reformed his MH into a machete. The vibrating took some energy to do, but Dalton was a one-man clearing machine on a mission. When the humanoids had cried out, it startled Todd. Not only was it loud, but he could see it as a strong defensive group tactic.

As they charged forward, he checked the overhead view. His eyes widened at the sea of red dots converging on their point. They kept popping in and out, most likely due to Evot losing track of them when they went under trees. If it had been a dozen or so dots, he would have thought their chances were good, but there were hundreds, and they were moving fast. As competent as the team was and as powerful as Dalton was, taking on hundreds of skilled fighters in their native jungle was a losing proposition.

"You've got to be kidding me," said Rick. "There's so many."

"Keep going," said Dalton. "If we must fight, we will, but we move as a team. No one is left behind."

Todd appreciated Dalton's cool head despite the war band about to descend on them. The first tribal member to appear looked like the others, except it had some type of white paint on its face. It carried a spear in one hand and a metallic blade in the other. What surprised Todd was how quickly it had scaled a tree.

The humanoid threw the spear at Dalton.

He blocked it, then fired his RSG.

The tribal member emitted a loud noise, then fell.

"Everyone we take down gives away our position," said Todd.

He got a good look at the attacker when he passed by. The mouth was unusually large, and the prominent display of jagged, sharp teeth unnerved him. One good bite from that, and there would be flesh ripped off. Dalton had picked up the pace, as had the sea of blinking red dots.

Seven hunters appeared in the team's path. Two climbed a nearby tree, and five waited on the ground. Three threw their spears at Dalton, but he knocked them away with his shield. Todd aimed and hit one of the two in the tree, while Rick took out the other.

The five on the ground charged.

Dalton ran into them like a bowling ball and bashed two.

Valerie spun into action on the left. She dodged a slash attack before hitting the attacker with her stun baton.

Brad struck one on the right, and Gizmo got another.

Dalton tapped the ones he had knocked back earlier.

"Not so bad," said Rick.

"The tribe has changed their path. They're not only coming here, but they're also ahead of us," said Evot over comms.

Rick shook his head. "Okay, maybe bad."

Valerie grimaced. "Yeah, we need to not be here."

"Agreed," said Dalton. "Let's move!"

Todd took a moment to catch his breath, then soldiered on. Dalton's pace was relentless, but so was the tribe's. Even with a head start, the tribe formed a crescent formation to the team's right. Dalton had already adjusted the group's path to head forward and to the left.

The second group of humanoids they encountered was larger, with six in the trees and nine on the ground.

Todd hit one in the right tree, while Rick got the other.

Valerie and Brad got two in the left tree.

Dalton dashed forward into the nine on the ground.

The ones in the middle tree hit him with their spears, but they bounced off Dalton's armor.

Gizmo appeared on the branch and struck both with a stun shot.

Rick and Valerie joined Dalton in the ground skirmish.

As Todd went to take a shot, a spear hit him in his right thigh. Searing pain shot through him, and he cried out and fell to the ground.

Brad rushed over while dodging another spear. He yanked the spear out, then applied the gel from the hub.

An attacker kicked Brad, sending him sprawling. It raised its sword above Todd.

He swallowed hard.

Gizmo jumped on Todd's chest and fired a stun blast.

The attacker faltered.

Evot appeared in humanoid form and pushed the tribal member back, then helped Todd stand.

"Thanks," he said.

Gizmo beeped at Todd.

"Of course," said Evot as she reformed into a fly swarm and assisted Brad, who evaded spears.

Todd winced as he picked up his SG-5. Dalton, Rick, and Valerie had taken all but two. The ones from the side and back had caught Todd off guard. While the team had engaged forward, these other ones sneaked in. It was a good tactic, but Todd did not want a repeat of it.

After the last two went down, Dalton scanned Todd. "Your suit protected you for the most part. The spear still penetrated but not too deep. Can you run?"

"It hurts, but I can try," said Todd.

Dalton took a moment, then pointed west. "We need to head that way. There's twenty ahead, fifty-six coming from the east, and thirty-one from behind us. Farther east are over one hundred more."

Brad shook his head. "We can't fight that many."

"Right, but we still have a head start. Follow me!"

Todd tried to keep up with Dalton, but the pain in his thigh made him stumble a few times. Rick and Valerie helped him move, but it slowed the group considerably.

They reached a mountain wall.

Todd studied Evot's aerial view. The third waypoint could be reached if they stayed along the wall. It would eventually lead to a slope toward the fourth waypoint, and they could get away. The problem was that some of the red dots had already massed at the third waypoint, and others came to pin them in.

He leaned against the wall. "There's a cave between here and the third waypoint. Maybe we can duck in there."

Dalton nodded. "I see it, but we don't know what might be in there. However, it's better than becoming a pincushion. Maybe I can seal off a tunnel or something, then chew through rock until we're high enough."

"You have the energy for that?" asked Brad. "That's a lot of rock. May as well cross over at that point."

Dalton furrowed his brow. "The only problem with crossing over too early is that if we do get stuck because I don't have enough energy, then there's no way out. At least here we have a fighting chance if that occurs."

"Worth a shot," said Rick. "I think we could probably take down a good portion of these assholes, but they would overwhelm us eventually."

"I agree." Dalton scanned Todd again. "How're you feeling?"

Todd sighed. "Hurts to walk, and I'm slowing the group down. Running on adrenaline at the moment."

"All right. I think the cave is probably our best bet, but we need to move now," said Dalton. "I'll carry Todd so we can move faster." He entered Scoutspectre mode and knelt. A small platform jutted out from his lower back. "Lean back on that."

Todd complied. The nanosuit extending over him was a strange sensation, but it kept his hands free. It reminded him of a child's seat. He had already reversed his backpack so it was on the front, but he could also use his SG-5.

"Just like that demon world except facing the other way," said Valerie.

"Yeah." Dalton stood and balanced himself. "Let's go!"

Todd grimaced, as each step shot pain through his leg, but it was better than trying to run on it. The plan was sound, but there were a lot of unknown variables. He did not think such a large cave would be uninhabited. They could be going from bad to worse. At least from his vantage point, he could cover the rear, but he also crippled Dalton's combat performance. Hopefully, they could reach the cave without issue.

Valerie kept up with the group's breakneck pace. The situation was tough. They were corralled, and the third waypoint at the base of the slope was now out of reach. While they could try to fight through, it was an open area. They would be riddled with spears at that point. If not that, then it would be a pitched battle with over a hundred warriors native to the environment.

The cave seemed like the best choice, but it was still an unknown. It might be a short cave or narrower as it went farther in. There could be vicious bugs or animals living there. Maybe the tribe pushed them toward the cave for a reason. She hated uncertainty, but out of a list of bad choices, it was the least bad option.

Valerie admired Dalton carrying Todd. She recalled when she had ridden on Dalton's back on the previous case. It was a handy piece of functionality. Rick looked more amped than usual, but she trusted he was ready to throw down with his life if need be. Brad had turned out to be adept with his

SP-8. Gizmo had also earned his keep. The stickbots had not come into play much, probably due to Brad not wanting to focus on controlling them in the middle of a frantic fight.

Along the way to the cave, the team had seen several tribal members, but they took the humanoids down quickly with a few stun blasts. She knew that would not work as effectively when they had to dodge dozens of spears at the same time. Other attackers came from behind but remained just out of range. If the group slowed or stopped, they would need to deal with that. Being hunted was not new to her, although the sheer number of hunters involved was.

After ten minutes, the team paused to the side of a massive cave entrance. In front of it stood a burly humanoid, larger than others of its ilk. Behind it were forty-two warriors, per Evot's count. Valerie's breathing ramped up. This was it. The final battle. Thankfully, the tribe did not open with tossing spears. She suspected they wanted to interact.

Dalton unloaded Todd and then switched to his official outfit as he faced the humanoid.

It barked at him and made unusual hand gestures.

"Okay...not sure what that means, but it's using some sort of sign language mixed with various noises," said Dalton over comms. He gestured at the team, made a circle, then pointed up the slope ahead.

The humanoid pointed back out into the forest, then at Rick's SG-5.

The ground trembled.

Dalton stared at the cave while everyone looked around.

Valerie's pulse quickened when a massive, clawed hand reached out of the cave and flattened three tribal members.

What walked out of the cave was something out of a nightmare. The creature was at least twenty feet tall and walked on four thick legs. It was like a lizard version of a centaur except with scaled skin. Its head reminded her of a dragon. It moved fast, and in just a short amount of time, it had not only crushed three humanoids, but it went to town on the others.

Dalton and the others moved farther to the left of the entrance.

The large humanoid they had been talking to, which she suspected was the leader, backed up and motioned at his fellow members. They formed a semicircle with their spears poking out. The ones from behind the team joined the leader.

It was an impressive sight as more and more of the tribe arrived and backed the leader. Unfortunately for them, their spears and blades could not pierce the creature's skin. It tore through them like tissue paper.

Dalton looked back at the team. "We need to help them."

"Shouldn't we escape while they're distracted?" asked Rick.

Dalton shook his head. "This thing is still in our way, and there are more warriors on the other side. I think if we help them, they'll let us pass. Although they attacked us in our first meeting, they didn't in this second encounter. I take it they are curious, and to be honest, they look like they need help. As for this monster, the fact it is on their turf means it has no fear of them."

"It's what Evaran would do, so no surprise," said Brad, swatting Rick's arm.

"Then let's kick its ass," said Rick.

The team fanned out and unloaded a barrage of stun beams on the creature.

It roared to face them.

Valerie's mouth went dry. If she were solo, this thing would slaughter her. Even with the team, it still might. The stuns had no effect except to piss it off.

It lumbered forward with outstretched claws.

Dalton peered back at the group. "Aim for its eyes and nose."

"What're you gonna do?" asked Todd.

"I have an idea. Trust me." Dalton ran toward the creature.

It grabbed him and lifted him off the ground.

He vibrated his suit, which caused the beast to shriek and open its clawed hand.

As the creature bent over in pain, Valerie and the others unloaded a hailstorm of stun blasts at its eyes and nose.

The beast roared again as it covered its face.

Dalton dropped to the ground and ran under the monster, then jabbed his stun baton into its underside.

The creature shook, then crashed. Its breathing went shallow as it stopped moving.

Dalton jumped on top of it and faced the tribe. After nodding at the leader, he jumped down.

The leader studied the downed creature, then spun around. He raised his spear and barked. The tribe reciprocated. The leader made a sign with his hands, and silence fell. He faced Dalton and pointed at the slope ahead.

Valerie got goosebumps when the tribe members ahead of them moved away from the mountain wall, generating a path to the slope.

Dalton motioned for the team to follow.

Valerie examined the warriors as she passed by. They were fierce, and she could not believe things played out as they did. Although there had been death, it seemed this hunter society had honor, and Dalton taking down what was probably a big threat to them afforded him some of that, which she suspected he had realized when he decided to incapacitate the beast.

She peered back after they were on their way. The downed creature would not survive this event, not with dozens of tribal members attacking it. Although the blades had seemed ineffective initially, they were quite effective on the underbelly. The creature must have been a persistent thorn in their side. The leader following the group seemed odd. She hoped he did not intend anything malicious, but he was probably more curious than anything.

After thirty minutes, they reached the fourth waypoint.

Dalton looked exhausted via her ARI, and he had carried Todd uphill all the way. Todd now stood with Rick's help. Rick and Brad appeared drained as well. Evot had rejoined them in human form, which elicited barks from the surprised tribal members following them. Valerie was tired too and longed for some well-deserved rest.

"Finally. We're here," said Dalton. "Everyone ready?"

"Yeah. Let's get off this nightmare Earth," said Todd.

Dalton made a slow wave at the tribal leader, then faced the mountain wall. He extended his right arm. Blue flames enveloped his fist and forearm.

The tribal members murmured.

A portal appeared on the mountain wall.

Dalton motioned for everyone to go through.

Todd and Rick entered first. Brad and Evot were next.

Valerie followed them but peeked back to see Dalton slightly bow to the tribe before stepping through. After he came through, the portal closed.

She surveyed the apartment living room they stood in. A man sat on the couch, his mouth open and eyes wide. The TV dinner he had been eating slipped onto his lap.

Dalton gestured at him. "Sorry. We're just checking for rats." He looked around at the others. "No rats here. Let's go."

Valerie struggled not to laugh. As they exited the apartment, she verified the man still sat there in shock. He might need to check his pants after all that.

They assembled in the hallway outside.

"Okay," said Dalton. "I think it's safe to say the hotel is out of the question. If Dynkara knew we were at the hangar, then they probably know where we're staying. We'll need a new place. Brad, find us a motel somewhere we can lay low."

"You got it," said Brad.

Dalton gestured at Evot. "Pick up our SUV and bring it here."

"Of course," she said.

"For the rest of us, let's wait outside, preferably somewhere out of sight," said Dalton.

"Just glad to be back," said Rick.

Todd grimaced as he massaged his leg. "Yeah, me too."

After ten minutes, they reached the side of the apartment building.

Todd sat against the wall with Rick and Brad while Dalton scouted the area.

Valerie took in some fresh air. It was not as clean as in the jungle Earth, but she was happy to be back. Todd grimaced and rubbed his leg wound, and she was sure he would get treated once they got the SUV back. She had been impressed with Brad. He was a survivor, and she suspected running from killer androids had helped hone that instinct. Gizmo had earned his battle stripes as well.

Evot had been helpful, and Valerie doubted they would have done as well without Evot's aerial views. Her ability to dig through obstructions also came in handy in addition to her retrieving information from the hub. Valerie eyed Rick. He had been a warrior on the battlefield, and she fought back-to-back with him in some of the fights. He even took on three warriors at once and prevailed with just his stun baton. His brutal, raw style appealed to her.

Dalton had been a solid leader as always. None of this would have been possible without him. He put the team first, and it showed in everything he did. She sat next to the others. Hopefully, they could relax in peace.

CHAPTER
NINETEEN

As Evot flew toward the SUV, she processed the recent trip. Parallel Earths were not new to her, as she had seen ten others, and technically, this Earth was one. Dynkara was advanced, and the robot guards had intrigued her. Brad's ability to control them was also impressive, although it did require some rewiring of the hardware.

Todd had been a capable second-in-command, and she saw Dalton taking him under his wing. He had done that with many a junior Scoutspectre and gave Todd a lot of respect. Rick had been as advertised, and his physical prowess helped when needed. His speed and strength were far above a normal human's, and on a planet like the one they came from, it was a good skillset to have.

Evot was curious about the blood bond between him and Valerie. Although Evot understood the causes and effects of the process and what was involved, it was another thing to observe and record the interaction. Rick and Valerie had an interesting discussion, then interaction earlier in the morning. Although Evot did not focus on their activities, it was recorded as part of her surveillance. Dalton would probably rate their actions as naughty.

Valerie had been fearless yet again when fighting. Like Rick, she was stronger and faster than a normal human, and she evaded multiple blows while counterattacking. She also tended to roll and flip around. In one move, she used a tribal member's shoulders as a launchpad to leap over another and hit them both with her stun baton.

The SUV came into range after twenty minutes.

Evot dipped down and scanned what was left of the burnt-out frame. Although anyone could have torched the car, she assigned a high probability that it was the same group that had attacked the team at the hangar.

"The SUV has been damaged," she said over comms.

"They torched it," said Dalton with a sigh. "Requisition a new one from New Orleans, and have it delivered to the motel Brad found for us. We're going to use an online ride service to get there."

"Of course," said Evot.

She contacted the Earth Ward's requisitioning system and used Dalton's credentials. Although she could hack in, there was no need, and this way would leave an audit trail—something Dalton always wanted. The SUV they would receive would not have the custom work of the previous one, but it would suffice until they got back to base. She put in another request for the same custom SUV that had been torched to be delivered to the base in Columbus.

"I have put in the requisition order for an SUV to be delivered to the motel Brad located. I also put one in for the custom one to go to our base."

"You're awesome, Evot," said Dalton.

"Thank you."

She enjoyed praise from him. When she was only an enhanced VI, he still treated her as a unique being. Now that she was an AI, she had context on those memories. In one case back in her original timeline, they were at an alien bar, and she was in her human form. Dalton had been drinking a green drink, and it got knocked over. She had caught it, but some had splashed onto her face. When she handed it back to him, he asked if she was feeling green, then laughed for 20.3 seconds. She understood now that he had been teasing her and it was a sign of affection.

"How's the situation at the hangar?" asked Dalton.

"Most of the group has left, but there's still a police presence, and Crayzo and a select few are around."

"Crayzo...he must be Dynkara's unwitting muscle here. See if you can get close and hear anything."

She was Dalton's eyes and ears, and he would be able to see and hear everything she did. That was one facet of their unique bond. There was a range limit, but within the framework of an advanced network, especially one with satellites, the range was effectively everywhere.

The area she flew over was right outside the hangar. There were several police cars and two black vans. Crayzo walked over to one of the cars and initiated a strange series of hand interactions with a police officer registered as Carl Breyers. She analyzed their custom handshake routine as a symbolic gesture of a special bond between the two. Perhaps the conversation would yield some information.

She flew over and landed on the edge of the hangar.

"Whaddup, dog?" asked Carl. "They said there's an Earth Ward inspector team out here. Dalton Kingston and his crew."

"Yeah, but underground somewhere. No way them bitches got past us. Know what I'm saying?" asked Crayzo.

They slapped hands.

"What's their deal?" asked Carl.

"Their card's been pulled, man. Real shit." Crayzo sucked on his teeth. "I heard they were here, so you *know* the click came strapped, man. Heard Dalton was some superstar. Burned his ride, though, you know?"

"Yeah," said Carl. He studied the hangar. "You seen that place down there?"

Crayzo shook his head. "Man, that's some hoodoo shit right there."

Carl snickered. "We got some guy, but he ain't snitching, and now some big dogs snatched him up." He sighed. "I gotta relieve someone."

"Keep grinding, man," said Crayzo.

They slapped hands again, and Carl entered the hangar.

Evot found their conversation fascinating. Although she understood the context of the discussion, the word usage and choice seemed strange to her. However, she knew slang differed based on geography. Crayzo still thought the team was underground, and he took credit for destroying the SUV. There was also more confirmation that parts of local law enforcement were involved.

She watched Crayzo for a bit longer, but he mostly sat outside and smoked something. Others came and went, and she calculated that he hoped the team would be found.

After a while, he drove off with some others. She did one final flyby of the area, then flew toward the motel.

After twenty minutes, she assumed human form when she arrived at the motel room. Todd and Brad were in the other booked room and were apparently fast asleep. A closed door connected the two rooms. Dalton sat at a small table, while Valerie and Rick relaxed on nearby beds. Evot sat opposite Dalton.

"Sounds like we know what Crayzo is up to," said Dalton.

"Yes. He thinks we're still there."

Dalton rubbed his chin. "They're definitely unaware of Dynkara. I'm guessing the only people who really know them are Septimus, Camilla, and Tiberius. Through them, everything else falls into place."

Valerie looked over. "They put out contracts via the Facilitator and then had agreements with local law enforcement to guard certain assets, like the hangar. They can also call on local muscle with ease."

"That's right," said Dalton. "It seems Dynkara agents can also do whatever's necessary, like having the Baton Rouge Crew watch the crime scene. Septimus may not have known about that incident. Plausible deniability."

"What a tangled web. I'm just glad to be back," said Valerie.

"Same here," said Rick.

Dalton waved a finger between him and Evot. "We need to process what we learned from the hub, then we need to put in an update to the Earth Ward systems."

"In case we don't make it, right?" asked Valerie.

"Protocol. The information is secured, and in the event of our deaths, it's released as determined by the council."

"Wish Inspector Sean had done that."

Dalton sighed. "The inspector arm is still new. We're feeling out what works and what doesn't. This is one protocol that should always be followed, and Sean was more old school in that regard. He kept everything close to him, and as a result, we had to go through what we did to get where we are."

Valerie stared at the ceiling. "Now imagine if we died, and someone got our notes about a giant beast, parallel Earths, robot guards, brutal tribal members, and rats the size of dogs."

They laughed.

Evot relished observing their conversation. Dalton was right that the protocol was still new and had not been fully adopted. By his using it, she calculated a high rate of adoption by the Earth Ward.

Valerie had created a hypothetical situation that ended with their laughter. Humor was hard for Evot to master. Valerie had phrased the situation as it would most likely occur if the team perished. While that would not seem funny, the image of someone being surprised as they read the case's notes seemed to be what was comedic. She suspected they would just be confused.

Dalton faced Evot. "All right, you ready to go through all that hub data?"

"I am, and I have organized it by logical topic."

"Okay. We can use external visualization. I have a headache, and I want to be able to have a cup of coffee."

Evot extended her hand and projected a hierarchal tree of topics. One disadvantage of exploring things in her unsecured space was that Dalton and Brad had to focus to enter it, and in the outside world, they lost control of their body. Although they could regain it once they were out, it prevented simple things, like getting a cup of coffee, using the bathroom, or even eating.

There was a lot of information to process, and Dalton had already begun expanding various nodes, which projected the node's data to the right. This would probably take a while, but she was happy to assist him.

Brad yawned as he slowly opened his eyes. For a moment, he thought he was still on the parallel Earth. The dirty ceiling suggested otherwise. The nearby alarm clock showed it was 5:30 p.m., and a sleeping Todd occupied the bed next to him. The room was quiet and smelled like sweat. Brad checked out the gel that had been dabbed over his wounds. He needed a shower and suspected the gel would come off if he did. Nothing a set of bandages could not handle. His underarmor would also need repair.

He sat on the side of his bed and rubbed his eyes. The nap had been refreshing, but he did not want to mess up his sleep cycle. He studied the fresh uniform neatly folded on a table across the room. A note sat on top of the jacket. He walked over and read it. Evot had washed his suit for him and left cleaning supplies in the bathroom. He grinned. She was always doing nice things for him.

He hopped into the shower. The gel took some effort, but it dislodged after a few pulls. It was an amazing substance, and it reminded him of super glue, except it did not take your skin with it when peeled off. The sheer amount of puncture and bite wounds alarmed him. They would take some time to heal. He did not have regeneration like Dalton, Rick, and Valerie.

After showering, Brad dried off and applied bandages before slipping on his underarmor. It amazed him that a quick spray from the showerhead could clean it. The technology was fantastic. He thought he would have to turn it inside out, but with all the holes in it, he just needed to hold it under the showerhead and let the water clean it up. It also dried fast in that when he set it outside the stall, it was dry and waiting for him.

He put on his suit and checked himself out in the mirror. His right cheek had a bruise, and he had a bump on his head. Despite the turbulent trip to the parallel Earth, he learned a lot more about the multiverse in general. He did a final check on himself, then eased open the door between the rooms and slipped inside.

Dalton looked up from his chair. "There he is."

Brad closed the door and sat opposite him. "Alive and well."

"You look a lot better," said Dalton.

"Trying. I'm still a bit queasy, but I feel like I'm on the last part of it. I think I'm just hungry."

Dalton smiled. "Excellent. Rick and Valerie went to pick up food, and Evot went with them. She helped pick dinner.

Rick wanted fried chicken, Valerie wanted jambalaya, and they found some place that serves both."

"Wow, that does sound good," said Brad. "I hope they bring enough back for everyone."

"I told them to go wild, but Evot already calculated an optimal amount."

"Sounds like her," said Brad.

Dalton gestured at him. "I know you'll probably downplay this, but I saw you put Gizmo on Todd. I couldn't reach him, and if you hadn't, we'd be in a different situation."

"I couldn't fight hand to hand, but Gizmo and I could shoot. It seemed like the right thing to do at the moment."

"And that's what I mean. You have a survivor instinct about you, yet you made sure the team was covered," said Dalton.

"Evot helped too," said Brad.

"Even so, I guarantee Todd is thankful you were there."

"It's cool."

Todd entered the room and rubbed his eyes. "My ears were burning." He sat on the side of the bed.

"We were just discussing Gizmo hopping on your chest when that warrior was about to cleave you in half," said Dalton.

Todd grinned. "Yeah, not my best moment." He slapped hands with Brad. "He had my back, though."

"It was chaotic out there," said Brad. "There's a hundred different ways one of us could have died."

Although Brad was sure Dalton noticed it, Brad's anxiousness had been cranked to ten ever since they went to the parallel Earth. The robot guards, while not as tough or efficient as android killers, still reminded him of his original Earth. Then when they left the hub, he almost became chow for flying animals and a brutal warrior tribe.

"I'm just glad to be back in one piece," said Todd. He motioned at Dalton. "I had to be carried like a damn kid in a car seat."

They laughed.

"Better that than dead," said Dalton.

Todd looked down. "I didn't feel like I contributed much out there. Brad had Gizmo and control of the robots. Rick had, well, he's Rick, and Valerie was an acrobat on the battlefield. You, of course, led the group, and Evot provided a lot of utility."

Dalton eyed him. "But you did contribute. You managed the group, which allowed me to seal the security portals and scout out the path we would take to the mountain. In combat, I watched you hit a moving target most would miss. Your marksmanship is second to none."

"Yeah," said Brad. "I shot at one of those warriors, and he dodged my shot, but you hit him."

Todd smiled. "Okay, now I do feel better."

They laughed again.

"Speaking of better, what's for dinner?" asked Todd.

"Rick, Valerie, and Evot are getting us fried chicken and jambalaya," said Brad.

Todd grinned. "That's what I'm talking about. What's the ETA?"

"Thirty minutes or so."

"Sounds good."

The calm atmosphere relaxed Brad. It was a far cry from the morning's hectic pace. It made it hard to believe that earlier in the day he had been fighting not only for his life but also for his teammates' lives. There was never a dull moment on this team.

"We have a lot of data to sift through tonight," said Dalton.

Brad leaned back. "That's more my speed. I think we have everything to tie it all together."

"We do, and I want to make sure everything is ready to go when I confront the Lightville council."

Todd's eyes narrowed. "You think they'll offer up the guilty?"

"I honestly don't know," said Dalton. "I have an Earth Ward rapid response team that will be in the area tomorrow morning. If anything happens, we'll have backup. I expect Septimus, Camilla, and Tiberius to put up a fight in some way. They may already have something in motion, or they may not even show up."

"Yeah, it sounds like we should go in prepared to fight," said Todd.

"That's the plan. I want to give them a chance to come peacefully first, though," said Dalton.

"Makes sense."

"Evot and I have already gone through a large portion of the hub data. I'll brief the team before we go over there."

"All right," said Todd.

Brad gestured at Dalton. "About those other Earths…I think I located my original one."

"I saw you marked that one as special," said Dalton. He eyed Brad. "You feeling a desire to go visit it?"

Brad laughed. "No way. Maybe if we went in the *Torvatta*, but I doubt Evaran would loan us his ship for that."

Dalton grinned. "Stranger things have happened."

Although Brad was intrigued with the idea of visiting his old world and potentially grabbing a friend or two, it was not a pressing priority for him. He did enjoy sifting through all the other Earths, though. Their signatures would be given to the Earth Ward, and they would probably assign it to the exploration arm of the organization. They investigated the various coordinates via a rift portal—something that was heavily guarded. If they ever decided to visit his original Earth, he would be interested in learning what they discovered, although it would be dangerous to visit.

Todd eased back onto the bed. "Well, I don't know about you two, but I'm ready to eat."

"Evot said they're on their way back now," said Dalton.

Brad's stomach grumbled. He was still a bit queasy, but jambalaya sounded good. He took a moment to appreciate where he was. The team was coming together for a good meal and had survived another case so far. Hopefully, the good luck continued when they confronted the Lightville council.

CHAPTER
TWENTY

Todd relaxed against the headboard of the bed. Dinner had been great, and the room smelled of fried chicken and spices. Brad had been a monster when it came to the jambalaya. After meat sticks, the meal had been a nice upgrade. Although they were only gone from this Earth for about two days, everything tasted better than he remembered.

Evot sat opposite Dalton at the table near the entrance, while Rick leaned against the wall across from Todd. Valerie rested against the other bed's headboard. It was a cozy atmosphere, and Todd appreciated the small moments of downtime. However, Dalton had furrowed his brow for the last ten minutes. He was going over everything and said he planned to update the team tomorrow.

Todd loved these types of meetings, as they were learning opportunities for him. Dalton was a natural leader, and Todd took mental notes regarding presentation and interaction. It was not only during meetings but also back on the parallel

Earth where, when against a litany of unknowns, Dalton always seemed to have a plan. Per his knowledge, it boiled down to assessing all known information and planning based on the team's state and abilities.

Dalton wiped his mouth with a napkin. "All right. We got some food in us." He motioned at Brad. "Some are still shoveling it in."

Brad grinned. "I can't help it. This jambalaya is awesome."

Everyone laughed.

Dalton used humor, and he knew it would work. He had told Todd that understanding someone's background, then doing research on them helped form a better mental image of that team member. Although Todd already did some of that, he did not have access to the suite of technological and information tools the Earth Ward had.

"Okay, no worries. You can listen in," said Dalton. "I wanted to go over what we know at this point and the plan for tomorrow. We had two goals when we came here. The first was to find out who killed Inspector Sean and his team. We did that, and we know it was a Dynkara robot agent. The second goal was to follow up on Sean's case. We've done that as well, and we've identified Dynkara and their plan to assimilate this Earth. That plan had phases, and in phase one, they replace people and make deals with others who will help them in their goal. Septimus, Camilla, and Tiberius Genucia have been identified as points of contact."

"Looking forward to seeing how they try to weasel out of this," said Rick, scoffing.

Dalton nodded. "We don't know who hired the Baton Rouge Crew, Damian Wu and the Star Lotus clan, or Crayzo due to the Facilitator's involvement and lack of an audit trail. It's not a stretch to think it was Dynkara via their robot agent, the same one that tried to kill Valerie and me. Unfortunately, we can't use those attacks as evidence since we have no proof of who ordered them."

"Can't we just ask the Facilitator to help?" asked Brad.

Valerie shook her head. "The contractors are anonymous. It's set up that way on purpose."

"She's right. That doesn't mean those people won't face consequences for attacking us, but we can't tie them to Septimus or the others," said Dalton. "However, we have records of their involvement with Dynkara via the information from the hub. That, we can get them on."

"Is there any proof of their involvement other than just being names as points of contact?" asked Rick.

"The hub information has that and more," said Dalton. "Septimus and the others were not only points of contact, but they also helped select who was to be replaced and which organizations to infiltrate. They also served as a go-between for corrupt officers nationwide, and all those payments—as hard as they were to track—are listed. It seems they thought keeping their information on another Earth was foolproof."

"No wonder there was such a rapid response at the hangar," said Todd.

"Right," said Dalton. "They know we went through and that we've scheduled a meeting with the Lightville council. Earth Ward is tracking various bank accounts thanks to Brad and Evot."

"We'll nail them to the wall tomorrow and then case closed," said Valerie.

Dalton sighed. "I'd like to think that, but I suspect Septimus and the others won't go quietly. They're hundreds of years old and not used to being subjected to law. There's also the issue that the Lightville council may defend them. We'll find out tomorrow, but if things go bad, we have a rapid response team that will assist us."

Todd understood Dalton's caution. Although the case now looked like a slam dunk, there were still some unknown variables. Still, if the team could handle a warrior tribe on a parallel Earth, then they could handle the Lightville council.

"Okay, that's about the gist of it," said Dalton. "Everyone, take the rest of the night off and relax. We'll head out at 10:30 a.m. tomorrow, so be ready to go by then."

Brad went to the bathroom, while Rick and Valerie exited the room. Evot also left and morphed into her crow form before the door shut.

"Scared them all away," said Todd, smiling.

Dalton eyed Todd. "I think we all deserve a break after the last few days. How're you liking the deputy position?"

"I like it," said Todd. "I've noticed you give me leadership of the team at times when you go off to scout and the like."

"That's on purpose, of course. This case and the previous one have given you experience that not many full inspectors can claim. You've had to deal with tough and strange situations."

Todd chuckled. "*Strange* is a good word. I looked at the training for a full inspector. It's gonna take a while."

"The coursework, sure. But field experience? I think you'll have that in no time flat. You know there are other paths available if any of those interest you."

Todd nodded. "I've looked at a few, but I think full inspector at some point is in my future. If not, then I'll have a backup in something."

"Good plan," said Dalton. "If you need assistance with anything, let me know. If you have a course that involves something specific in the field, we'll try to include it."

"I appreciate that," said Todd. "This is a lot better than being a bouncer."

They laughed.

Todd grinned. "Pays better too."

Dalton raised a finger. "Don't forget all the amenities that come with the job."

"Healthcare, pension, allowances, and the sheer size of the organization are a big draw," said Todd. "A couple of years ago, I would have said no way would I work for the Earth Ward. Funny how life turns out sometimes."

"I hear ya."

Todd was happy where he was. He recalled being worried he would not find enough work to cover the taxes on his property. Money was no concern when it came to the Earth Ward. They had a ton of it and paid people who they believed in quite well. Each team had its own contract splits, and Dalton's was odd in that he took none of it. Even with Rick added, they just upped the overall contract amount, so the split was still generous.

Todd had a hunger to be a full inspector, but he did see some other roles in the Earth Ward that intrigued him. One position dealt with identifying and assessing threats. His experience with the Faith Militia would come in handy there. The greatest aspect of the Earth Ward was he kept his pay wherever he went, and after fifteen years, his pension kicked in. His future looked bright.

Rick sat on a concrete parking lot bumper with a beer in his hand. Dinner had been great, and he loved hearing that the team had everything needed to confront the Lightville council. It was dark out, and despite the bugs swirling around the lights outside the motel doors, it was a nice night to have a beer, especially with Valerie as his drinking bud.

He recalled the sinking feeling earlier in the morning when it was his time to watch. Everything had seemed peaceful, but there were murderous trees and animals everywhere. One slipup, and that was it. It was an unforgiving Earth, and he was thankful to be back on his. That other Earth did not have fried chicken.

"Mr. Thinker over there," said Valerie.

Rick grinned. "Just happy to be where I am."

"On our Earth or on the team?"

"Both," said Rick. "I was thinking how just this morning we were on a brutal parallel Earth. Now we're swigging beer after some awesome fried chicken and jambalaya. What a swing of events."

Valerie sipped her beer. "Yeah. I'm not too surprised Dalton reached out to you to join the team. You were tough on our first case." She swatted his arm. "I can't be the only muscle here."

"Uh-huh," he said, smiling.

"Seriously, though. It would have been a lot different back there on the parallel Earth without you."

Rick frowned. "Those warriors were fast and tough. They'd have overpowered me if I didn't have my enhanced abilities."

"Same here. And there were hundreds, even if we only saw around fifty or so. They would have eventually ground us up," said Valerie.

He looked out across the mostly empty parking lot. "I'm just glad Dalton invited me to the team. I much prefer this to what I was doing."

Valerie eyed him. "Your ex-slayer group. How's that doing now?"

"I'm sure we'll hear about their war with the Faith Militia." He shook his head. "Damn idiots. I gave them a refuge, then they turned it into headquarters for a war."

"You think they'll be successful?"

Rick grimaced. "Maybe. They've got fighters for sure and a solid network of informants. Plus, they already know the enemy and terrain. What they don't have is numbers. In their area, yes, they control that. Outside of that…good luck."

"And you know there'll be blowback."

"Yep. Sure as shit will happen too. Innocents will get caught up, families split." He sighed. "There was no need for all that."

Valerie stared at her beer. "Why didn't you stop them from forming it? It was your group, I thought."

He scowled. "I formed a council to run things in case I ever got wiped. As a sign of trust, their vote could overrule me, and that's exactly what happened. Dalton's invite couldn't have come at a better time."

"Well, I'm glad you accepted. I like this team. It's like a little family. Dalton's the dad, Evot's the mom, I'm the sexy daughter, you're the tough older brother, Todd's the responsible brother, and Brad's the baby."

They laughed.

"Yeah, I don't know about being the oldest," said Rick. He clinked beers with Valerie. "But I get the gist. The team's solid, and I like the casework. In time, the name "Executioner" may be replaced by "Inspector." Who knows?"

Valerie gazed into the sky. "You check out the paths available in the Earth Ward? They have so many."

"I saw some of them. I'll take a deeper look after this case. Maybe the Earth Ward needs an executioner."

"Possibly," said Valerie. "As for me, I'm not sure I'd be an inspector, but they do have paths more suited to my skills."

"You mean being a spy or intelligence agent or something."

She grinned. "Yeah. But for now, I like where I'm at."

"In the Earth Ward or here right now?"

Valerie hopped up and then climbed up to the roof.

Rick was not sure if he had offended her somehow, but there was a blood bond between them. Maybe he had said something without thinking, which would be par for the course. As he reviewed their conversation, an object landed on his head. It took a moment before he realized it was Valerie's pants. His pulse quickened. A few seconds later, her shirt hit him. His heartbeat increased. He set them to the side and looked up.

Valerie still had her underarmor on. "You coming up?"

"Uh…"

She moved back onto the roof.

Rick stood.

Her underarmor flew off the roof and crashed into him.

He gulped.

Valerie peeked over the edge. "We have some unfinished business…unless you're not interested. What we did on the parallel Earth was just a warmup."

He tossed her stuff back up and then scaled the wall. The roof was dusty but private for the most part. His eyes widened when he saw Valerie in the nude.

She pushed him. "You're a tough guy, huh? Prove it."

"I…you sure this is cool?"

She slapped him. "Less talk. More action."

He grabbed her and pulled her in close. "Oh, hell yeah."

CHAPTER
TWENTY-ONE

D alton went through his thoughts as he drove the team to Lightville. It was 11:00 a.m., and the trip so far had been quiet. The previous night had been good, and the team appeared to be in high spirits—Rick and Valerie more so than the others. As discreet as they thought they were, Evot had been circling overhead. While Dalton avoided observing, Evot had some questions on their activities. Dalton let her know they were having a private moment, so it would be best to ignore what she saw.

Regarding the presentation to the Lightville council, he had gone over it multiple times now. He was not sure how they would react. Perhaps they would be supportive of their family, or maybe they would agree that justice needed to be served. Either way, the facts would be presented, and if things went south, an Earth Ward response team with two vans of elite agents was on standby just a fifteen-minute drive away. He hoped they would not be required, but this was a delicate situation.

The team was geared up and ready for a fight. Rick had on his executioner outfit, while Brad had his stickbots and Gizmo powered up and prepared. Todd was cool and calm as expected, and Valerie had checked her weaponry several times throughout the ride. After the trip to the parallel Earth, they were prepared for anything.

They entered Lightville and, after ten minutes, arrived outside the city council compound. Everyone disembarked.

"Evot, you'll need to be in human form for this," said Dalton.

"Of course," she said as she complied.

"Everyone else, be alert, but let's keep things calm."

Everybody nodded.

"All right, let's get this show on the road," he said.

They walked up the stairs and then were escorted inside to the inner chambers, where they stood before the council.

Dalton did a quick survey of the room. Septimus, Camilla, and Tiberius were absent—replaced by flat screens that showed their faces—but the rest of the council was there. Based on the environment data displayed, Dalton suspected they were in a corporate office of some type.

"Inspector Dalton Kingston," said Marcus. "It's only been four days since we last met. I'm surprised you asked for another meeting with the full council so soon. How can we help you?"

Dalton moved his hand out in an arc. "We appreciate that you took the time for this meeting." He raised two fingers. "We came to Baton Rouge with two goals in mind for this case." He lowered one finger. "One. Find out who killed

Inspector Sean and his team." He raised the finger back up. "Two. Investigate his case and take it over as needed. To that end, we now have enough information to resolve both. Evot, show the robot we encountered outside the Fringe."

Evot projected an image of the robot.

Dalton pointed at it. "This robot attempted to kill Valerie and me outside the Fringe." He gestured at Brad and Evot. "They were able to peek into the robot's internals, and that's when we learned it had killed Inspector Sean and his team because they were getting close to the robot's employer's point of contact here in Baton Rouge." He cast a quick glance at Septimus's screen.

Septimus scowled.

"I see," said Marcus. "I wasn't aware there were robots advanced enough to do that. We have Amelia, and you have Evot, but I would think this other robot is from someplace else."

Evot projected an image of the hangar.

Dalton gestured at it. "You're right. The robot is not from this Earth. It's from a parallel one."

The council members murmured among themselves.

"The image Evot is showing is of a hangar here in Baton Rouge that leads to this other Earth. We went to investigate and were attacked, forcing us to go through," said Dalton. He shook his head. "It was not a pleasurable experience there, but we learned of Dynkara and their plans to assimilate not only our Earth but multiple other parallel Earths. This robot was an agent for them. Dynkara has phases, and they were in phase one on our planet, which is replacing people with duplicates, forming alliances, and removing potential threats. The end phase deals with a world war and their stabilizing presence to unite the world."

Julius drew his head back. "Are you being serious? Parallel Earths?"

Dalton motioned at Evot. "Show the slideshow I put together last night."

"Of course," she said.

Dalton studied the council as they looked on in shock. The hub images were meant to reveal the advanced nature of Dynkara. The other images showed the surface world and the brutal tribe and murder trees.

"As you can see, Dynkara operates underground hubs where they have portals to other Earths. They call our Earth 743. I sealed the portal to our Earth, though, so they won't have any more contact here now."

"How did you get back?" asked Portia. She motioned at the images. "And why were you on the surface?"

Dalton raised his arm, which erupted in blue flames. "I can open a portal back to this Earth at any time if in another timeline. I can also permanently seal portals, like I did to the one that led to our Earth."

The council sat back.

"That's a very…unique set of abilities," said Marcus.

"And handy when you're stranded on a parallel Earth or need to shut a portal down," said Dalton. "Nonetheless, we couldn't portal back at that depth, so we went to the surface. The nearest point to jump back without appearing underground was a mountain eighteen miles away. That's why you see images of a brutal landscape."

Marcus's eyes widened. "I'm amazed your team survived that. That places looks dangerous."

Dalton grimaced. "Yes, and it was dangerous to investigate this case too." He motioned at Todd, Rick, and Brad. "They were ambushed by Damian Wu of the Star Lotus clan." He circled a finger around. "We were all assaulted at the crime scene by the Baton Rouge Crew. You already know about the robot attacking Valerie and me. At the hangar, Crayzo, leader of the South Boyz, and corrupt local law enforcement attacked us."

Julius studied Dalton. "Dynkara didn't want you discovering them, it seems. You mentioned from before that Inspector Sean and his team were investigating a Lightville contact. Did you find out who it was?"

The room fell silent.

Dalton faced Septimus's screen. "We did. The robot was protecting Septimus. He is Dynkara's point of contact here on this Earth. He has helped them identify targets to be replaced, organizations to infiltrate, and potential threats to deal with. The robot learned that Inspector Sean was about to be given Septimus's name, so Sean and his team were eliminated. However, Septimus's interactions with Dynkara were stored on the parallel Earth, and we now have that data. Oh yeah, I forgot to mention, Dynkara blew up the hub after we left. Security measure."

Camilla's and Tiberius's screens went blank.

Septimus sighed. "You're too damn thorough. I'm impressed." He laid a hand on his chest. "Really, I am. That was a very detailed presentation."

Marcus stared at Septimus's screen. "You admit to this?"

"Why not? At this point, it doesn't matter," said Septimus. "It's time for a new direction and leadership for lightmires, and Dynkara invested in that vision. *My* vision."

"What madness is this?" asked Julius, standing. "Why did Camilla's and Tiberius's screens shut off?"

"I didn't do this alone," said Septimus, smirking. "For too long, this council has hidden. Yes, we have money, but we don't use it to live. No, we invest in isolating ourselves. We have the power and ability to rule this planet. The old way is dead. My way is not."

Portia's eyes narrowed. "If you weren't happy, you could have worked with us."

"Exactly," said Adrienne. "This is not the way to do things."

"I tried…but Father and Uncle are hell-bent on maintaining the 'hiding like peasants' tradition established in the Roman era. Those who dare to think differently are outcast," said Septimus. "Felix and the other outcasts have the right idea, but they're too weak."

"You're confident in telling us this as if it has no consequences," said Dalton.

Gunfire erupted outside the building.

Septimus smiled. "Who's going to report it?"

"You would attack your own family?" asked Marcus, rising.

"Out with the old…in with the new. You chose your side. Now live with the consequences of that. Isn't that what you tell Outcasts? Well, now *you're* the outcast."

Septimus's screen went blank.

"We're being jammed," said Evot.

"I can confirm," said Amelia.

Marcus rushed over to Dalton. "Who's attacking us?"

"My guess…Crayzo along with Dynkara resources," said Dalton. "I assume your security forces are on their way."

"They would be, but Septimus knows our security apparatus as well as I do."

"Then he knows how much time he has. Are there any secure exits or rooms here?"

Julius stepped around the table. "We have a subterranean network we can use."

"Can Septimus access it?"

Amelia shook her head. "Only the entrances to it. I locked them out just now, but they've already come in. Everything else inside is secured. There is a safe room we should go to."

"And Septimus will expect us to do that," said Dalton. "Amelia, can you take us there?"

"Yes."

"All right, here's the plan. Evot, get outside this jamming area and contact the Earth Ward rapid response team. Todd, Rick, and Valerie will cover the rear. The Lightville council will be in the middle. Amelia, Brad, and I will take point," said Dalton. He entered Scoutspectre mode and spawned his shield and stun baton.

"What is that?" asked Marcus.

"Something you want in the front," said Dalton. "Amelia, lead on."

As they exited the room, Dalton focused on sensing things around him. Whoever attacked was getting close, which meant they broke through the compound's security with ease. Not too hard to do when everything was known about them. Septimus's plan to eliminate everybody as a last resort could work, but he underestimated Dalton's team.

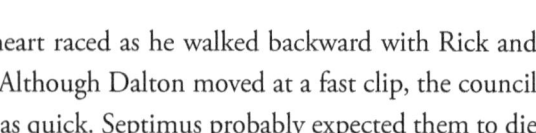

Todd's heart raced as he walked backward with Rick and Valerie. Although Dalton moved at a fast clip, the council was not as quick. Septimus probably expected them to die outright or while trying to get to the safe room. It was hard to fathom that Septimus, Camilla, and Tiberius would try to kill those they had known for centuries. That was family drama taken to a whole new level.

They arrived at a stairwell. Todd notified Dalton that he would hold the area until the group reached the underground entrance. Rick and Valerie assumed positions to the sides of the doorway into the stairwell, and Todd waited farther back on the edge of the stairs. He could step down to break line of sight and would rather fight a pitched battle there than have whoever was coming shoot down and potentially hit the group.

After ten minutes, the attackers came into view.

Most looked like the ones from the hangar. They carried assault weapons, and a select few wore tactical vests. Todd aimed his SG-5 and shot through the door, stunning the first gang member to appear. Gunfire erupted in the small area, which caused him to step out of line of sight.

"Let them come in," said Rick.

Todd nodded.

A moment later, two attackers rushed through the doorway.

Rick hit one in the head with a stun baton.

Valerie got the other.

"Grenade!" said Todd.

Rick batted the grenade back out as it sailed through the door.

An explosion occurred outside.

"We're entering the subterranean network now," said Dalton over comms.

"Okay. We're on our way," said Todd. He motioned at the bodies. "Let's use them to plug up the doorway, then we can go."

Once they stacked the bodies, Todd and the others began to descend. It did not take long for the other attackers to fire down the stairwell's gap.

"Stick to the sides!" said Todd.

Although the bullets from above could not reach them, it still made the trip unnerving. The shooting stopped when the gang members ran down the stairs. It was now a race to the bottom. Todd listened in as Dalton ran into some of Crayzo's crew below, but they were not equipped to deal with Dalton.

After a hectic ten minutes, they reached the bottom.

Todd pulled on the door. "It's locked!" he said over comms.

"Try now," said Amelia.

He yanked the door open and ushered Rick and Valerie inside. Once they passed through, he joined them and closed the door.

Bullets hit the other side.

"Holy shit, we cut that close," said Rick.

"Yeah, stairwells suck to fight in," said Valerie.

Todd pointed at the door. "Let's hope this holds. Dalton and the group are not too far ahead. Let's go!"

As they hustled away, Todd focused on the green line that appeared on the ground thanks to his ARI. Even with all the chaos happening around him, he appreciated the new technology and what it could do. After they had gone down a few hallways, an explosion echoed in the distance.

"I think that was them blowing the doors," said Valerie.

"Yeah, I'm sure Septimus planned on that," said Todd. "We're not too far away from the others."

After five minutes, they reached a side room.

Todd's eyes widened at the massive circular door. It was thick and resembled a vault door. The Lightville council had already hurried into a comfortable lounge area filled with cabinets. A trail of blood drops stained the ground. Someone must have been hit.

Dalton motioned Amelia in and faced the council. "We're going to seal this door. I'll stay in contact via Amelia. It seems the jamming signal doesn't penetrate this deep. We'll clear out the remaining attackers down here, disable the jamming signal, then deal with Crayzo and the others. I assume those bullet wounds can be healed."

Marcus stepped forward. "Yes, they can." His gaze burned into Dalton. "I can't believe this is happening. He would attack his own family. His own family!" He sighed. "We… we thank you for all you're doing. If you weren't here, I suspect we'd be dead."

"Earth Ward's got your back," said Dalton.

Marcus nodded.

The door whooshed and sealed shut.

"All right," said Dalton. "Brad is hooked into the network down here and will give us a heads-up on who is coming and from where thanks to the sensors in the hallways. Unfortunately, they've disabled the connection to the outside world regardless of the jamming. As you also saw, we had to deal with some attackers from the other entrance that leads outside. There's eight more coming from the outside entrance and ten from the stairwell."

Rick shook his head. "Damn, eighteen. There's not a lot of places to defend down here."

"Yes, but there are side rooms. Let's get the eight coming from the outside entrance first, then we can deal with the ten. I'll take point and camouflage into a side room. You four, draw them down, I'll pop out, and we'll sandwich them."

"I like it," said Valerie.

They moved to the hallway.

Dalton vanished as he slipped into one of the side rooms.

Todd set up out of line of sight with Brad, Rick, and Valerie at the end. The plan was solid, but anything could happen.

The assailants stormed down the hallway.

After a moment, Dalton said, "Okay, they're past me. Get their attention."

Todd and the others peeked out and released a volley of stun blasts.

The lead attacker and three others crumpled.

Dalton stepped out and fired his RSG at one, then entered Scoutspectre mode and charged the remaining three.

Todd hit another one who had turned to face Dalton, and the last two tried to run past Dalton.

He bashed one, then stunned the other.

The one on the ground raised his hands.

Dalton tapped him with his stun baton, then joined the team.

"Went well," said Todd.

Brad chuckled. "They sure didn't expect Dalton."

Dalton entered official mode. "Yeah, but now we have ten more to deal with. This won't work with them since they're coming from the stairwell, and there are no side rooms until the vault room."

"They're already there," said Brad. "Four are outside the door shooting at it; the other six are in the hallway."

"How spaced out are they in the hallway?"

Brad updated everyone's ARI to show a camera view of the hallway.

Todd glanced at him. "Could your stickbots land on their hands and make them drop their weapons?"

"Sure, but they'd be detected on the way to them."

"Unless I take them and toss them at the gang's feet," said Dalton. "They wouldn't shoot, and if they drop their weapons, I can begin the fight while Todd, Rick, and Valerie rush in. I assume Brad will need to stay behind to focus on the stickbots and Gizmo."

Brad grinned. "That might actually work." He handed Dalton his stickbot belt.

Todd smiled as Dalton vanished. The approach was different, and the team had a solution. He missed having these types of battle meetings, and there was no shortage of fighting. The ARI had a view from one of the stickbots Dalton carried on his shoulder. It showed him sneaking up to the men.

There were now five inside the room and five outside.

Dalton grabbed five stickbots in each hand. After a moment, he tossed them at the men.

They danced around and tried to knock away the stickbots.

Todd stifled a laugh as they called the stickbots "silver bug things," but some of the men did drop their weapons. Others tossed them to the side to focus on the stickbots that ran wild across their bodies and poked them.

Dalton broke camouflage and entered Scoutspectre mode. He attacked those in the hallway.

Todd, Rick, and Valerie charged and burst into the vault room.

As each stickbot jumped off, Todd, Rick, and Valerie fired stun beams at the men. The remaining two tried to melee, but Rick smacked one in the head with his baton, and Valerie kicked the other to the ground, then hit the back of his head with her baton.

Todd went to help Dalton, but he had already subdued the five he had engaged.

"Damn, you didn't need our help!" said Rick.

Dalton entered official mode. "Well, it helps when you have a shield that can clear a path."

Brad walked up with Gizmo. "Looks like I lost another three stickbots. Damn. Down to eight now."

"We'll get more and upgrade them. This has been a good field test for them."

"Agreed. What now?"

Dalton gestured at the sealed door. "Let's put the weapons in there. We can't tie these men up, but we can lock them in a room."

Valerie bent and grabbed a man under his arm. "Where to?"

"I've marked a room in your ARIs that should be big enough," said Brad.

"Todd, coordinate here. I'm going topside to scout the situation," said Dalton. He paused. "You did good. All of you did." He took off.

"All right, you heard the man. Rick, Valerie, you two can relocate the bodies. Brad, communicate with Amelia that we need the door open, then we can move the weapons."

"You got it, boss man," said Rick, smiling.

They laughed.

Valerie slapped Todd on the back before dragging a man away.

Todd knew Rick was teasing, but he was glad there was no friction with him being in command. Valerie seemed to have accepted it without issue, and Brad appeared relieved he did not have to mess with leadership. Todd's former slayer unit would not have fared well in this fight. He would have most likely been counting his last breaths for trying to battle eighteen enemies. This team was unique, though, and he loved every minute he was part of it.

CHAPTER
TWENTY-TWO

Valerie studied the stairwell. It had only been an hour since they had come down it; now they waited to go back up. The weapons from the gang members had been stored in the vault, and she and Rick had moved the men into a side room at a breakneck pace. She cracked up when Rick got a kick out of her posing the men in suggestive positions. She loved playing around—something he did not seem to mind.

Dalton had camouflaged and gone up top. With Evot not back yet and the jamming still in place, his camouflage ability was the next best thing for reconnaissance. Brad had tried to connect to the cameras above, but they had all been broken. Valerie tapped her foot as she looked up.

"Anxious?" asked Rick.

She exhaled. "Yeah. Ready to put these guys down."

"Me too," he said. "I won't relax until whoever is attacking is down and the place is secure."

Brad raised a finger. "Not to burst anyone's bubble here, but Septimus, Camilla, and Tiberius are still somewhere out there if they're not here. We may have to go get them."

"Then we'll get them," said Todd. "They've made their intentions known, and once that gets out, it's just a matter of time."

Rick slapped hands with him. "Hell yeah."

"Dalton's coming," said Valerie.

"You sensed him?" asked Brad. "I didn't."

She shook her head. "Heard him."

Dalton appeared before them. "I confirmed Crayzo's up there with about thirteen of his crew. He's lounging around in one of the side rooms. However, the place is packed with his crew and also seven guys wearing full tactical outfits."

"Dynkara?" asked Todd.

"Definitely. I sensed their alternate timeline signature."

Rick extended a finger. "I take it they don't know their portal back is gone forever."

"I suspect they were here for the long haul. Most likely placed for events just like this," said Dalton.

"What about the jammer?" asked Brad.

"It's outside in a truck."

Todd ran a hand over the back of his neck. "We need to hit that first, then."

"My thoughts exactly," said Dalton. "I've updated the map in your ARIs. You should see where I marked anyone I came across. The plan is that I'll sneak out and attack that jammer. When I do, I'll hook up with Evot and go from there."

"What should we do?" asked Todd.

Dalton raised a finger. "Hang tight for the moment. Once the jamming device is down, I'll rejoin you all, and we can provide a second front when reinforcements arrive."

"I can use my stickbots to get an idea of what's going on with Crayzo and his men," said Brad. "I could even update our ARIs like you did."

"Like what you did earlier," said Rick.

"Yeah, although that means I'll need to be somewhere safe. Thankfully, the jammer can't affect my connection with the stickbots."

"You need to go in the vault, then," said Todd.

"I like it," said Dalton. "All right, get the stickbots going, then move Brad into the vault. I'll be back."

"Be safe."

Dalton vanished as he went up the stairs.

Rick puffed his cheeks. "All this waiting. I want to kick some ass."

Valerie loved his tough persona. He spoke his mind, and his actions reflected his character. It amazed her that she knew of Executioner as a cold-blooded killing machine with no personality, while the man before her was still a death dealer but with a personality she liked. They still shared a blood bond, and although they had already fooled around, she would not mind another go.

He glanced at her, and she smiled.

"There'll be plenty of ass-kicking, I'm sure. Just wait," said Todd.

It pained Valerie to have to wait for the action to begin, but Dalton was being cautious and for good reason. There were twenty heavily armed men up top, with seven of them likely seasoned fighters. Her main concern was the others getting hurt because when Dalton came back, it was go time.

Valerie escorted Brad up the stairs to the door leading to the interior. She pushed the door open slightly.

Brad's stickbots jumped off his belt and ran through the crack.

His stickbots were fast and hard to detect, and if not being focused on, they were invisible. As she walked with Brad to the vault, the stickbots updated the mini map with live positions of the men upstairs.

"Your stickbots are so cool," she said.

Brad chuckled. "Yeah, but takes some effort to control them all."

After fifteen minutes, Brad had been moved to the vault, and the others waited back at the bottom of the stairs.

During that time, Valerie had observed the movement patterns of the assailants upstairs. The Dynkara guys seemed to hold specific points, while Crayzo's crew walked randomly. Crayzo stayed in his room.

Dalton contacted them. "All right. Jamming is down, as are the two guards nearby. I took out another one farther away, and it seems there's more members out here. I've contacted Evot, and the Earth Ward rapid response team has joined up with the Lightville police. Apparently, Crayzo's crew has struck other places in town. I see smoke. Nonetheless, reinforcements are arriving in numbers, so I'm coming to you now."

"I hope everyone is safe," said Evot over comms.

"Good to hear your voice," said Todd.

"I should hope so."

Valerie grinned. Evot always injected a sense of light-heartedness in a tense situation. Everything seemed better with her around.

After another ten minutes, Dalton had rejoined them. "It's pretty crazy up top and outside. However, Evot is providing aerial surveillance, so we have an advantage out there. The combined Earth Ward and Lightville force will be here shortly. Once they engage, we'll make our move."

Valerie scrunched up her face. "Don't you think it's odd that no one's come to check down here?"

"I assume that since they think the jamming is still in effect, they believe communications are a no-go. Crayzo probably gave the eighteen attackers the benefit of the doubt and time to deal with us, but you're right. I expect he'll send someone to get a status update. That means we need to make our move shortly."

Rick cracked his neck. "Let's get it on."

The sporadic sound of gunfire outside echoed in. With Evot's and the stickbots' surveillance, Valerie had a good tactical overview of the area. Her heart raced as they went up the stairwell. It was fight time.

Rick's adrenaline surged as he followed Dalton. Although waiting to move was the safer option, Rick wanted a tougher and riskier fight. He loved the ARI's tactical overview—something he wished he had long ago. However, that type of equipment was expensive, and there was no Evot or stickbot equivalent outside of maybe drones, but they were loud.

When they reached the top, Dalton faced the group. "Based on the layout, we're in the southeast corner of the building. Crayzo is in a room to the west, and there is a heavy security guy at each corner of the building, two with Crayzo, and one patrolling. I'm going to take out the heavy guard outside this door, then go north. I'll eliminate that guy, then dig in and cause a commotion. Once the others come for me, you three come out and hold the entrance. I should be able to keep the east hallway clear, but you'll need to take down the heavy tactical guy in the west and handle whatever comes from the west hallway."

"We got this," said Rick.

"We're ready," said Todd.

Valerie pulled out her SP-8 and stun baton. "Let's get on with it."

Dalton vanished and opened the door. A moment later, he dragged in an unconscious man and closed the door. "No life-monitoring system, so we should be good. I don't know what their check-in pattern is, but it won't matter in a few minutes. Okay, out."

Rick studied the downed man in the stairwell. He probably did not even know what hit him. Dalton could appear behind someone, then stun them before they realized. It would not take Dalton long to reach the spot and take out another guard. Then it was on.

Rick's heartbeat ramped up when Dalton signaled for them to move out five minutes later.

"All right, you two ready?" asked Todd.

"You know I was born that way," said Rick.

Todd laughed. "All right. Let's go."

They burst into the room.

Rick rushed over to the left side with Valerie. They hit the tactical guard with a stun blast on the way. Todd went to the right side and peered down the hallway leading to where Dalton was. Per Todd's visual in Rick's ARI, Dalton had pulled the northwest guard out of position. That left the two guards in Crayzo's room and the one patrolling, who was en route to Dalton. A horde of gang members also converged.

"Fire down your hallway!" said Todd. "We need to relieve pressure off Dalton."

Rick went to the right of the west hallway entrance, while Valerie got the other side. He peeked out.

A gang member ran toward him. A shot later, and the man was down.

Shouting from the others was followed by the men coming down the hallway.

Rick nodded at Valerie, then they both hit two men each. They ducked when a hailstorm of bullets flew past them. The situation was tight, but Rick loved it. They had penned Crayzo's crew into an L-shaped hallway, with Crayzo's room off to the side. Rick wished he had a grenade or an explosive of some type.

Every time he or Valerie tried to take a shot, the men fired.

"We're keeping them back, but we can't shoot at them," said Rick.

"I'm moving to Dalton's position," said Todd. "He's going to advance west and fight at that corner. When he does, engage in close-quarters combat."

"Got it," said Rick.

When Dalton crashed into the other end of the hallway, the men focused on him.

Rick and Valerie charged into the west hallway and into the thick of the fighting. He counted seven gang members and the heavy tactical guy.

The gang members switched to knives.

Rick used his stun baton and SP-8. A shield would be much better in times like this. He was used to dual wielding blades, but that would be lethal.

The first gang member tried to jab him in the gut.

He stepped back and hit the man's hand with his baton.

The member cried out as he fell.

Another stabbed Valerie in her upper thigh, causing her to wince as she backed up.

She slapped the knife out the attacker's hand, then roundhouse-kicked him into the scrum.

Dalton and Todd dealt with the tactical armor guy and two gang members. Todd had taken some hits. That left three in the middle.

A gang member punched Rick in the face.

He shook it off and fired with his SP-8, downing the man, while Valerie got another. The last one tried to run, but Rick shot him.

Rick and Valerie rushed over to Dalton, who had assumed a defensive stance with his shield. Todd stood behind him and tried to angle in a shot.

The tactical guy unloaded a burst of assault weapon fire, but Dalton's shield held.

Valerie slid into one of the gang members, while Todd yanked another back, then slammed the man to the ground. A tap later, and the man was out. Valerie had taken down her person as well.

The tactical guard pivoted, but Dalton bashed him from the side. He tapped the guard in the neck, which caused him to pass out.

"Fun fight," said Rick.

"Yeah, it was almost too easy," said Valerie, rubbing the wound on her leg.

"Let's not get cocky," said Dalton. "You got stabbed in the leg, and Todd and Rick took some hits. We still have Crayzo's room, and notice that reinforcements haven't arrived inside yet."

"I'm fine. Let's go," said Valerie.

"All right, let's pay Crayzo a visit."

Rick did a final survey of the downed crew. It was obvious they were not skilled fighters. The tactical guards might have been, but Crayzo's crew seemed more geared toward shooting wildly and using knives. The fight was easier than the ones on the parallel Earth. Then again, those fights involved more than a few fighters. Even with the easier fight, the team had still been roughed up.

They reached Crayzo's room.

Dalton entered with his shield out front.

Rick followed him in and examined the room. Crayzo sat in a chair with his sneakered feet on the desk, his dreadlocks swishing as he moved his head. Two gang members stood on either side of him, with two tactical guys out front with weapons aimed.

"Hold on, playa!" said Crayzo. "Dalton Kingston."

"Inspector Dalton Kingston, Earth Ward, to you," he said. "Your unlawful attack here will have consequences. Stand down."

Crayzo laughed. "Yeah, sure. I was surprised to see your ass. Pulled some magic shit at the hangar."

"And now I'm here with my team," said Dalton. "You're under arrest, and there is a large contingent of security forces about to converge here. Give up now, and there will be no need to add any more charges to the already exhaustive list. You can even cooperate and validate what information we have."

Crayzo stood. "Bitch, don't tell me what to do! This is Crayzo you're speaking to. You know why they call me Wild C?"

"No, and I don't care."

Crayzo pulled out a pistol and fired at Dalton, who raised his shield and blocked the shot.

Rick and Todd fired on the gang members on the left, while Valerie got one on the right.

The two tactical guards unloaded on Dalton as Crayzo jumped over the desk.

The remaining gang member went for Valerie.

Dalton charged forward and bashed the heavy guard on the left, while Todd engaged the other.

Valerie ran toward her attacker. She ducked to the side, then flipped backward into a kick that hit him in the face. She stunned him, and he passed out.

Crayzo tried to flank Dalton and shot at him.

Rick slapped the gun out of Crayzo's hand and shoved him back over the desk.

Valerie yanked the assault weapon from the tactical guard Dalton fought. He tapped the man in the neck with his baton.

Todd had already disarmed his attacker. He pushed him to the ground, then stunned him.

Rick jumped over the desk and grabbed Crayzo from behind when he tried to stand. "What do you wanna do with this trash?"

Dalton eyed Crayzo. "Stun him. He can get picked up like the rest."

"Screw you!" said Crayzo.

"I think it's you who's about to get screwed," said Rick. He glanced at Todd. "You know what to do." Rick pushed Crayzo against the desk, where he flopped over.

Todd tapped Crayzo in the head.

Rick looked around. "That went well."

"Sure did," said Dalton.

Rick studied the men on the ground. It looked like a tornado had hit them. That was about what it felt like when running with Dalton sometimes. He was an unstoppable force. They still needed to handle Septimus, Camilla, and

Tiberius, who most likely would be entrenched. Crayzo had been used as muscle and fodder as well. Whether Crayzo knew that or not was unknown.

Dalton raised a hand. "It seems reinforcements have cleared outside."

"Hell yeah," said Rick. "Time for operation cleanup."

CHAPTER
TWENTY-THREE

Dalton had been impressed with the team. Together, they had assaulted a heavily defended area against armed opponents. He was proud of their cohesion even if they sustained several injuries during this last part. Although everyone had a few hits on them, they seemed to be doing okay. Todd had a bruise on his cheekbone, and Valerie had a minor knife wound in her upper right thigh. Rick had a black eye, but he seemed to relish in the violence.

Brad had led the council outside, where Marcus and Julius were to meet up with the Lightville security commander and the Earth Ward rapid response captain. Dalton had Todd, Rick, and Valerie clear out the bodies and weapons. Although stun was used inside, a quick look around outside the council's compound showed that lethality had been implemented to some degree.

Dalton observed the council's reaction when they had stepped outside. Marcus and Julius were grief-stricken. They had pointed out downed Lightville officers and called them by name. As part of a small city, they knew the law enforcement side intimately. Dalton's team assisted the cleanup crew.

Dalton joined Marcus and Julius, and they rendezvoused with Captain Herk of the Earth Ward rapid response team and Commander Vitus of the Lightville defense force. Herk wore the expected black tactical suit of the rapid response unit. His dark-skinned head was shaved, and his scars and steely gaze despite the carnage suggested he had seen some battles. Vitus had on a white two-piece outfit with several prominent badges on it. His tan skin was typical of lightmires in Lightville, and he had dark slicked-back hair with a part.

Dalton shook their hands. "I'm glad you two came. It was pretty hairy here."

Vitus frowned. "We would have come sooner, but our station got hit with two RPGs. It was hell responding to that, and if Captain Herk and the Earth Ward hadn't arrived when they did, we might not be standing here."

"It was a bad situation, sir," said Herk, glancing at Dalton.

"Just call me Dalton."

"Yes, si—Dalton."

Marcus pointed at several corpses. "It seems even with a response, there were still many casualties. I dread to see that list."

"It will take a while to compile," said Vitus. "Captain Herk mentioned the Earth Ward will help provide security until we're ready to resume operations. I'll help coordinate that."

Julius glanced at Herk. "We greatly appreciate that."

He gestured at Dalton. "It was his call."

Julius nodded. "Still, the Earth Ward has shown itself as an ally today. If Dalton and his team had not been inside, the council would have been gone. Septimus would have been able to spin any lie he wanted without consequence."

Vitus scowled. "Septimus was behind this? The people we fought looked like gang members."

Marcus sighed. "It's a long story, and we'll need a debriefing. However, in summary, Septimus, Camilla, and Tiberius tried to eliminate the council and our law enforcement in one shot. That would have left them legally in charge of things. They used Crayzo and the South Boyz, along with some additional help, as the muscle."

"That's barbaric!"

"I know," said Marcus. "However, they didn't plan on Dalton's team and the Earth Ward to get involved. Septimus appears to be the ringleader, and his mistake began with the killing of Inspector Sean and his team."

Herk glanced at Dalton. "They're responsible?"

"It goes much more beyond that," said Dalton. "I'll make the case file available to all here so we're on the same page, and I can help with any debriefing. However, we still need to capture Septimus and the others."

Julius growled. "They'll be at Tiberius's office downtown. I recognized the backdrop on their screens from the meeting earlier."

"We talking a secure building?"

"It's really the top five floors. There is building security, and I can only imagine he has other security aspects we're not aware of. He knows of Amelia's abilities, so he probably would have some defense against that."

Dalton rubbed his chin. "They must think that with the jamming, they won't get any updates, so they're waiting for a signal that would only be relayed if Crayzo had been successful. If we're going to hit them, it must be now."

Herk looked around. "We have our hands full here, but we can get another unit out from New Orleans if necessary."

"It will probably take them some time to get there," said Marcus.

"Then that's too late," said Dalton. He scrunched up his face. "I'll take my team."

"Without knowing what's there?" asked Vitus.

Marcus gestured at Dalton. "Their team just took down Crayzo and some heavy-duty mercenaries. I think they can handle this."

Vitus looked Dalton over. "After we get everything settled here, we can try to send some assistance. I wouldn't underestimate trying to arrest Septimus and the others. They have tech, money, and power. Besides, I thought you were an investigative team, not a fighting unit."

Dalton grinned. "It's a mix. Since I take on the harder cases, sometimes you need a group that can fight."

"Got it."

"Their team is tough," said Herk. "On my end, I'll get a unit over there even if it will be late."

"Sounds like a plan," said Dalton. "I'll leave it to you all here, then."

He shook everyone's hands, then communicated for the team to meet at the SUV. After they assembled, he went over the plan.

"So outta the frying pan and into the fire," said Rick.

"Something like that," said Dalton. "When we get there, Evot will perform surveillance. If there's a helicopter on the roof, she'll disable it. I have no doubt they'll be tracking everyone entering the building. Since it's downtown, they'll probably know as soon as we arrive."

"Lots of places for ambush," said Todd.

"I know. Brad will infiltrate any systems once we arrive. That should give us an idea of what's going on internally, while Evot handles external. Based on the map, we can park a bit away in a parking garage, then walk over. Before that, though, we'll formulate a plan based on Evot's and Brad's information."

Brad flashed a thumbs-up.

"Let's go," said Dalton.

They climbed into the SUV and drove off.

It was risky to try to catch Septimus and the others off guard, but they probably felt safe in Tiberius's building. Reinforcements would come too late, and Dalton did not want anyone to escape. If city, county, or state law enforcement got involved, it would get even messier.

As they drove, Dalton kept an eye on Evot's scanning. He was not sure what to expect when they arrived.

After twenty minutes, they parked in an underground parking garage several streets away from Tiberius's building.

"Okay, Evot, do your thing," said Dalton.

"Of course," she said.

"I love seeing what she sees," said Valerie.

"Makes reconnaissance so much easier," said Todd. He gestured at Brad. "I guess we need to get you in close to touch the building's systems."

Brad grimaced. "Yeah. I already checked for wireless access, and it looks like there is none. They probably designed their security with Amelia in mind."

"Then it's walking time."

Dalton scrutinized the area around the building as Evot flew over it. There was a helicopter on the roof, and she made quick work of disabling it. Morphing into a swarm and ripping the wiring to shreds was easy. There were other buildings of varying heights nearby that could have threats, but Evot did not detect anyone on the roofs.

"Looks like an everyday, normal building," said Rick.

Dalton furrowed his brow. "Which is what they want everyone to think. All right. I'm going to get Brad close to the building and see what he can access. Once done, the rest of you can come. Be ready to go."

Time was of the essence, and every minute was one where Septimus and the others could have learned of what happened. They might already know and have evacuated. They could also be there and provide plausible deniability of any involvement when law enforcement reached out. Doing something that showed they were somewhere else when everything went down would be the sort of thing Dalton would expect Septimus to do. Either way, the team was going in.

Brad grinned as he rode piggyback on Dalton. Valerie had mentioned that it felt odd when Dalton's nanobots covered her, which Brad now understood. What surprised him was how effortlessly Dalton moved through traffic and people to reach the side of Tiberius's building. Brad could see how someone could get into all sorts of trouble with camouflaging.

Thankfully, the trip to the building had been short. Along the way, he had scoured for available tech, and when he did, he kept a hand over his eyes. Dalton said the glowing eyes would appear through camouflage unless covered, and the sunglasses were not enough. People would freak out if they saw a set of blue eyes floating in the air. As for the tech he found, there was the usual assortment of cell phones and the like and even a few laptops.

When they had approached the building, he tried to connect to its system, but there was not much at that distance. However, once they reached the side of the building, he was able to detect the nearby internal systems. The top floors had no cameras. The building's security system was simple and could be easily overridden, although it would not do much to help the team. The top floors were low tech, and he suspected that was on purpose. Someone like Amelia could blow past a high-tech defense.

A checkpoint with a metal detector existed on the bottom floor. It was manned by six guards, with two at the detector and four scattered around. Another security guard stood next to the elevator. They all wore normal work outfits, and their sidearms were holstered. A quick check of the elevator system showed it could be shut down electronically, but there was also a manual shutoff on the first floor of Tiberius's block. That would probably be shut off at the first sign of the team approaching.

Tiberius's black box approach for his floors impressed Brad. He had expected there to be computers or even cell phones, but he could not detect any at this range. Without a central system hooked up there, he was blind.

"How's it looking?" asked Dalton.

Brad sighed. "Not so good. Some security downstairs, but Tiberius has his floors locked down. Elevator will probably be disabled when we enter as well."

"Then we'll need to deal with security and hike it up ten floors."

"Looking that way. On the plus side, the security doesn't look like they could stop us if they wanted to."

Dalton placed his hand on his chest. "We have jurisdiction, so there's nothing they can do legally to stop us. However…I expect they'll try."

"Yeah," said Brad.

"Why not use the stickbots to investigate Tiberius's floors?" asked Evot over comms.

Brad looked up. "Could, but how are they getting in?" He focused on the slightly open window Evot highlighted.

"I can take them there, and they can enter," she said.

"That'll work," said Brad. "There's still the distance aspect. I'd need to be at least at the same level."

Dalton peered up. "I can get you there, and then Evot can do the transfer."

"You're gonna scale the wall?"

"You're surprised?"

"I guess I shouldn't be at this point," said Brad.

He gulped when Dalton placed his hands on the wall. Little suction cups with tiny spikes emerged across his front. Brad's mind reeled as Dalton climbed with ease. He was a fountain of surprises. It made Brad wonder how well-known Dalton's name must have been. If he wanted to find you, he would, and there would not be much to stop him. Not even a building.

After ten minutes, they reached an area to the side of the open window.

Evot swooped in and grabbed Brad's belt from his extended hand, then she placed it near the window.

Brad concentrated as the stickbots came alive and jumped onto the windowsill. The room inside was empty, so he had them enter. It did not take long to have them fan out and find the local network. One of the stickbots plugged into an available Ethernet port on the wall. Brad smiled, as he could now see inside the local network. Although he could access the building's systems earlier, it only connected to security and maintenance systems. This network was specific to this floor and whatever business operated it.

"You in?" asked Dalton.

"Yep," said Brad. "Moving to a port near the stairs. The connected stickbots will act as a relay for the other stickbots."

"Sounds good," said Dalton.

Brad only had eight stickbots, and now one was nearby and served as the base one he connected to. He ran the other seven to a room near the stairs while making sure they were not seen. The floor seemed quiet, and he only saw a few offices with people in them. One of the stickbots plugged itself in, and he had the remaining six enter the stairwell.

The stickbots navigated the difficult terrain with ease. The stairs were no issue, and after a few minutes, they had gone up two levels to the entry floor for Tiberius's offices. The bots wiggled under the closed door. A guard stood nearby, and the long hallway led to various side offices. Brad navigated one of the stickbots behind the guard and ran it into an empty side room.

A quick check of the area showed there to be a desk but no computer or cell. Various bookshelves and a filing cabinet filled the rest of the room.

"They really went low tech up there," said Brad. "There's no network to plug into so far."

Dalton sighed. "Go figure. Can you have the other stickbots go to the other four floors?"

"Sure can."

Brad focused and had four of the six stickbots go to each floor. Like the first floor, there was a sealed door they could crawl under. The second and third floors were mostly empty, but the fourth floor had some activity. He found a room where Septimus, Camilla, Tiberius, and a robot argued about something.

Dalton smiled. "Oh yeah, that's the good stuff. Looks like Septimus isn't too happy with Dynkara. Probably just learned that their coup attempt failed."

"What's next, then?"

"We'll assemble the team out front, then go up and arrest them," said Dalton. "There doesn't seem to be as much security as I expected up there."

The stickbot's feed went blank.

"What just happened?" asked Dalton.

"Looks like the robot detected the stickbot and shot it," said Brad. "I'm moving the other ones back. Damn, down to seven now."

"All right. Time to get the others over here," said Dalton.

Brad checked with Evot while Dalton explained the situation to the others. Evot had been circling overhead and looking for any signs of additional security. She had spotted what she thought was a rifle jutting out from a window across the street, but upon closer inspection, there had been nothing.

This should be a simple arrest, but the presence of a Dynkara agent might be an issue. There could be others around, but the stickbot had been compromised. They already searched for more, and the one on the eleventh floor was crushed while trying to flee.

He sighed. Now he only had six left. After this was all over, assuming he was still alive, he had some ideas to improve the bots. For now, the focus was on arresting Septimus and the others.

CHAPTER
TWENTY-FOUR

D alton disengaged his camouflage mode when he spotted Todd, Rick, and Valerie crossing the street. The side alley had proven to be a useful hiding place, and Brad seemed relieved to be on the ground again. His ability was powerful, and Dalton appreciated having it available. After Evot lost her servbot, he was anxious about putting her in harm's way, although she could probably have done the interior reconnaissance.

Everyone assembled around Dalton.

"Watching the stickbot feed was awesome," said Valerie. "Doesn't look like much is going on up there, but at least we know those bastards are there."

"And they know someone was trying to spy on them," said Todd. "I'm sure whatever security measures they have in place are active now."

Dalton motioned with his hand. "Let's play it cool. Remember, we're an Earth Ward inspection team. The law is on *our* side."

Rick smirked. "I don't think they care much about the law or who's on what side."

"I agree, but we still need to act professionally," said Dalton. "If it gets heated, then all bets are off. Everyone understand?"

They nodded.

"What about that rifle thing Evot thought she saw?" asked Brad.

Dalton looked up at the building across the street. "Evot didn't find anything on a closer scan, so I trust that. Let's move."

He did a final check to make sure everyone was geared up, then proceeded to the front of the building with the team. The entrance looked like every other one on the street. It would be hard to know anything nefarious was going on by appearances.

When they entered the building, the security guards at the booth ahead stared them down.

Dalton extended his badge wallet. "Inspector Dalton Kingston, Earth Ward. We're here on official business."

A tan-skinned man in a light-gray uniform raised a hand. "Sorry, sir, the building is shut down."

"That's fine," said Dalton. "What we're here for doesn't require the building to be open."

The guards drew their batons.

"No one is to come through," said the man.

"On whose authority? We have jurisdiction here."

"None of my business or, frankly, yours either."

Dalton walked over to the mantrap and pushed through.

The guard rushed in front of him. "I'm warning you. Don't do this."

"You're obstructing our case, which has legal consequences. Are you sure you want to do this?"

The man hesitated as another man walked up.

Dalton sighed and glanced back at the team. "I guess we do this the hard way."

He entered Scoutspectre mode and formed a stun baton from his MH. In one swing, he struck both guards, who dropped to the ground.

The other five, including the elevator guard who had rushed up, drew their weapons but were hit by stun blasts from the team.

"Septimus must have something on them to have them act like this," said Todd.

"That or they don't believe we are who we say we are," said Rick.

Dalton nodded. "Both possibilities."

"The elevator has been shut down," said Brad as his eyes flashed blue. "Looks like it's walking time!"

"Great," said Valerie.

Dalton waved forward. "Let's go. And stay alert."

He stepped over the two downed men and checked the other five. The team had been quick in disabling the guards. They probably did not expect the team to whip out stun weaponry. Without any technical link from Tiberius's floor to the lobby area, Septimus and the others probably would not know the status of the team until they went upstairs.

They entered the stairwell and ascended.

Dalton concentrated on trying to sense anything ahead, but it seemed quiet. Once they reached the fourth floor of Tiberius's offices, things would heat up. When they arrived outside the sealed door, Dalton vibrated his hand enough to disable the manual lock. He motioned for everyone to stand back, then raised his shield and opened the door.

A gunshot rang out.

Dalton charged in and bashed the shooter against the wall, then stunned him.

A robot similar to the one they fought before appeared in the hallway and fired a laser at Dalton.

He blocked it, then ran forward. He could not allow the robot to shoot again since the team's underarmor and suits would not stop a laser shot. He bashed the robot, which caused it to drop its weapon. While grabbing the robot's left arm, he kicked the body to the side, severing the arm.

Todd, Rick, Valerie, and Brad shot stun beams at the robot, which made it fritz. They stood over it.

"Yeah, I think we'd all be dead if you weren't here," said Rick, gesturing at Dalton.

"This is the one that was arguing with Septimus," said Dalton. He narrowed his eyes. "They're not too far away. Let's move."

A few guards tried to stop the team as they progressed, but they were easily handled. Dalton suspected Septimus probably had a contingency plan. If it was to fly away via helicopter, that one would be dead. It might have been the robot, but that did not pan out.

When they reached the double doors to a conference room, Dalton morphed into his official suit and faced the group. "I don't know what to expect here, so be alert."

"Seems too easy," said Todd.

"Agreed," said Dalton.

He pushed open the doors and surveyed the room. The left side was all windows and provided a good overview of the area outside. Septimus sat at a big desk at the back, with Tiberius standing to his right and Camilla to his left. An open area separated the two groups.

"And here he is," said Septimus, clapping. "The Earth Ward's lapdogs."

"You're under arrest for aiding a dimensional threat against Earth and for a lot of other things as well. Come quietly, and this won't escalate," said Dalton.

Septimus laughed. "Sure, sure, surrender to the Earth Ward." He looked out the window, then back at Dalton. "I don't think so."

"You're awfully confident," said Dalton.

"You have no idea how powerful Dynkara is. I do, and if you did, you would be helping me."

Dalton smiled. "I know how powerful they are, and if you truly knew the powers that existed here on Earth, you would be helping *us* against Dynkara."

"Maybe so," said Septimus. He gestured at Valerie. "But when vampire trash like that is allowed in, it's not a good look for the Earth Ward."

Valerie bared her fangs and hissed.

Dalton scowled. "Dynkara must have brainwashed you because your family almost died."

Septimus extended his hands off to the side. "Tiberius and Camilla are my family. My *only* family. We've had to suffer through centuries of inept leadership and decisions that always ended badly for us three. No more. We'll take our rightful position as the leadership of Lightville."

"Yeah, that's not happening. The fact we're here should tell you that," said Dalton.

"There's still time."

Dalton's senses flared when he detected a fast-moving projectile. Its trajectory would hit Todd. Dalton narrowed his eyes. Everything slowed. He entered Scoutspectre mode, and once his shield spawned, he stood in the bullet's path while bumping Todd away.

The window shattered.

Dalton flew backward as the bullet hit his shield.

Todd's eyes widened. "What the hell?"

"Sniper!" said Valerie.

Rick steadied Dalton, then the team retreated to the hallway as Septimus and the others exited via a side room.

Todd licked his lips. "That woulda hit me!"

"But it didn't," said Dalton. "Evot is already engaging with the sniper, and you can see what she sees. She said she disabled the weapon, and the sniper is on the run now. I guess her first detection of a rifle earlier was right, but whoever the shooter is, they knew she was around and evaded her closer scan."

Valerie scowled. "I know him. Marksman, aka Viktor Sokolov." She glanced at Dalton. "I can get him."

"We shouldn't split up," said Dalton.

"Trust me," she said. She peeked into the room. "Septimus and the others have run off. You need to go after them. I can nail Viktor as long as Evot helps me locate him while you and the others capture Septimus."

Dalton studied her intense expression. "All right. Go, but Todd goes with you. I expect updates."

Valerie swatted Todd's arm. "Let's go!"

"We'll get him," he said. "Count on it."

They took off down the stairs.

Dalton studied the now empty conference room. He focused and sensed that Septimus and the others were on the run.

"They're getting away," said Brad.

"Not for long," said Dalton.

Rick scrutinized the room. "Then we need to move." He shook his head. "Can't believe Todd almost got sniped. You saved his ass."

Dalton grimaced. "Yeah, but I didn't plan on a sniper being present. I should have scouted that building after even a hint of a sniper. That's on me."

Rick laid a hand on Dalton's shoulder. "Man, you can't account for everything."

"I can try," said Dalton. He motioned forward. "Let's get these assholes."

Valerie hustled down the stairs with Todd behind her. Viktor Sokolov's appearance had surprised her. He was known for sniping hard-to-reach targets, and he possessed a kill list that rivaled her own. As a fellow assassin for hire, she had run into him a few times at neutral places where assassins could go. She was sure her joining Dalton's team irritated Viktor.

Why he tried to snipe Todd remained a mystery. Even now she sensed his raging heartbeat. Although he appeared calm on the way down, she knew he was freaking out inside. If Dalton had not pushed Todd away, he would be dead. Just like that.

She and Todd reached the ground floor and burst out of the building. Navigating the street was no obstacle as they hurried to the building Viktor was in.

"All right," said Valerie. "Evot shows three exits to the building. She can cover two while hovering at an angle. If you can cover the front entrance, then we have Viktor trapped."

"You're going in alone?" asked Todd.

"If we both go, there's a chance he might escape, and even with Evot tagging him, he could probably evade her. Plus, I know Viktor and his tactics."

Todd scowled. "I'd like a piece of that asshole."

She touched his shoulder. "I'll get him, and you can slap the ties on him."

"Okay. Good luck. If he comes out this way or any other ground entrance, I'll chase him down."

Valerie squeezed his arm and entered the building. If Viktor did try to escape and ran into Todd, it would be a tough fight. While Todd was a capable fighter, Viktor was on another level. She had heard he even gave Daedroulds a run for their money in close-quarters combat, which was rare for a human unless they were enhanced.

She rushed to the stairwell. The elevator would be too slow, and time was of the essence. Viktor had probably already moved on, but she would be able to capture his scent and track him. When she reached the fourteenth floor, she peeked into the hallway.

A robust man with a tray of food sauntered down the corridor. He had a manila folder tucked under his arm, and the strong odor of lasagna filled the air. She sighed and entered.

The man paused as he looked at her.

She gestured at the open door at the end of the hall. "Whose office is that?"

"Do I know you?" he asked.

She flashed her badge wallet. "Associate Inspector Valerie Simmons, Earth Ward. Now, whose office is that?"

"Uh…Kyle Deamus's."

"Has anyone been in or out of there other than him?"

The man gulped. "He's not in this week. They're rewiring or something. Technician was in today."

Valerie's eyes narrowed. "I see. And did this technician have a weird accent and carry a long case?"

"He did, actually. You know him?"

"Yeah, but he tried to kill my friend. Go to a side office."

The man's eyes widened before he dashed away.

She shook her head and continued. The food's aroma filled the area, and although she could now detect the faint odor of what she thought was Viktor, it had competition from a microwaved lasagna meal. Her senses went into overdrive, as Viktor often left surprises if his position had been compromised.

When she got to the room, she paused outside and peered in. The end of a sniper rifle lay inside near one of the windows. Evot must have landed on it and used her swarm to eat through. While she was powerful in that regard, she was also vulnerable. Thankfully, she was not harmed, but she did make Viktor leave, which was good.

Valerie scrutinized the floor for signs of a trip wire. She grinned when she saw a thin line across the space between the desk and the wall. The line was hard to detect, but the incoming light made it easier to see. She followed the wire to the side, where it went up the wall and to a rectangular container. That was most likely some type of gas. He liked to paralyze his victims that he didn't snipe and talk to them before killing them.

She concentrated on his scent, which led out of the room and down a hallway to another stairwell on the other side of the building. She reached the stairwell and put her ear to the door. It was quiet. After entering, she looked up. He had apparently decided to go higher. That was a distracting move since most would probably suspect he would have tried to flee the building by going down. Unfortunately for him, she had enhanced senses.

She hustled up the stairs and paused at the landing to ensure there were no traps. A level later, she stood outside a door. Based on his scent, he had recently been there. She pushed the door open and stepped back. Nothing happened. She peeked in but yanked her head back when a bullet flew past her.

"Ah, so they sent you. Valerie Simmons. Ex-assassin. Traitor," said Viktor.

She scowled. "Sorry you feel that way." She activated her comms with Todd and Evot, then whispered, "I've found him. Come when you can."

"Not just me…there are others. You betrayed the code," said Viktor.

She laughed. "There's no official code. It's just an unofficial agreement for how things operate. The rules are broken all the time and then used to justify whatever."

Viktor sneered. "Perhaps. But working with the Earth Ward as part of an inspector team? Not assisting the Star Lotus clan in freeing their members that were detained? You've fully stepped out of the world."

"And I don't care. I do what's best for me, and right now, that's apprehending you since you took a shot at one of us. I have to ask…why Todd?"

"He was more valuable dead than alive. You, Dalton, Brad, and Rick were worth more alive and have things of value to certain people. The last thing I need is capturing you four, then Todd deciding to be a hero. Easier to take him out," said Viktor.

Valerie grimaced. "Contract work. Great." She watched as Evot entered as a swarm of flies in a nearby room. Todd was on his way up as well. "I'm going to guess the Facilitator was involved. I never figured you the type to work with the likes of Septimus."

"I suspected he was the contractor," said Viktor. "All I had to do was watch that room for your team, pull them over here, then I was free to capture or kill them. Kill Todd first, then maim Rick on the way over. Brad would have been knocked unconscious by the gas, and Dalton would have been stunned. Easy pickings. Unfortunately, there was an unknown variable."

"Evot."

He scoffed. "Whatever that was. Not much on it but enough to know it had detection abilities. In the past, you would've worked with me on this."

"That's the past. This is the present. Also, you would not have stunned Dalton."

Viktor cried out.

Valerie took that as her cue and rushed into the hallway with her SP-8 and stun baton out. Evot had swarmed around Viktor and caused him to drop his sniper rifle. Valerie took aim.

Evot moved away.

Viktor went to grab his rifle, but Valerie hit him with a stun shot. He shrugged it off and stood, pulling out a knife.

Valerie wrinkled her brow. The stun should have downed him unless he had a counter to stun weaponry. It would not surprise her if he had planned for that. She aimed at him.

He rolled forward and knocked the pistol out of her hand, then tried to kick her.

She dodged and slammed her heel into his knee.

He grunted as he crumpled.

She tried to hit him with her stun baton, but he stabbed through her forearm. She dropped her baton as searing pain ripped through her. With great effort, she dove for her SP-8 and shot him in the face when he lunged at her.

He crashed next to her and lay still.

She dropped her SP-8 and struggled to move.

Evot assumed human form and rushed over to Valerie as Todd entered from the other end. "You are being paralyzed."

"Only for a bit," said Valerie through gritted teeth. "It's his MO. I'll be out when he awakes."

Todd slapped wrist ties on Viktor. "And he'll be in custody."

Valerie lay back and stared at the ceiling. The poison ravaged her muscles. This must have been what Brad and Rick went through. It was not her smoothest fight, and Viktor wore some sort of armor that seemed impervious to stuns. His face was not, though. If she had been alone, she would probably awaken in a torture room somewhere.

Evot held her hand. "We're here for you. I had planned on shooting him with your pistol, but you did it."

Valerie forced a smile. "I couldn't let you have all the fun."

Todd grabbed her other hand. "Just relax. We got your back."

Valerie hated feeling weak. She was thankful Todd and Evot were there and had her covered. It was one of the benefits of being on a team. Although she wanted to talk to them, her throat had already lost control. They rolled her onto her side, so all she could do was stare at the wall. She probably would only be out for an hour or so, but it meant that she, Evot, and Todd could not assist Dalton and the others. She hoped they were doing okay and were not having any issues.

CHAPTER
TWENTY-FIVE

Rick noted the fire in Valerie's eyes when she left. She looked like she was ready to murder someone. Todd resembled someone who had recently shat himself. Given that he was almost sniped, that was understandable. With Evot assisting Valerie and Todd, that left Dalton, Brad, and Rick. The open room ahead of them now had a breeze wafting through, and the floor was covered in shattered glass.

Dalton led the way forward with his shield facing the busted windows.

Rick grimaced as he looked across to another building. He hoped Valerie and Todd handled Viktor. The guy was a threat, and it appeared he had some history with Valerie. Probably an assassin thing.

They reached the end of the room and paused before the door to a side one.

Rick was thankful they were past the windows. Although Viktor may be on the move, that did not mean there were no other snipers out there. Rick gripped his SG-5. Viktor had been unexpected, and Septimus might have more tricks.

Dalton moved into the room and rushed over to a door on the other side. He tried to open it, but it did not budge. He vibrated his hands at the hinges and then kicked the door in.

Brad drew his head back. "This stairwell is not in the building layout."

"I'm gonna guess where it leads to isn't either. Could be a trap," said Rick.

"I agree, and I can sense Septimus and the others now," said Dalton. He advanced down the stairs with his shield raised.

Rick put away his SG-5 and pulled out his dual stun batons. Like Valerie, he was adept at fighting with them. Hopefully, she and Todd were okay. Rick focused back on the group's descent. Dalton moved at a fast clip, but Rick had no issue keeping up. Brad, on the other hand, looked like he was about to keel over, so Rick slowed some to let him catch up.

After reaching two levels below ground, Dalton paused at the final door. "I'm sensing something, well, *somethings* from the parallel Earth."

"Robots," said Brad. "I detect five of them."

"I suspect they're waiting for us."

Rick puffed out his chest. "They're in our way."

"Yeah, and before we go in, know that my armor can handle laser shots and lesser projectiles. If there's five robots with laser guns, it could get dicey. Stay out here for the moment, but if you want to see, Brad can put a stickbot on my shoulder," said Dalton.

Rick and Brad nodded as Brad placed a stickbot on Dalton's shoulder.

Dalton opened the door and stepped inside.

Rick studied the room. A door sat at the back, and between that and the group stood five robots similar to the one they fought upstairs.

"Nice, a panic room," said Dalton. He gestured at the door. "And that's where I'm sure I'll find Septimus and the others."

"You're correct," said Septimus over a speaker. "And, yes, it is quite a nice panic room."

"There's no need for all this," said Dalton. "Surrender now, and the Earth Ward may take that into account."

"May?" asked Septimus. "No, they would make an example out of us. I must warn you, though…if you somehow defeat the robots and get in here…you won't like it."

Dalton talked over local comms. "Brad, see if you can find out what he's talking about. He's using a speaker, so there's tech here."

"Got it," whispered Brad.

"I'm going to disable the guns, then, Rick, it's time to fight."

"Hell yeah," said Rick, quietly.

Dalton charged the first robot.

It shot a laser at him, which he blocked. The other four fired lasers, but they did not affect Dalton's armor.

Rick was amazed at their speed. He wanted to jump in, but he knew if they shot him, he'd be dead.

Dalton vibrated his hand and dashed around the room, hitting all of the weapons. "Now!"

Rick entered and attacked the nearest robot.

It dodged his strikes and stepped back. Another one kicked him off to the side.

He hopped up, his teeth gritted. Even with his tough suit, he felt that kick. These robots had strength. He extended both batons.

"Bring it on!" he said.

The first robot rushed forward while the other tried to flank him.

He ducked and swept his leg at the approaching robot.

The other one went to knock him down.

He was ready this time. He lay on his back and used his legs to catapult the robot over him. After it crashed into the wall, he rolled over and hit it with both stun batons.

It stopped moving.

He scooted back and used the wall to stand. His eyes narrowed when he saw that the other robot had broken off and went after Brad. Dalton handled three robots by himself, which was impressive. Rick went to help Brad.

When the robot came within a few feet of a startled Brad, he extended his hand. "No!"

The robot froze.

Rick had thought the robots required internal rewiring to be affected, but it seemed not in this case. It could be that Brad required more focus if there was no hacking since it looked like he used everything he had in him to prevent the robot from moving. Gizmo and the other stickbots were deployed but standing still. Rick tapped the robot with a stun baton.

It crashed to the ground.

Brad exhaled and wiped the sweat from his brow. "Thanks. I was gonna have Gizmo shoot it, but my focus was on not dying."

"It's cool," said Rick. He glanced at Dalton, who stood over three lifeless robots. "Looks like playtime is over."

"So is Septimus's ability to listen in there," said Brad.

They assembled around Dalton.

"Find anything?" asked Dalton over comms.

"Yeah," said Brad. "We can speak freely. The robots were their eyes and ears. As for the door, it's a sliding one that can only be opened from the inside. They also have explosives all around this room and throughout parts of the building, with an electronic trigger system."

"You disabled it, I suppose."

Brad nodded.

Rick grinned. "Then all that's left is getting in there and arresting them."

They went to the sealed door.

"How are we doing this?" asked Rick.

Dalton motioned for them to stand back.

It always amazed Rick when Dalton used his vibrating ability to cut through things. In this case, he started two feet from the door's top-right edge. He moved his hand into the metal all the way up to his shoulder, then slowly moved down.

After ten grueling minutes, Dalton stepped back. "All right. All that's left is to kick. Be ready to fight."

Rick gripped his SG-5, while Brad wielded his SP-8 and Gizmo stood at attention.

Dalton focused, then kicked in the partially cut-out section, which flew into the panic room. They rushed in, then Dalton raised his RSG at Septimus.

Septimus, Tiberius, and Camilla sat on comfortable chairs, sipping wine and eating snacks. It was definitely not what Rick expected.

"So…it's come down to this," said Septimus, glaring at Dalton. "You ruined everything. Our sources assured us the Earth Ward was incompetent. Yet here you are."

"I'm glad to be a disappointment, then," said Dalton. "Surrender peacefully, and I don't need to stun you."

"Do you hear yourself?" asked Septimus. "Why do you work for the Earth Ward? You could work for Dynkara and secure yourself a spot in the new world order."

Dalton morphed to his official outfit. "I don't do what I do for power, and I couldn't care less about a new world order."

"Your loss." Septimus raised his right hand, which held a detonator. "I guess in the end, neither of us wins."

Tiberius and Camilla winced as Septimus pressed the button.

"Oh…about that," said Dalton. He gestured at Brad. "Did you forget what he can do?"

"I was assured he couldn't breach this!" said Septimus.

Brad grinned. "Maybe before we went to the hub. Unfortunately for you, I disabled the one there too."

Tiberius shook his head. "Well, I'm not going down without a fight." He grabbed the pistol from his holster.

Rick took aim and fired.

Tiberius slumped to the floor.

"Technically, he did go down without a fight," said Rick, smirking.

Dalton eyed Camilla. "Should we expect something from you?"

She sighed. "No. Just do whatever you're going to do."

"All right." Dalton motioned at Rick. "Use the ties."

He walked over and signaled for Septimus and Camilla to stand and turn around.

Camilla did so, and Rick applied wrist ties to her.

He gestured at Septimus.

"Make me," he said, glaring at Rick.

"You sure about that?" asked Rick.

"I got this," said Dalton. He waved for Rick to step aside.

Dalton walked over with his stun baton. "When you wake up, you're going to face justice." He tapped Septimus on the forehead.

Septimus crashed back into his chair.

"And that's that," said Rick.

"Sure is. Let's get them back to Lightville." Dalton pointed around. "I'll get Septimus; you get Tiberius. Brad, if Camilla tries to run, stun her."

"My pleasure," said Brad.

Gizmo beeped at Camilla, who stepped back.

"Don't worry. He has orders to stun only if you make a break for it."

"Great," she said.

Rick put wrist ties on Tiberius, then lifted him up. As they walked out of the panic room, Rick went over the fight.

The robots were a nice touch, and he suspected that if it had been a regular inspector team or even a purely human one, there'd be corpses on the ground. The explosives were so Septimus and the others would not have to face justice. Thankfully, Brad was present. Rick was not in a hurry to experience a building falling on him.

They reached the stairs and ascended.

Rick was glad the perpetrators had been caught. They had built an elaborate web of deceit that involved a power from another reality. He laughed to himself. These cases were crazy, but he loved every minute of it.

Dalton studied the chaotic scene outside the Lightville council compound. Security officers assisted Earth Ward personnel with moving bodies, questioning witnesses, and escorting Crayzo's crew to a temporary holding area. A few officers roughed up the gang members, and given the amount of casualties, Dalton understood their raw emotion. There was even a small FBI presence along with a local police unit from Baton Rouge. That would need to be dealt with carefully.

Earth Ward's Captain Herk was busy with Lightville's Commander Vitus in dealing with all the activity. Julius sat on a curb and consoled Portia. Septimus and Tiberius were in a special van, while Camilla was with the other prisoners. Dalton had ordered an Earth Ward cleanup crew to Septimus's building, as advanced robots, even downed ones, were not something anyone from this Earth should come across.

Todd directed Rick, Valerie, and Brad to help where needed. Dalton appreciated Todd taking charge and could see him running his own team in the future. Valerie appeared to be recharged since the paralysis agent had worn off, and she now moved as if she had a new set of legs. Rick was bruised up, but he seemed to work through the pain, which Dalton expected. Evot was nearby in her human form and provided technical assistance. All in all, the team made an impact on the cleanup.

Dalton joined Herk, Vitus, and Marcus. "You three appear to have things in order."

"I brought up additional units once the initial assessment was done," said Herk.

"I saw it," said Dalton. "Evot updated me."

"I figured."

Dalton glanced at Vitus. "How's Lightville outside of this area holding up?"

Vitus scowled. "Lots of confusion and anger. I've already given a statement, but this is going to require some time to heal. A lot of good officers died today. There were also innocent civilians killed."

Marcus growled. "And I'm partly responsible for not seeing the threat."

"I wouldn't say that," said Dalton. "Septimus covered his tracks well and even had protection from Amelia if she were to somehow get involved. He worked with a powerful ally with immense resources. This isn't on you. This is on

Dynkara and Septimus, Tiberius, and Camilla for assisting them."

"What do we do with them?" asked Vitus, looking at Marcus.

He gestured at Dalton and Herk. "They're the Earth Ward's. For the record, Lightville will officially open talks with the Earth Ward to become a member. We may even permit the opening of an office here to coordinate better. I also suspect they have the resources to put away people like Septimus long term."

Dalton cast a sidelong glance at Herk, then faced Marcus. "We do, and I appreciate your willingness to work with us. I know it's not easy when family is involved."

Marcus spit on the ground. "They're not family anymore!"

Dalton could almost feel the pure hatred radiating from Marcus. To have his own children and family try to kill him must have really messed with his head. The wounded council members made it even more of a mess. Septimus, Tiberius, and Camilla were now outcasts. Marcus knew the Earth Ward would punish them hard, and he seemed okay with that.

"They'll be going to our dimensional prison for holding, and then we'll go from there," said Dalton.

Marcus raised his head. "Whatever you need to do. I trust you'll do what's right. You've proven that."

"Yes, you have," said Vitus.

Dalton appreciated the vote of confidence. Having Lightville work with the Earth Ward would be a big boost to the Earth Ward's abilities. He was sure they would work out some type of healing program as well, where Earth Ward employees with critical needs could be handled. In return, Lightville would receive a lot of recognition and support for whatever they wanted to do. Lightmires would officially join the nonhuman political world as a powerful faction.

"Also, we're going to get rid of some of our more archaic laws, like nonhumans not being allowed in the city after sunset. There's a lot of changes coming. We'll even reach out to Felix," said Marcus.

"It's a new chapter," said Dalton.

Marcus looked over at Julius. "We're going to do it right this time." He eyed Vitus. "This can *never* happen again."

"It won't," said Vitus. "Septimus didn't only hide from you but from our eyes and ears as well. I suspect there were some on the force who supported him. We'll get to the bottom of that. You have my word."

Marcus shook hands with Herk and Dalton, then laid a hand on Vitus's shoulder before heading for Julius and Portia.

Vitus motioned at a group of workers. "I need to handle some things. Excuse me." He shook Dalton's and Herk's hands and then left.

"Big win for the Earth Ward but at a great cost," said Herk.

"Yeah," said Dalton. "There's a lot of work to do here, but having Lightville in the Earth Ward fold is a good thing."

"Definitely. First the Ogben coven, then the Tanner pack, and now Lightville. You're making quite the name for yourself."

"You've read the cases?"

Herk nodded. "My daughter attends the WildHaven Institute, and she mentioned there were some new Ogben coven witches enrolled. I thought she was joking, but then I saw what you did to bring them on board from the Earth Ward internal news. I have to say…that is one of the last factions I would have ever expected to join the Earth Ward, yet here we are with Lightville joining up. Crazy."

Dalton smiled. "Whatever works."

"All right, I better get back to it," said Herk. He extended a hand. "It's been an honor to work with you."

Dalton returned the handshake. "Likewise."

Herk took off toward two prisoners who had gotten into a scuffle.

Dalton surveyed the busy area. It would take time for things to settle down, and he would need to write up the after-case reports. It still bothered him that an inspector and his team had been killed and that he lost a friend. It showed how dangerous the job could be, but it needed to be done, and he was more than qualified to do it.

However, it was the team that made him genuinely enjoy what he did. They would be returning to their base once the area had been fully secured and everyone cleared out. Dalton did not know how long that would take, but he craved a good night's rest.

CHAPTER
TWENTY-SIX

Todd studied the base's landing pad out back as he awaited Ranasa's arrival. It was 11:00 a.m. on the day after all the events in Lightville. Although he was glad Ranasa was visiting, thanks to Jake being kind enough to fly her up, he was still shaken from almost being sniped. If Dalton had not been present, Todd would have died. He sighed. He had been so close to death and had not even known it.

This would be Ranasa's first visit to the new base. She had already been to Todd's house, and he had shown her Louisville as promised. The drive to the base would have been longer, but thankfully Jake had an opening in his schedule. Todd remained surprised the Ogben coven had let her come, but it seemed things had calmed down there. With their new agreement with the Tanner pack, the whole area she was in was more stable.

His heartbeat ramped up at the familiar whine of Jake's stealthed ship landing. A moment later, it decloaked and the back door wound down.

Ranasa ran out with a large bag on her side. She dropped it once near Todd and gave him a big hug.

He took in her fruit scent and held her close. Although they had not been intimate or even officially in a relationship, all indications implied it would go that way. He loved being around her and her no-nonsense approach to life.

Jake peeked out with a big grin and did a two-finger salute at Todd before going back inside the vessel.

A moment later, the ship took off.

"Glad you're here," said Todd, smiling.

"Yeah, me too," she said and swatted his arm playfully.

They laughed.

Todd grabbed her bag. "They have a room set up for you here. Place has a ton of rooms, come to think of it."

"This is a big place from above. I look forward to checking it out," said Ranasa.

They walked toward the sliding door entrance.

Evot landed in crow form, then morphed into her human form. "Hello, Ranasa. It's good to see you here."

"You too, Evot. You're looking good!"

Evot smiled. "Thank you. I have slightly changed my appearance to appear more pleasing visually since our last meeting. My hair is redder and my skin is lighter. I also made minor facial and body adjustments."

"It's working for you," said Ranasa with a grin.

"Thank you again," said Evot. "Are you planning on staying in Todd's room?"

Todd cleared his throat. "You assigned and prepared her room already."

"Yes, but I have calculated Ranasa will spend more time in your room."

Todd's eyes widened. "Uh, let's just get her to her room, and we can go from there."

Ranasa chuckled.

"Okay," said Evot. She glanced at Ranasa. "I would like to allocate some of your time for discussion while you're here."

"Sure. What about?"

"Relationships."

"Oh…okay."

Evot smiled.

Todd gestured forward. "All right. Maybe we should get moving."

Although he loved Evot's innocence, he suspected she was going to ask about his and Ranasa's relationship. That was fine, but they had not really defined it yet. It would be better for Evot to ask Ranasa about it in private. What Evot's end goal was remained unknown, but Todd figured it had something to do with Brad.

"Evot is so much fun," said Ranasa once they reached her room. "It's so interesting that you get to work with her."

Todd set her bag down near a table. "Yeah, she's unique. Brutally honest, which is good, but sometimes her timing can be off in that regard."

"I get it," said Ranasa. She explored her living area. "Wow, all this for me? I love it!"

Todd pulled out a cold soda from the fridge. After cracking it open, he took a seat. "It's all yours, and you're welcome to stay as long as you want."

"Really?" she asked, sitting opposite him.

His pulse quickened. The thought of her being interested in having her own room when she visited indicated she might be up more often. He would enjoy that.

"Sure. I'll stay up here if you're around, and if not, I still have my house for between cases."

"Then I have multiple places to visit."

Dalton knocked on the open door.

"Hey, Dalton," said Ranasa.

"Hey yourself," said Dalton, waving at her. "Am I interrupting anything?"

Todd shook his head. "Come on in."

Dalton stood before them. "I hate to be the bearer of bad news…but your property was attacked."

Todd sat up straight. "What? By who?"

Dalton faced the TV on the wall.

It flashed on and showed an aerial view of the burnt-down remains of Todd's house.

Todd jumped out of his chair. "What the hell?"

"It happened last night. Firefighters got to it but were too late. Local police are investigating," said Dalton.

Todd huffed. "Any leads?"

"Our drone picked up this."

The screen showed a burned metallic T standing upright.

Todd sighed. "Figures. I knew they would come; I just wasn't sure when."

"What is that?" asked Ranasa.

"It's a steel T doused in gasoline, then lit on fire. It stands for *traitor* and is used by the Faith Militia."

Ranasa stood next to him and ran her hand along his back. "I'm sorry."

"I need to head down there," said Todd.

Dalton pointed outside. "Jake is already on his way back."

"I'm going with you," said Ranasa.

"All right," said Todd. He glanced at Dalton. "I guess I'll miss the get-together later today."

"Yes, but it's understandable," said Dalton.

Todd looked at Ranasa. "I'll grab some things. Meet you out back in ten."

"Okay," she said.

"I guess I'll need to make my room here a bit more permanent," said Todd.

"Not a problem," said Dalton. "I'll have Evot do whatever needs done."

"I appreciate it," said Todd.

His stomach churned as he hustled to his room. He figured the Faith Militia would strike at some point. It seemed they chose this last night to do it. The T structure that was lit on fire was something he had seen and also helped erect in the past at various places. The Faith Militia in the area was now fully committed to removing him. It was not safe to live there anymore.

Thankfully, he had a spacious room with all accommodations at the new base. Although he had weighed spending a month on and off there, it was now permanent. Rick had already moved in, so maybe it would not be so bad. If Todd had been at his house with Ranasa during the attack, he had no illusions they would be alive.

Todd's eyes narrowed. He was in a new chapter in his life, and his property was a casualty of that. Although he would miss his house, he was not tied to it. Hopefully, the underground bunker was okay, but the Faith Militia would know of it. It depended on how accurate they were in their attack. Either way, he would not let the incident taint his new direction.

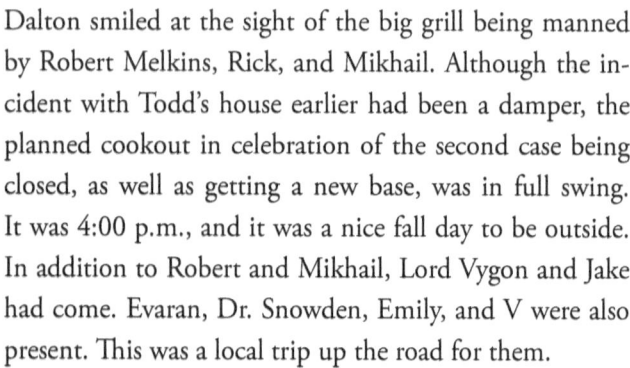

Dalton smiled at the sight of the big grill being manned by Robert Melkins, Rick, and Mikhail. Although the incident with Todd's house earlier had been a damper, the planned cookout in celebration of the second case being closed, as well as getting a new base, was in full swing. It was 4:00 p.m., and it was a nice fall day to be outside. In addition to Robert and Mikhail, Lord Vygon and Jake had come. Evaran, Dr. Snowden, Emily, and V were also present. This was a local trip up the road for them.

Dalton cracked up as Evot and V danced around in their cat forms, much to Emily's and Valerie's delight. Dr. Snowden and Brad chatted off to the side.

Lord Vygon and Evaran approached Dalton. He nodded at them both.

"Interesting case," said Lord Vygon.

"I'll say. It definitely was not what I expected," said Dalton. He glanced at Evaran. "You ever heard of Dynkara?"

"I have not," said Evaran. He raised a finger. "However, the concept of a multi-timeline society is not uncommon, and I have run into them before."

Dalton wrinkled his brow. "How often?"

"I registered several hundred thousand in my travels before coming to Earth."

"One that messed with Earth recently too," said Jake, joining them. "A society of psychopaths from multiple timelines. Yeah, not fun."

Dalton's eyes widened. "Doesn't sound like it. As for the Dynkara portal to this Earth, I permanently sealed it. Hopefully, they can't come back, but I know it's possible."

Evaran studied him. "Yes. If they possess a large enough rift crystal, they can punch through timelines, especially since they have been weakened recently."

"There's still some cleanup here to do," said Lord Vygon. He gestured at Dalton. "We're following up on the list of hundreds that have been replaced. It seems they've gone into hiding. The Dynkara agents are also difficult to find, which is odd, considering their robots should stand out."

"Hopefully, Septimus can help with that. If not him, Tiberius or Camilla," said Dalton.

"We'll see," said Lord Vygon. "They have a new home in our dimensional prison. Despite that, I've been personally handling the relationship with Lightville. I expected some pushback due to ancient vampire and lightmire history, but they seemed to ignore that past, which made things easier."

Jake smiled. "I suspect we'll get an employee discount of some type for their healing services."

"Yeah, but they're also giving us slots for free treatment," said Lord Vygon. "Obviously, high-priority cases will use those."

"I think this will be a good relationship for the Earth Ward," said Dalton.

Evaran half smiled. "You are a natural ambassador."

"To be fair, the cases sorta lean toward new allies if completed," said Dalton.

"True, but your success rate and reputation show that the Earth Ward is serious. I see it growing rapidly with you investigating cases. The *Torvatta* chose well."

Jake grinned and motioned at Dalton. "Yeah. It used to be people asking me if I knew Evaran. Now some are asking if I know you."

"I don't seek fame," said Dalton.

"I know," said Jake. "Still, you're getting more known after each case."

Dalton sighed. "As long as there are cases to be resolved, that'll remain my focus."

"As it should be," said Evaran. "As for Evot, her servbot has been repaired and can be integrated whenever you are ready."

"No time like the present," said Dalton.

"Very well. Follow me," said Evaran.

Dalton notified Evot to come along. V decided to join them as well, and they both arrived in their humanoid forms.

After five minutes, they were on board the *Torvatta* in the medical bay dimensional room.

Evot rushed over to the servbot controller on the counter.

"You should be able to connect to it now," said Evaran.

Evot focused, and the servbot morphed into a cat.

"It appears to be functional," said Evot. She hugged Evaran, then high-fived V.

Dalton laughed. "I'm glad you're back to two servbots."

"I'm surprised she was able to be hit," said Lord Vygon.

"Brad showed me why it happened," said Evot. "I was too predictable. The robot used an efficient algorithm against me."

"That must have been an interesting fight," said Jake.

Evaran raised a finger. "I adjusted the coating of the servbot controller. It should be able to handle laser shots now. It is still prone to injury from projectiles, although I made it hard enough to handle small arms fire. I can do the other one while I am here."

"Thank you," said Evot, smiling.

Evaran bowed slightly. "If you wish to transition to a body at some point, we can help with that as well, assuming Dalton is okay with it."

"It's not my decision," said Dalton. "I'm used to Evot's main processor in me, but that's her call."

Evot smiled at Dalton. "I like where I am now."

"Very well," said Evaran.

Dalton looked around. "Whew. I haven't been here in a long while. It still feels like yesterday when I was dying on Heristacan and you all saved me."

"Query. Would your team be interested in seeing that event?" asked V.

"I don't know. I've never asked them. Maybe I should while the *Torvatta* is here. They'd love the holo room." Dalton pointed at Evaran. "Assuming that's okay with you."

"Of course it is."

Dalton nodded. "Wait here."

He walked outside and cleared his throat.

Everyone focused on him.

"V has suggested there may be interest in watching when I first met Evaran and the gang. Evaran is okay with it, and we could use the holo room."

"Oh, hell yeah," said Rick.

Brad laughed. "Like you have to ask if we want to see that."

"Yeah, no kidding," said Valerie.

Emily swatted Valerie's arm. "Let's do this!"

Everyone filed into the *Torvatta*.

Lord Vygon joined Dalton outside. "You have a great team, and I'm proud of what you've accomplished since you arrived."

Dalton eyed him. "You getting sentimental on me?"

"Not at all. Evaran and the gang recently finished a trip with me, although I was dropped off twelve thousand years ago. I'm just enjoying *this* particular moment in time."

"You know something about the future, don't you?"

Lord Vygon sighed. "I can't say. What I can say is…let's enjoy this moment while we can."

Dalton understood Lord Vygon had some insight into future events, and he had alluded that things might be rough. This was another example to add to that list.

"Have you seen the footage of my trip with Evaran and the gang already?" he asked.

"Some," said Lord Vygon.

Dalton slapped him on the back. "Then let's enjoy it. As Emily said, let's do this!"

THE END

NOTE FROM THE AUTHOR

I hope you enjoyed *Lightville*, Book 2 of *The Inspector Dalton Files* series! This book introduces the team's new base and takes them to Baton Rouge, Louisiana. This case takes place a month after their last one.

Rick Westmoreland is added to the team, which adds a great dynamic. Everyone received some new equipment, and Brad got some new gadgets. Things heated up between Rick and Valerie, while Todd stepped up as a deputy inspector. Evot had to contemplate her existence somewhat, but Dalton was there for her as always. He likes the direction the new team is going, and this case was a good test for them.

A major faction is introduced in the lightmires. They have always been around, but they try to avoid interaction with powerful factions when they can. Their decision to join the Earth Ward is big, and it's all thanks to Dalton's team.

There is also another world involved in the case. You haven't seen the last of Dynkara. Their reach is long, and there are remnants left on Earth.

As always, there are hooks to *The Evaran Chronicles*. Emily joins up with half the team in the first scene. Since the team is in Columbus, Ohio, which is where Emily lives, it's just a stroll down the road for her. Dalton is one of her closest friends, so she doesn't mind popping in from time to time.

If you liked the book and have the time and inclination, a review would go a long way in helping out this indie author. If you do submit a review, I'll put in a word to Dalton should you find yourself being replaced and about to be cremated by Dynkara! Want to be notified about new book releases? If so, you can sign up below.

WWW.ADAIRHART.COM/MAILINGLIST.ASPX

I will only send you emails about new book releases, major updates, and the occasional newsletter, usually once a month. I dislike getting spammed too, so I will use this sparingly to keep you in the loop.

ABOUT THE AUTHOR

I have been dreaming about fictional worlds since I was a kid. I devoured anything related to fantasy and science fiction. I developed a setting over the last twenty years and struggled to find a medium I could express it in. I discovered I enjoyed writing, and it is a passion of mine now. Exploring my setting through the written word has been an awesome journey.

I work in the information technology field and have my master's degree in it. It has helped me to shape some of the concepts I write about. I also enjoy keeping up on futurology and science in general.

I live in central Ohio and enjoy walking, reading, gaming, learning, listening to music, and trying to keep up on my never-ending list of TV shows and movies to watch. If you want to contact me, you can do so on my website at

WWW.ADAIRHART.COM

You can also reach me on

Facebook...........................fb.com/AdairHart
Goodreads.....www.goodreads.com/AdairHart
Email..............Adair.Hart.Author@gmail.com

ACKNOWLEDGMENTS

This was a great journey for me, but I wouldn't be here without the help of others. I would like to thank the following people in no particular order:

My editor, Miranda Miller. She is amazing to work with and I continue to grow under her watchful eye!

My cover artist, Tom Edwards (tomedwardsconcepts@ gmail.com), for an awesome cover. He made Dalton and Evot look good while they do a holosketch.

My family and friends who helped encourage me along the way.

My proofreader, Paula, for providing a professional service.

My formatter and interior designer, Colleen Sheehan (www.ampersandbookinteriors.com), for helping me make my pdf interiors shine.

BOOKS

You can see all books in *The Inspector Dalton Files*,
The Evaran Chronicles, and *The Earthborn* series at

WWW.ADAIRHART.COM/SERIES/AllBOOKS.ASPX